SPECI

This bo

# THE ULVERSCROFT FOUNDATION
(registered charity No. 264873 UK)

ˉstablished in 1972 to provide funds for
ˉ1, diagnosis and treatment of eye diseases.
.amples of contributions made are: —

A Children's Assessment Unit at
Moorfield's Hospital, London.

•

Twin operating theatres at the
ēstern Ophthalmic Hospital, London.

•

A Chair of Ophthalmology at the
Australian College of Ophthalmologists.

•

Ulverscroft Children's Eye Unit at the
ˈrmond Street Hospital For Sick Children,
London.

ı help further the work of the Foundation
ːing a donation or leaving a legacy. Every
ˌbution, no matter how small, is received
ı gratitude. Please write for details to:

**ˌ ULVERSCROFT FOUNDATION,**
**ˌe Green, Bradgate Road, Anstey,**
**Leicester LE7 7FU, England.**
**Telephone: (0116) 236 4325**

**In Australia write to:**
**ˌ ULVERSCROFT FOUNDATION,**
cⁱᵗ  ˌe **Royal Australian and New Zealand**
**College of Ophthalmologists,**
**94-98 Chalmers Street, Surry Hills,**
**N.S.W. 2010, Australia**

# THE IMMORTAL WOUND

The Saxons face increasing opposition as Arturo secures his garrisons and his army strengthens. But Count Ambrosius poison's Arturo's wife, Daria, who was pregnant with the warrior's child. However, he subsequently meets and marries Gwennifer. Arturo faces many bloody battles against the Saxons — culminating in the most ferocious clash of armies yet, the Battle of Badon Hill . . .

Books by Victor Canning
Published by The House of Ulverscroft:

BIRDS OF A FEATHER
THE BOY ON PLATFORM ONE

THE ARTHURIAN TRILOGY:
THE CRIMSON CHALICE
THE CIRCLE OF THE GODS
THE IMMORTAL WOUND

VICTOR CANNING

---

# THE IMMORTAL WOUND

## Book Three

*Complete and Unabridged*

# ULVERSCROFT
*Leicester*

First published in Great Britain in 1978

This Large Print Edition
published 2012

The moral right of the author has been asserted

British Library CIP Data

Canning, Victor.
The immortal wound.
1. Great Britain- -History- -Anglo-Saxon period,
449 – 1066- -Fiction. 2. Historical fiction.
3. Large type books.
I. Title
823.9'12–dc23

ISBN 978–1–4448–1244–2

Published by
F. A. Thorpe (Publishing)
Anstey, Leicestershire

Set by Words & Graphics Ltd.
Anstey, Leicestershire
Printed and bound in Great Britain by
T. J. International Ltd., Padstow, Cornwall

This book is printed on acid-free paper

– With love –
'To the one who wept
when the dream ended'

# The Coin of Hadrian

In full company they came riding across the flat headwater meadows of the infant Tamesis river and breasted the growing slope to the wide mouth of the wooded valley at the head of which lay the Villa of the Three Nymphs. It was a day of high summer, the blue sky cloudless. Early morning rain had lacquered the beech and ash trees and brought the valley stream into a foaming spate above which dragon and damsel flies hawked and hunted the gnats. At the head of the company rode Arturo on the White One, the mare's long mane and tail swirling in the strong breeze, her hocks mud-splashed, while at her de loped the great hound Anga.

Arturo held himself stiffly in the saddle to ease the slow-dying pain in his left side and to lessen the chafing of the tight bandages of coarse linen strips that bound his midriff. But for him the nag of the arrow wound meant little against the growing pride and joy which filled him at this time of triumphant return. Behind him rode Lancelo carrying the wind-streamed red and white banner of the White Horse, and following them came the full company of Companions, their red and white scarves and war helmet crests tossing and swinging. Every man among them was straight-backed with pride and tight-lipped with deep pleasure at the thought of the long, hard weeks of the progress they had made down the Tamesis river to Londinium and then of the long return which had taken them, fighting and triumphant, through the lands of the Regni to give taunt and despite to the Saxon people of the south-east. There was not a man among them who did not give thanks to their God or gods or find silent prayer for bosom friend or stout flankman in cavalry charge who rode no longer with them. And not a man among them now who, with the prospect of ease and leisure so near, would not have turned at Arturo's command and ridden east again to harry the Jute and Saxon men. Yet with the prospect of comfort and rest so near in this friendly territory there was no relaxing of their hard-taught discipline. The slow-moving baggage train was shielded by two ranks of protecting horsemen and along the rising valley sides flanking patrols threaded their mounts through the thinning trees. Arturo came in triumph but with no lessening of care.

Arturo himself, glancing skywards, seeing there for the first time a slow circling of hawks and kites, frowned as he watched them. The bite of sharp instinct born of grim campaigning suddenly roused him. He reined-in and called a command to Lancelo.

A command horn blew, the sharp notes wickering and echoing from side to side of the valley. The company halted and its flanking troops formed a herisson about the baggage train. The outriding patrols on the valley sides changed formation and strung themselves in a wide protective bow across the front of the company.

At Arturo's side, now, Lancelo, his eyes skyward, said, 'When the carrion birds gather they come for feasting.'

Arturo nodded. 'Stay here. I go forward with Gelliga and his troop.'

Lancelo raised the command horn to his lips and at its call the dark-bearded, sweet-singing Gelliga with his second-in-command, fresh-faced, giant-handed Borio, came riding up with their men.

With a glance at the far sky and its circling birds of prey Gelliga said, 'Maybe the wolves have taken but a single cow somewhere and the carrion wait for the pickings.'

Arturo said nothing. He put the White One to a trot and rode forward through the thinning wood and the troop followed him. After a while they came out of the trees into the wide, sloping bowl of the valley which rose to the Villa of the Three Nymphs from whose goddess-protected fountain rose the source of the stream that watered the valley. He reined-in his mount and raised a hand. The troop spread behind him in a half moon and, as they did so, the feasting carrion birds rose in alarm from the slaughtered cattle and swine whose carcasses littered the stock pens. A thin plume of smoke rose still from the smouldering ruin of a thatched cart shed. The dead thorn fences around the crop strips were gapped and the high standing barley and bean vines lay trampled and flattened where horsemen had rampaged wantonly through them.

Tight-lipped, Arturo raised his eyes to the villa itself. Long days of restoration he and his fellows had laboured to make the old Roman villa inhabitable again. The red tiled roofs were gapped and the gaunt fire-blackened timber frames of eating hall and sleeping quarters still smouldered. Sword-sharp anxiety coursed through him. For the crops and the cattle and the wanton destruction of the villa he cared little. He had come riding back in triumph, waiting for the moment when free of the forest he would raise his eyes to the villa and see standing at the top of the wide steps that led down to its lower terrace the

4

figure of his wife Daria, the woman whom the gods had gifted him. Daria of the bright eyes of the blue bell flower, of the lips redder than any thorn berry and hair like polished black serpentine . . . Daria who carried his child. As he would have kicked the White One into a gallop he was halted by the appearance of two horsemen who came round the eastern edge of the villa, picking their way over the rubble of the long eating hall, and began to ride down towards them.

Behind him Gelliga said, 'They come in peace, my captain.'

The two men rode down to them slowly. One was elderly and the other a young man. They carried their shields slung over their shoulders, their swords were at their sides. They were warcapped, their tunics and gartered hose worn and marked with rough living, their hair long and lank over their shoulders.

Lancelo said, 'They are Cymru men and they ride the cavalry crossbreeds of Ambrosius but wear not the blue scarves of the Sabrina squadrons.'

Arturo said nothing. The destruction he saw before him he knew could be at Ambrosius's orders. For that, slaughtered cattle, spoiled crops and sacked villa, he cared nothing. But if harm or death had come to

Daria, he swore to the gods that Ambrosius should pay the debt with his own blood.

The two men came down to them and now Arturo saw that the cloth of their belted tunics was crudely striped in greens, yellows and reds. The elder man — who was much the same age as Arturo's own father, Baradoc — wore a bronze torque about his neck, partly hidden by his unkempt beard. The young man at his side carried the other's features with a faithfulness that marked him as a son.

Reining-in before them the elder man raised a hand to touch his brow in friendly greeting. Then, smiling, he said, 'Arturo, son of Baradoc of the tribe of the Enduring Crow, let my first words be of happiness. Your wife, Daria, is safe and well and awaits you at the villa.'

'May the gods be blessed for that. And you, too, if it is so because of your protection.'

The man smiled. 'The gods it seems have fated me to bring happiness of this kind first to your father and now to you. You do not know me?'

Smiling now from the joy which was in him Arturo said, 'Aye, I know you now. My father has spoken often of you and of the time when you would have carried off my mother into slavery when you raided her uncle's villa in

6

Aquae Sulis many years ago but since you were of the Ocelos tribe, all of whom are distant kin to his own, he denied you the right since he claimed that my mother was already betrothed to him.'

'Aye, he tricked me to save her, not knowing that he spoke the truth then of their love. Yes, I am Cadrus of the Ocelos.' He pulled aside the front of his tunic and showed, tattooed on the brown skin of his shoulder, the symbol of the goose with the golden feet. 'And this is my son Anwyl who would take service with you. He brings with him my blessing and ten good men, mounted and armed who wait in the woods beyond the villa. For myself I go back to my own lands in the hills west of Gobannium and Eurium beyond the Sabrina for I campaign no more with Count Ambrosius.'

'Whose work this was?' Arturo waved a hand over the dead cattle, stricken crops and the ruined villa.

Cadrus smiled. 'You should have foreseen it. You are not only banned from all his lands and those of your own Prince Gerontius, the blood price on your head for any man's taking — but you have made Ambrosius a figure of shame by drawing some of his best men from him. Aye, and now you have marched your warriors east to Londinium and south about to taunt and fight the Saxons while Ambrosius has stayed close to Glevum and Corinium and seen his own men grow restless for action and loud with complaint. To ease their grumbles a little . . . ' He half turned and held out a hand towards the ruined villa, ' . . . he sent a wing of the Sabrina cavalry to destroy all you have created here and to take your wife captive. And would have taken her if we had not ridden ahead and saved her.'

'For which you have my thanks yet may well suffer from the hands of your own king Vortigern with whom he is leagued.'

Cadrus shook his head. 'Vortigern is dead. There will be no levies from his lands beyond the Sabrina until Ambrosius or some other proves his worth — '

'And that man.' Anwyl, despite his father's frown, broke in sharply, 'is you, my lord Arturo. The news of your great progress has run fast before you. Men speak openly in the barracks of Corinium that now there is only one way to manliness and true action against the Saxon kind, and that with the companions of Arturo. And I . . . ' He stopped suddenly and looked at his father.

Cadrus smiled and with a cock of his head towards Arturo said, 'My wolf cub has much to learn, not least that he steps out of place from over-eagerness. But take him and his men and see them blooded. They are all of the Ocelos and will serve you well when you have schooled them.'

'I take them willingly. But now I would go to my wife wherever you have lodged her.'

Cadrus wheeled his horse about and pointed up the long valley slope. 'She waits for you.'

Looking upwards Arturo saw that Daria now stood at the top of the courtyard steps waiting for him. He gave an order to Lancelo and then urged the White One into a canter towards the villa.

Standing on the steps, the sound of falling water from the spring that filled the broad basin of the fountain of the three nymphs making quiet music for her ears, Daria waited for the coming of her husband. The eager breeze moulded the soft stuff of her blue woollen gown about her body and, against the constraint of the yellow band about her head, lifted and toyed with the fall of her ebony hair. One hand ran nervously with pleasure along the amber beads which strung her neck and the sun dully fired the bronze clasps which ringed the dusky skin of her arms. Gown, beads and armlets were all tokens of his love, all plunder spoil sent ahead of his coming, but none so dear or precious

9

as the gift which she held now for him, that life which in the last few days had begun to move with increasing vigour beneath her heart, the child of his begetting.

As Arturo rode towards her a command horn blew below, the notes long and compelling. The company broke line and formation and moved to make camp in the lower meadow, men and mounts moving with an ease and assurance which had never been there during the long training days of the past, a sureness never to be perfected by drills, a sureness which only came from campaigning.

At Daria's side, Ansold, her father, seeing the companions disposing themselves below, said, ' 'Tis battle that puts the final temper to a sword. Born of hammer, fire and water it may be, but true virtue it must find against its own kind.' He spat with the wind and grunted something else to himself.

Daria smiled to herself, knowing his envy. Great swordsmith though he was, he had longed to follow Arturo as had done Lancelo, her brother and Arturo's banner-bearer and righthand man. Arturo reined-in at the foot of the steps and the horse tang of the White One came to her on the breeze as her eyes marked Arturo's bearded face. He had lost weight and his skin was dark and tight-stretched like the leather of a worn belt. Yet the shine in his eyes was the old shine and for a moment his lips showed pale and pink in the purse of a private smile for her. But she knew the pain and wound stiffness in him as he dismounted, came to her and took her hand and kissed it, saying, 'You wear my gifts.'

Remembering sharply the boasting boy she had long ago first met on a rain-swept Dumnonian moor, she smiled with the happiness that flooded her and answered him in the teasing manner which was always open love play between them.

'There is no gift, man of the tribe of the Enduring Crow, greater than your safe return. So — you have moved against the Saxon kind at last. May the gods make you content enough to stay by my side until you are whole again.'

'The wound is clean and heals fast.'

'That I would see for myself.'

She took him by the arm and led him across the courtyard, through the rubble and desolation, to her room in the south wing of the villa, the walls fire-scorched, the roof gapped and its beams roughly propped with newcut timbers, and then out to the open portico. Here, untouched by fire, a great growth of yellow roses rambled up the pillars, surviving still from the days, long distant now, of the peace and prosperity of the villa before Rome had withdrawn its last active legions from this its most northern province, budding and blooming through the days when the ill-starred Vortigern had made federation with Hengist and Horsa to aid him against Scot and Pict only to find them with the passage of years not allies but land and plunder-hungry pirates. Close to the roses stood a table and two stools, the table bearing an earthenware jug of wine and drinking beakers.

Daria poured wine for him, but before she could pass the beaker, he put his arm around her and kissed her and the trembling in her body was matched by the shaking of his own hard frame.

Releasing her, Arturo said, 'Now tell me that you and the boy are well.'

Smiling against the certainty in him, she said, 'The child and I are well, my lord. To know that it is a boy you must — ' the tip of her tongue flicked teasingly between her full red lips, ' — as usual have had private word from the gods.'

Soberly Arturo said, 'It is a boy. In a dream the gods have promised it.'

'*Aie* . . . those dreams of yours. Then there can be no doubt. Now drink and then strip.

Your wound to me is of more account than anything else.'

Arturo hesitated, then grinning and shrugging his shoulders, he began to strip to humour her, saying, 'From Sorviodunum I rode ahead alone to the Circle of the Gods one night. There after Prince Gerontius had outlawed me I buried beneath one of the standing stones a gift from my mother which I would make a gift on his birth to my son. As I dug in the dawn light one, whom I thought to be a homeless wanderer, took bow and arrow to me for the sake of plunder. The arrow missed its true mark. I killed the man with my sword to find he was my uncle Inbar, long cast out of the tribe for his villainies . . . a wanderer who would have killed me, less for the blood money, than for the joy he would have taken in the grief of my mother and father.'

'And the gift?'

Dropping his short cloak to the portico balustrade Arturo reached within his shirt and pulled out the silver chalice which his Roman mother, Tia, had given him when he had left the tribe as a youth to go to Isca Dumnonia to serve with the cavalry of Prince Gerontius. As Daria took it, he said, 'There is a story to it which I will tell you the day that our son is born and I place it between his hands.'

Daria smiled. 'A story, no doubt, of gods and magic.'

Running the back of his hand down the soft bloom of her cheek, Arturo grinned. 'In truth, yes. But not one of my dreaming. Would you doubt the word of my mother Tia?'

'Never. But yours often.' As she spoke Daria turned the silver chalice in her hands. It was little larger than a drinking goblet with handles each side curved and worked in the shape of rams' horns. One of the handles was badly bent and the bowl was marked with dents and had become tarnished from burial in the ground. Around the outside rim ran a continuous key pattern and on one side, in bold relief, was a large round boss in the shape of a circular wreath of bay leaves enclosing the outline of a human eye. As she turned it in her hands Daria was thinking that although she had often said she doubted his words there was in them a passion and conviction which could not be ignored. There could be no doubt of his belief that he was marked for greatness by the gods to whom he always looked for signs of approval — and found them, though others might not be so convinced — before taking any great action. This belief was a flame in him which burned strongly, never wavering or dimming. But for

14

her he was her husband and man. The wish was suddenly strong in her that the child should be a boy. For that she would pray, but to her own God.

At the sight of the wound she was relieved to see that it had begun to heal cleanly. As she washed and fresh salved it, Daria gave him the news of Count Ambrosius which old Ansold had gleaned by secret visits to nearby Corinium. Ambrosius would have marched eastwards at mid-summer against the Saxons. But Prince Gerontius at Isca had sent only scant and poorly trained levies, and from the now dead Vortigern had come no levy but a straggling of small chief's and independent young warriors. So Count Ambrosius had sat tight, too wise and cautious to mount a great campaign with a doubtful force.

Sipping his wine and listening Arturo felt at once contempt and compassion for the man. Ambrosius dreamt still of the past glories of the Empire and was impatient to rid this country of Pict and Scot and Saxon kind and call himself Emperor. He lacked no passion for that end, but the glory would be forever denied him. Caution inhabited the centre of his heart like a frightened harvest mouse huddled in its grass nest high in the summer corn, scenting the rank of hunting marten or polecat. There was scorn in him at

15

the pettiness of the man who, hearing of his own small progress with a handful of men, could give vent to it by raiding the villa and destroying crops and cattle. There would be no joy in the hearts of the gods at such smallness of spirit. *Aie* . . . already, he knew without arrogance, that they looked else-where to place their favours. Although his own progress had been from lack of men no great affair, he knew that their eyes were on him. They had fought no great battles for he lacked men as yet for these. But the men would come, and come quickly now as the noise of his name spread and the story of his long-spanned foray was told and re-told and carried far and wide, from hearth to hearth and town to town. And what bard or traveller was there who would not add his own wonder touches? Then let it be so. There was a power in the sword which showed only in the heat of battle. But there was a power in the word which worked without let and spread fast like bright morning over the land.

At his side Daria said, 'You smile. But I doubt it is from the pleasure of returning.'

For a moment he would have told her the truth of the smile, but then not wanting the gentle mockery which she alone had the privilege of offering, he said affectionately,

'Then you are wrong. I smile because the gods have been good to me in linking your life with mine. As lovers we lay in the uncurling bracken together and the high larks sang our happiness. As man and wife I have lain at your sleeping side and your soft breath has touched my cheek like a silk-winged moth. I smile because each day I have wakened beside you the morning light borrowed brightness from your opening eyes. And I smile now because — '

'Because, my Arto — ' Daria interrupted him, ' — you have finished your wine and it fills your head with fancies.' She leaned forward and kissed him on the brow, and went on, 'My lord, I am content to see you back. You will rest and recover, and that will be all my happiness.'

Arturo said nothing, but the smile went from his face and slowly he shook his head and then said flatly, 'No, there is no rest for me, not for many a long year.' With a gesture of his hand down the valley to the ruined crop strips and to the carrion birds that still fought and bickered over the dead cattle, he said angrily, 'The gods arranged this welcome for me. You think it was to daunt me? No — it was to show me clearly their will. Tomorrow at sunset we ride for Corinium. No man now, not even Count Ambrosius, can offer injury to Arturo and his companions without knowing that it will be returned in full measure . . . fire brand for fire brand, slaughter for slaughter.'

Eyes widening Daria said, 'You would move against Corinium where Ambrosius numbers a hundred and more men for each one of yours?'

'Against Corinium, no. I have no quarrel with honest citizens and work folk. But against Ambrosius and the Sabrina cavalry which are camped outside it. Their food stores and their cattle shall know fire and slaughter. Their barracks and their eating halls shall be gutted and left roofless. And when all is done there will be those of the Sabrina squadron who will hide their smiles and their joy and will ride to join me. Under the sky nothing happens by chance. The gods rule the world. Mark their signs, read their message and obey it, and their favour is with you until the day they justly decree the last grain of sand has fallen to the bottom of the hour glass.'

Tight-lipped Daria held back the protest within her. When the madness of the gods touched this man, her lover, husband, father of her child to be, she knew that there was no crossing his purpose. She lifted the wine jug and refilled his beaker.

When they had ridden out long weeks ago to make their progress down the Tamesis river into the Saxon lands they had numbered two troops of twenty-four horse each and a remount section of six horses — scarce sixty horses and fighting men. They had lost and won men and horses along the way and now mustered three troops of thirty horse and a remount troop of ten horse. The company of companions had grown and with it, too, had the baggage train and the men who manned it. The growth would continue almost each day.

At sunset the next evening they paraded for their foray against Count Ambrosius. Arturo took with him but two troops, and there was not a man among them who did not know the hard country ahead of them, and knew, too, the cavalry camp of the Sabrina Wing at Corinium. Many of them had come from there to join Arturo, discarding the blue neck scarves of Ambrosius for the red and white scarves and war helmet plumes of Arturo. Durstan, the first of the companions who had been outlawed with Arturo by Prince Gerontius, led one troop with Garwain as his second-in-command. Black-bearded Gelliga with Borio as his second-in-command led the other. The rest of the companions stayed to guard the villa camp with Anwyl, son of Cadrus, and his ten men. Cadrus himself went with Arturo, not claiming the honour as a return for the service he had rendered him, but pointing out that Corinium lay on his route to Glevum where he must cross the Sabrina to reach his homelands. Before they set out Pasco, the broad-minded priest who had shared all their past campaigning, sitting on his sturdy dun pony, made prayer for them and kept it short for one of his virtues was never to give warriors more measure of admonition than he sensed their mood would take.

'You fight now,' he called in his high voice, 'to free this land from the tyranny of strangers and the covetousness and pride of those of your own race who see only in victory a bloody licence to oppress their own people. To be such is to be less in the eyes of the gods, and the Father of all gods, than the creatures of this earth — for where is there fowl or fish or four-legged beast that makes war to enslave its own kind? In victory be merciful. Be less than that and when you die your spirits shall wander unshrived for evermore in limbo.' He touched his brow and raised a hand in blessing, piping loudly, 'Holy Christos and His great Father and timeless

Dis and fierce Badb and gentle Coventina give you protection and comfort as long as you move in the ways of truth and honourable brotherhood and companionship.'

As he finished speaking Lancelo at Arturo's side blew the command horn and the horsemen moved away to flanks and centre and breasted the steep slope behind the villa.

Standing beside the courtyard steps Daria watched them go. Arturo had given her his love and protection. But neither to her nor to any other woman had she not come into his life could he ever truly give himself. The gods had claimed him long before she had met him on the rain-swept Western moors beyond the Tamarus river, the old, fierce gods of this country — not hers to whom out of respect for her and others like her among his company he paid respect. Ambrosius dreamed of the past glories of the Empire and ached to clear this country of its foes and then take to himself the imperial purple ... Aye, and then maybe turn his eyes southwards to Gaul and beyond, brooding in a dream of restoration of all the provinces that Goths and Vandals now held. The dream was void of reason for time could not be turned back. Only Arturo held the true dream; to clear this land of its invaders, to make it one country and to give its peoples peace and prosperity under the sign of the White Horse. For this end the old gods had claimed him. With any woman or man who loved him and gave him their companionship and trust but did not read his heart aright there must always be the fierce, intermittent ache of loneliness. There was no doubt in her mind that though he loved her she was less to him than his love of country, than his love of the gods who, he had no doubt, shaped his destiny, and — the truth of this more easily borne — less than his desire for their child to be a boy. The dream the gods gave him called for a son to follow him and to make fast the bright future for which he laboured now. With this she was content, but she knew she would be less than a woman truly in love not to have grieved in the dark stretches of night when she lay alone for that part of him which was forever beyond her understanding and cherishing.

Three nights later as she lay on the furs of her couch while the quiet of the valley was broken now and then by the call of nightjar and owl, Arturo and his companions raided the cavalry camp which lay a little off the Glevum road to the north of Corinium.

They had waited in the thick woods some miles from the camp, the woods which had once sheltered Arturo and the now dead horsetrader Volpax in the days when they had made horse stealing raids on the cavalry picket lines for mounts. They came down on it in the hour when sentries and guards yawn and rub their eyes and nod with sleep, when the fighting men off duty were filled with dreams or sunk in the lingering stupor of the past evening's wine and mead drinking, when the brazier fires of the picket watches along the horse lines burn low; and they came, spread wide across the heath and meadow land in a great front of two lines of horses shaped like a crescent moon. They bore down on the camp, with no shout or war cry, with only the pounding beat of hooves drumming the hard ground in a rolling tattoo of endless growing thunder. They came, the extended double rank of horses and warriors, sweeping from the north like the onward rush of a great tidal wave, fiercer and swifter than any of the great bores which from time to time swept up the broad channel of the not far distant Sabrina river, and they overwhelmed the camp in a wave of destruction. But no companion killed unless to protect his own life. Arturo had given this order for among his own men were many who had come to him from the Sabrina cavalry wing. They lit the heath and straw torches they carried from the picket fires and took flame to huts and brushwood stockades. They stampeded the picket lines, setting the hobbled and tethered Sabrina horses rearing and kicking and squealing with panic so that they broke free from their tethers to run or stumble or roll loose into the camp to add confusion to confusion. They fired corn sheds and stores and set ablaze the year's new hayricks and burst through the folding pens of sheep and cattle to send them stampeding into the night and the surrounding countryside from which — since town and country folk never hesitated to take the gifts the gods sent — less than a third of them were ever recovered. They swept round the great blue tent of the Praefectus of the Sabrina Wing (Praefectus because Count Ambrosius clung to the names and ranks of the old Roman formations) slashing the guy and straining ropes so that it collapsed like a stricken monster over the cavalry commander as he lay in his bed and trapped him there until long after the great crescent of Arturo's men and horse had wheeled at the far end of the camp and swept back and through the camp again as the fires of destruction now turned night to day. As they went the horns of the crescent curved more sharply inwards and the charge took ahead of it all loose and stray mounts herding them northwards into the night as booty.

They left behind them firmly planted in the earth, so that it was the first thing the Praefectus saw when he wormed his way out from under the loose tent cloth, a tall standard pole driven into the ground by Lancelo as he galloped by. From it in the freshening night breeze flew the banner of the White Horse, snow white and blood red, streaming in the wind. Tied to it was an old piece of vellum on which Arturo had written — in the Roman tongue as a touch of mockery to the imperial dreams of Ambrosious — this message:

Arturo and his Companions of the White Horse thank Count Ambrosius for the courtesy of his virtuous concern for the well-being of all those at the Villa of the Three Nymphs who do now humbly return it in somewhat fuller measure — Arturo, War Duke of Britain.

Later the following afternoon in the fortress at Glevum which was Ambrosius's headquarters the Praefectus of the Sabrina Wing stood stiff-faced before his commanding officer and watched him as he read the message. Ambrosius, wearing a red cloak over a well-polished cuirass, raised a hand and smoothed one of the greying wings of hair which tempered his growing baldness. After a

25

moment or two he lifted his head. From the large, severely lined face a pair of narrow-lidded faded blue eyes fixed the Praefectus coldly. He raised a hand and eased the cloak more comfortably on his left shoulder and then said in a quiet, bitter-edged voice, 'So, he calls himself Dux Bellorum. In jest or in earnest?'

'I know not, my lord.'

'And maybe neither does he. But no matter. He has made a fool of you, a laughing stock of the Sabrina Wing, and a mockery of me. More than that wherever men sit and drink and gossip, wherever pedlar or pack-man stops to beg crust or drink at farm or hovel, the story of this night's work will run and grow and grow and grow!' With each repetition of the word 'grow' he thumped the table before him angrily with his fist, his face stiff with anger.

'Maybe, my lord. But he should not live long to enjoy the pleasure of it. I wait but your order to take my men to the villa.'

Thumping his fist on the table Ambrosius almost shouted, 'You are a fool, Corbulo! By the time you get there he will be long gone. No, go back to Corinium and I wish you joy of the looks and laughter of the townsfolk — which you have well earned. Go!'

Without a word Praefectus Corbulo saluted

26

and left the room to seek the staff officers' quarters and the ease of a large goblet of wine which, whether earned or not, he badly needed.

Alone in his room Count Ambrosius picked up the tattered piece of vellum and read the message once more. Then slowly he began to smile to himself and shake his head. Dux Bellorum, he thought . . . and all the message in the Roman tongue. That at least was courtesy . . . By Mars, the man had spirit to match his courage and arrogance and he dreamed high. Well, that were no failing given the right schooling to go with it. What should he do? Smoke him out wherever he might now seek to lodge himself? Or let him run under whatever favour the gods might show him? And then use him? More and more men were beginning to be drawn to him. Did they sense that he had that divine afflatus, that magic which he himself had never known? Well, then why not let him run until his power and his followers had grown and then cut him down and step into his place, grieve for his loss, honour him in death, and then gather into his own command the army which he would have created . . . Aye, even leave his men the White Horse banner under which to fight for him still, every man going into battle knowing that his ghost rode ahead of them,

27

that his magic armoured and protected them still.

He reached forward and beat with his bare knuckles on the hanging gong which stood on the table. When the guard outside the room came he gave him an order. Then he rose and went to the window. Looking westward over the partly refurbished Glevum walls he could see a great loop of the Sabrina river and beyond the rise of the wooded hills that rose and died in the mist haze of summer, a mist that hid the mountains of Cymru . . . mountains and valleys which were full of fighting men who could be drawn across the Sabrina by a leader with the magic and appeal of an Arturo.

He turned as the guard came to the door and announced the Decurio Aulus Venutius, the troop commander of Ambrosius's personal mounted bodyguard, a Roman of full blood still although his family had been domiciled in Britain for eight generations, a proud young man who shared Ambrosius's imperial dreams and served him faithfully without questioning or seeking for the reasons behind any order given to him.

Ambrosius sat down while Venutius stood before him, a young man in his early thirties, sandy-haired, clean shaven, a pink and white complexion which the sun never affected, something a little plump and boyish about his face still, the pale jade-coloured eyes frank and marking a seeming guilelessness which masked, as Ambrosius knew well, a ruthless devotion to him and his aspirations. Venutius sensed — though no open words had ever been spoken between them about it — that his fate and the promise of future power and position would wax or wane with his master's. Like a good cavalry man he never questioned orders, nor would he tolerate any questioning of his own. He wore now a short off-duty white tunic waisted with a soft leather belt dyed blue with woad, the colour matching the neatly tied cavalry scarf about his neck, a pleasant-seeming young man who could be trusted under the greatest stress never to show the full truth of his real nature.

Gently Ambrosius said, 'You know my faith in you?'

'Yes, my commander.'

'Three nights from now you will desert from your command here in Glevum. You will take your horse and arms and ride south and find Arturo of the White Horse. You will join him as so many of the Sabrina Cavalry Wing have done. You will give him faithful and loyal service. Aye, if it comes to it you will die at his side in battle as any of his other companions would do. You will love and

29

honour and obey him in all things.'

'Yes, my commander.'

'All this you will do — until one comes to give you my wishes.' Ambrosius leaned back a little in his seat and felt beneath his toga for the belt which he wore around his under tunic. His hand came free from the belt pouch and he tossed on to the table between them a coin. It lay on the boards, shining dully in the sunlight which came through the window. 'Whoever comes will bring the coin with them so that you will know he comes from me. You will do whatever is ordered. And think not that my messenger will come only once. Time will show how long my need for an ally in Arturo's camp will last. But when that time is past you will come back to stand first at my right hand.'

'Yes, my commander.'

'Good. Take up the coin now and look at it for I would have you know it well.'

Venutius reached out and picked up the coin. He knew it already, though not in detail, for when Count Ambrosius was in counsel he often absently took it from his belt pouch and toyed with it as though the play of his fingers over it aided his thoughts and decisions. It was an aureas of the Emperor Hadrian, a gold coin much worn. Still clear on one side was the head of the great Emperor and on the other a seated goddess figure wearing a Phrygian cap and holding in her left hand an upright spear with the words — *Roma Aeterna* — encircling her, and the rim was marred in one place by a deep nick in the soft metal.

Venutius handed the coin back and said quietly, 'I shall remember it and wait for it, my commander.'

Ambrosius took the coin and, fingering it in thought for a moment, suddenly smiled, and said, 'Then go and become a good Companion.'

'Yes, my commander.'

Decurio Aulus Venutius saluted and left, and Ambrosius sat slowly fingering the gold coin of Hadrian and said quietly to himself, 'Rome Eternal . . . Rome Eternal . . . '

# The Camp above the Cam

Four days after the raid on the Sabrina cavalry camp they left the Villa of the Three Nymphs. They took with them the few cattle which had escaped slaughter and the small supply of food and grain which was left to them. The ruined crops, so near to the point of harvest, meant that they faced a lean winter. They loaded the wheeled carts and the few pack animals with the most vital and precious of their household and warfare gear. What they could not carry they left to the settlers and the people of the district who had befriended them. Arturo rode ahead with Durstan, his friend of the old Isca days who had been outlawed with him by Prince Gerontius, and Gelliga was left in command of the progress of the slow baggage train and the full complement of cavalry troops. Daria pressed to be allowed to ride ahead with Arturo but he forbade it. She was near four months gone with child and rode a quiet pony. When she tired of that, she was carried on one of the baggage carts and always close to her hand were her brother, Lancelo, and her father, Ansold.

They went south over the Tamesis river and then across the country of the headwaters of the Abona river which flowed through Aquae Sulis and finally found the sea at the mouth of the Sabrina estuary. They crossed the lands of the old Belgae tribes to reach the northern limits of the territory of the Durotriges. Here they swung sharply due west. As he rode Durstan smiled to himself for they were now retracing almost exactly the path he and Arturo had taken in the days when they had escaped from Isca Dumnoniorum after being outlawed by Gerontius.

He said now, 'This place you have chosen will bring you no favour with Gerontius, nor that of King Melwas of the Summerlands in whose country it lies.'

'We shall see. But since — no matter how remote it is at the moment — they both fear the threat of any Saxon approach from the East they will take some comfort from knowing that we stand first in their path.'

'It will be many a long day before the Saxons thrust so far West.'

Arturo smiled. 'Long days become long years. But well within our lifetime you will see it. The gods will favour them to give us the trial of proving our manhood and right to hold what is our own.'

'The gods have told you this?'

Unexpectedly Arturo grinned. 'They had no need. Hengist and the other Saxon leaders might now be content to sit and hold what they have south and east of Londinium and northwards along the Saxon shores — but each spring more of their countrymen arrive in their long keels. And they are land and plunder-hungry men. A bucket can only hold so much water. The Saxon bucket is almost full and must soon overspill.'

'This place we go to has already been marked by Gerontius. Your own father works on it still?'

Arturo shook his head. 'The work was hampered by Melwas. He wants no fortifications overlooking his country.'

'What greeting then can you expect from him?'

Arturo shrugged his shoulders. 'All those who stand against me — even in good conscience — must know that the gods are with us. All that is needed is courage and patience. The rest is in the hands of the gods.'

Durstan said no more. There was no man in the company of the Companions now who would say or argue more once Arturo said that the gods were with him. The gods of his country had Durstan's reverence but he sometimes wondered . . . aye, occasionally felt sure . . . that the will of Arturo was more often than not remote from any dictation of the gods. Arturo lived in a dream of his own creation, the great dream of a Britain freed from the faintest taint of Saxon intrusion. But, by the gods, one had to admit that once set on course there was no stopping him. The thought occurred to him that although — perhaps unknowingly — Arturo took the name of the gods in vain they looked kindly on his presumption and, so far, had given him their favour.

Late in the afternoon of the fourth day of their travel they came to the borderlands of the Summerlands held by King Melwas. Here the country was gentler. For the most part men worked their plots in peace, game was plentiful and when the gods gave good harvest only the improvident had to pull the drawstrings of their trew tops tight in winter to still their bellies' grumbles. But the roads were still broken and ruined for the days were long past since the last Roman *mensor* travelled them with a surveying detachment of legionaries to keep them in good state by the enforcement of local labour. Men now used the old tracks and ridgeways and the ancient pathways over down and through deep forest. Long before sunset they reached the edge of the smooth downland and following it saw slowly rise from the green country ahead a great hill which stood on its own in a sweeping bight of the downs. A long loop of a river called the Cam curved around the foot of its westward flanks to run away to the north through the heart of the Summerlands on its way to the Sabrina sea. They rode up the mount, following a track from the north-east, through the thin skirting of trees around its base. Finally they came out on to the great ridge-backed plateau of its crest, the whole of whose perimeter was enclosed by a triple line of ancient earthworks and ramparts long neglected and falling into ruin.

On the top of the plateau ridge, where stood the remains of a Roman shrine to the god Mars, raised there to mark the conquest of the hill fort by the westward thrust of the legions when they had first come to the country over five hundred years before, Arturo and Durstan sat their horses, slacking their reins so that the mounts lowered their heads and grazed the sweet grass. To the north-west lay the Summerlands, the country of King Melwas. In the still lucid light of early evening they could pick out the green slopes of Ynys-witrin, the glass isle, at whose foot Melwas had his summer quarters for he delighted in the abundance of game and fish which filled the rivers, streams and meres and the wide spread of marshlands. And far beyond the glass isle, backed by the sun sparkle on the waters of the sea, there stood up, too, the great knoll of the raven god Bran.

That night, as Durstan slept rolled in his heavy cloak, Arturo kept watch with Anga at his side, and he was full of content. This hill above the river Cam would serve all his wants for some time to come. The plateau too was large enough to house more men and horses than he would have under his command for a long time to come. There was room too for the growing of crops and the building of shelters for which there was plenty of timber to be cut from the steeply wooded western side of the hill. For water there were two spring-fed wells, one within the perimeter and the other a little way down the slope on the north-east side. As he sat there listening to the call of a little owl from the wooded slope and the steady cropping sound of the hobbled horses as they grazed in the warm night, he knew that the coming winter would be hard, and made harder if he found turned against him the anger of Prince Gerontius and King Melwas. They could harry and plague him at a time when the real hardships up here would be hunger and the fast need for warm quarters. There was nothing he could do to appease Gerontius, but the Prince would never move against him into

King Melwas's lands unless Melwas gave leave. The first thing he had to do was to make some sort of peace with the King — and a man who came suing for peace, no matter for how short a period, must bear gifts and the promise of more. The main body of the Companions would not arrive for at least another three days. The peace must be made before they arrived. To ride with only Durstan as companion to King Melwas was to offer the man the chance of treachery. Chewing on a sweet grass stalk he considered the wisdom of this move. Should he wait for his people to come and then lodge here in open contempt of Melwas or should he sweeten the man by riding without companions to seek his peace? As he pondered this the sky to the north-west was suddenly and fiercely afire with the burning streamer of a falling star which curved earthwards and finally burnt itself away high over the summit of Ynys-witrin. Without doubt he knew that the gods had spoken.

They rode into Ynys-witrin the next morning over the long causeway which spanned the marshes at its foot and were halted by the guard at the stockade which blocked the entrance to the small settlement. Arturo asked for an audience with King Melwas. A messenger was sent to the King and after a long delay — deliberately prolonged, Arturo was sure, to stamp upon them his authority and power — they were conducted through the settlement to the edge of a wide mere on whose bank had been built of withy poles and rush thatch a long hall which Melwas used as his hunting lodge. Children played and frolicked about the water's edge and a guard of long-haired, half-naked marsh warriors armed with swords and spears formed a half circle about a rough wooden table outside the hall. Here Melwas sat, bareheaded, the sun firing the red tints in his fair hair, wearing a short cloak of otter skins across his shoulders, his chest, tanned brown, bare to the top of his trews. The man wore no finery, and carried no mark of kingship; a man who had twice Arturo's age, a man powerfully built with a large, pock-marked face, whose eyes were hidden as he bent over a fishing net spread on the table and his fingers worked skilfully with waxed thread repairing a hole in it.

Arturo and Durstan dismounted and Arturo, standing at the head of the White One who blew gently through her nostrils not liking the smell of rotting fish and offal that came from the midden at the nearby water's edge, dropped a hand and touched Anga's head, as the hound, sensing some stress in the air, began to growl low and deep in its throat. The growling stopped at Arturo's touch and Melwas raised his head to show grey-green eyes, the skin about them deeply creased from years of sun glare on the waters and marshes of the Summerlands.

Unexpectedly Melwas smiled and said, 'So at last I meet Arturo of the White Horse, son of Baradoc, outlaw of Prince Gerontius, thorn in the side of Count Ambrosius and — ' his tongue flicked between his lips like a lapping cat's — 'the scourge of the Eastern long-keel men. All these to so many. And what are you to me?'

'One who comes in friendship and asks for sanctuary on the hill above the Cam until such time as I can turn against the Saxons again.'

'And if I refuse, and hold you now to send to Prince Gerontius?'

Arturo smiled. 'Would I have come, King Melwas, had that thought held truth in my mind?'

'But it may be the truth in my mind.'

Arturo shook his head. 'No, for last night the gods spoke to me and gave sign that I should come to you. I could have stayed on the hill until my company arrived and defied you — but I am here and make you the gift of friendship.' Arturo stepped forward, ignoring

40

the tensing of the Melwas warriors who stood around, and drew from within his surcoat a cloth bundle which he put on the table before King Melwas. He unwrapped it to display the gifts he had brought, all of it plunder taken from the Saxons; an old Roman gold chain, two bronze arm bands with their bosses intricately worked in enamels that flashed with kingfisher brilliance, a silver ring fashioned in the form of a snake, its coils studded with small emeralds and its eyes two bright rubies and, last of all, a small bronze wine flagon whose handle was shaped in the form of a hunting dog which stalked a pair of finely modelled duck which adorned the spout. It was no surprise to Arturo when Melwas picked up the flagon first and ran his fingers over the moulding of the dog and the ducks.

Melwas looked up at Arturo and his eyes were suddenly shrewd beneath their busy, sandy brows. 'Fine gifts . . . aye. Well then, you shall have my leave to stay on the hill if you add to them one other.' He glanced from Arturo to Anga who sat on his haunches at his side, and went on, 'Two days ago I lost my best hound to a boar. Give your hound the word to come to me and serve me and, even though Gerontius and Ambrosius give me commands and threats to deny you winter

41

sanctuary, I will defy them. *Aie* . . . give me the hound and you can take back these other gifts.'

For a moment or two Arturo said nothing. The noisy, happy cries of the children bathing and playing by the mere filled the air. A heron flapped low and clumsily across the water and at his side Anga snapped at a bluebottle which teased his muzzle. Then slowly shaking his head Arturo said, 'No, my lord. There are three things which the gods deny any man the right to gift to another, a virtuous wife, a horse which was the first to carry him into battle, and a hound which would stay by his dead body till death for itself gave it release to follow him into the Shades. No, my lord — you ask too much.'

Melwas was silent for a while and then, with a shrug of his shoulders, he said indifferently, 'Then my young warrior, Arturo, it seems that the gods have betrayed you and have sent you here to rid themselves of you.' He raised his right hand and pointed his forefinger at Arturo. With the movement, each of the men in the half circle about him lifted his spear and held it poised ready to throw. Melwas went on, 'They wait but one word from me.'

Arturo dropped a hand so that it rested on Anga's head and he answered in a level voice,

'There may come a day when the gods will desert me, King Melwas. But this is not the day. Give the word and you shall see the spears turned aside from me in full flight.'

Melwas's lips tightened and his brows almost hooded his eyes as he faced Arturo's defiance, then suddenly he gave a great shout of laughter and smacked the table before him with his fist and cried, laughing, 'Lower your hackles, you fighting cock. You think I would tempt the wrath of the gods by the death of one they love so much? But know this, for a hound such as yours I would trade any of my wives — though to be fair none of them are virtuous. The hill is yours and we will drink to it.' He turned and shouted to his womenfolk who stood bunched about the doorway of the long hall to bring wine and at this his bodyguard lowered their spears.

As they rode back to the hill fortress through the early afternoon Durstan said to Arturo, 'The gods were truly with you.'

Arturo nodded 'As they always are. But also a man has his own wits. Gifts are made freely as we gave our plunder. But no man of pride names the gift he wants. The mind of Melwas was open to read. He did but follow a humour to test me.'

Durstan said no more. Close though he

was to Arturo, the first of the companions, he knew that there would never be any man with a true reading of his nature. Well, it would be a story to tell the others when they arrived, and in his mind he began to hear the telling as he would give it . . . nay, sing it, for it deserved the rise and fall of rhythm and the stamp of rhyme. Arturo and the Spears of Melwas The spears that were thrown only to be miraculously turned aside in mid-air by the gods . . . when the mead flowed the stamp of feet and thumping of fists on the boards would set the wonder alive to spread through all the land long after all that lived today were dead and dust.

★　★　★

Within the week the full company had arrived at the hill and every daylight hour was spent in establishing itself there. Trees were felled to make living quarters, stables and cattle pens. Furrows were turned to make crop strips across the gentler slopes of the hilltop and the little of seed corn left was sown. They cut late hay and carted it from the free land to the south and each day game was hunted along the downs and river valleys for fresh meat and also for salting against the winter. Deer, boar and small herds of escaped or abandoned kine, swine and sheep roamed in the woods and heaths.

There was a small settlement of King Melwas's people nearby and Arturo gave strict orders that none of them was to be molested nor the goods or cattle taken. As the weeks passed traders and pedlars were to learn of the camp on the hill above the Cam and found that they could come and go freely to offer their wares. But even so, it was clear that the winter would bring lean times. Leave was given to any man who asked to go back to his own people so long as he returned well before spring. Few asked for most preferred to tighten their belts and stay with Arturo. If there were any doubts in Arturo's mind about the near starvation they would have to face as the months passed he showed none of it. The future was in the hands of the gods and there would be no favours from them for any man who doubted their powers. And already the gods were on their side for warriors hearing of the camp began to drift to them and most of them came carrying a grain or roots sack across their horses' backs. But of all the men who gathered to him Arturo was most content with the first to ride up the hill only a few days after his company had come to rest there. This was Decurio Aulus Venutius, the commander of Ambrosius's personal mounted bodyguard.

He was escorted to Arturo by Gelliga who still could hardly believe that such a high ranking Sabrina officer should choose to join them. Arturo was sitting on a rock outside the rough shelter which had quickly been made for himself and Daria. Daria, refusing to over-cherish herself, was away with some of the other women gathering hazel nuts from the hill slopes to be ground into flour for the winter.

When Gelliga had left them taking Venutius's horse to be watered and fed in the lines, Arturo said, 'And what brings Aulus Venutius to my side?'

The plumpish, fresh-complexioned face of the man creased into a smile. 'Aulus Venutius grew tired of being barrack-bound and bodyguard to Count Ambrosius. I am a cavalry man and, like my horse, have grown stale and restless for the need of action.'

'All I can give you here is a tight-belted winter of hard and cold lying.'

Venutius shrugged his shoulders. 'After the winter comes the spring. I am tired of keeping sword and armour bright for ceremonial parades.'

'No matter your rank in Glevum you will serve here as a trooper.'

'That will be no hardship. There are many

here who have known me as such. Although I am of full Roman blood this is my country and my family have served it faithfully for many generations. I have no more love for the Saxons than you, my lord.'

'You know the mind of Count Ambrosius and the working of his thoughts?'

'Yes, my lord.'

'Then we will talk about this soon. But for now go to Gelliga and he will assign you to a troop and your duties.'

That night, as Arturo lay by Daria's side in the darkness, she said, 'Your Venutius gives up a good deal to come here. Your name and your force grow. Ambrosius could have sent him.'

'All things are possible. But had I been Ambrosius I would have sent someone of lesser rank and importance.'

'Maybe that is how Ambrosius has reasoned.'

'Then I will keep that in my mind too.'

Smiling to herself Daria went on, 'Maybe the gods will give you a sign to prove him faithful.'

Arturo laughed gently. 'They have no need for I have already decided to put him to the test. If he comes to kill me — and what else could Ambrosius wish? — then he shall have his chance, and soon.'

Four days later on a day of great heat, as though summer were making a last gesture in defiance of the onthrust of autumn, Arturo rode down from the hill to the river Cam with a party of men to set osier traps in the river to take the eels which with the coming of autumn were now beginning to run seawards. He took with him Venutius. When he had seen the men set to their work Arturo rode up the river to a spot where it broadened into a wide pool, its far side thickly matted with tall mace reeds and beyond them a tangled scrub growth of willows and thorns.

Pulling up the White One Arturo nodded at the pool and said to Venutius, 'It is too long since I had a proper washing.' He dismounted and began to strip free his clothes. 'Keep guard on me.'

Naked he dived into the pool and swam for a while. Then he came back to stand below the bank where he reached to the pool bed and began to scrub himself with handfuls of sand and small gravel as he had used to do in the moor streams of his own tribelands in the far west. Above him Venutius sat his horse, sword hanging from his belt and his long cavalry lance held upright, and said, 'In Glevum the Roman baths are still in use for as far as he can Count Ambrosius keeps all the old observances.'

Arturo laughed as he stepped naked out of the water and began to dry himself on his under shirt. 'Aye . . . but he puts the cart before the horse. First there must be fighting to bring peace — then with peace a man has a just need for comforts.' As he spoke — naked and defenceless, an easy mark for the swift dipping and thrust of Venutius's lance, a quick heart blow and then an easy escape for the man — he heard Anga snap at a worrying fly and his eyes held his companion's.

Green and guileless were Venutius's eyes as they watched Arturo and he said, 'The wound in your side, my lord, has healed clean. Is it true it came from your uncle Inbar?'

'It is. He was a man of many parts, courage and craft and greed. The gods twisted his nature at birth.' He turned away from Venutius and bent to recover his clothes, knowing that he was fair mark for a swift downward thrust of the lance to spit him through the heart if the nature of this man, too, had been twisted at birth But no thrust came.

As they rode away and began to breast the rising ground to return to the camp Durstan, bow in hand, the arrow still strung in it ready for use, stepped free of the scrub on the far side of the pool and watched them. His brow was beaded with sweat but not from the heat of the day. One muscle movement of Venutius's spear arm and the arrow would have been winging towards him . . . *Aie*, but even so, the risk had been great. He could hear Arturo saying, 'If he raises his lance and your hands are not steady and the arrow flies not true — then the gods are no longer with me.'

That night as they lay together Arturo told Daria of the testing of Venutius, and she said, 'And you mean to try him no further?'

'No. To do so would be to doubt the gods. If he is here for mischief it is not against my person. Maybe he comes to read my mind and plans and then to return to Ambrosius. But I think not.'

A month later, when the first of the fierce autumn gales blew hard to set the browning tree leaves spinning and flighting through the air and the first prick of green from the winter corn began to stipple the worked soil of the crop strips, a party of pedlars and traders came into the camp to barter their salt and seed and cloths and their leather hides and rough pottery wares for the few young foals already dropped by the mares of the cavalry mounts and the little that now remained in the companions' war-chest of their Saxon plunder. Venutius, who had been made horse-master and put in command of the fodder stores for all the cavalry mounts — and was proving hard and demanding of any companion who grew idle or careless over the care of his beast — was wrapping a dressing of strong herbs over a festering cut in the right forehock of a stallion. As he squatted at his task he heard someone come up behind him and glancing over his shoulder saw one of the pedlars. He gave the man a nod and bent again to his task. The pedlar stood watching him until he had finished his work and then, as Venutius faced him, smiled, and said, 'The bellies of horses and companions will be full of loud grumblings before this winter is out.'

Venutius grinned. 'Maybe, but the remedy is tight belts, tight girths and a patient notching away of the days to spring.'

Looking down the picket line of horses the pedlar, who was middle-aged, thick-bearded and warmly clad in a heavy woollen surcoat over strong leather trews, said, 'It is known that you have more mounts than men. I have done well this year and have a mind to change from shank's pony to a good beast to carry me comfortably. Sell me one of your spare mounts and I will pay well.'

Venutius laughed and shook his head. 'We part with nothing but the foals . . . aye, and with those reluctantly.'

The pedlar said, 'I can pay you in coin which will buy you corn and fodder to keep a dozen horses from dying through winter lack.'

As he spoke he reached into the wallet of his surcoat belt and flicked a coin through the air for Venutius to catch. Looking down at it Venutius's face stiffened as he saw the sun-glitter rise from the golden face of the aureus of the Emperor Hadrian, one edge of which was deeply nicked. Then, without a word he tossed it back to the pedlar. They faced one another in silence while about them the air was full of the sound of the bartering going on in the camp. A horse whinnied high, and there was a sudden bright burst of laughter from a handful of the few women who still stayed with their men in the camp. For a few seconds it was in Venutius's mind that he could have wished that he had come to the companions as a free man for he had grown to admire and respect the spirit of them all. He said sharply, 'Speak that which you have come to speak!'

The pedlar, scratching at his thick beard, said, 'The lady Daria carries the child of Arturo. He longs for a boy and, if it is true the gods favour him, then it will be a boy.'

'Boy or girl, what matters it to Count Ambrosius which she drops?'

'I am not in his counsels. Like you I do his bidding. But his mind is not difficult to read sometimes.' He waved his hand around the hill top. 'This is a beginning. Come spring Arturo will move again and more men will come to him and suddenly a handful of deserters becomes an army. Armies have leaders, and given enough victories the leaders become kings. Kings have sons so their deaths solve no problems when a line of inheritance is secure. When Arturo dies — ' he winked, ' — god-willed or Ambrosius-willed — then our noble Count would have none alive with right to claim his place.'

'Then why not have Arturo killed now — before there is any army to win victories?'

The pedlar shook his head. 'Even a simple man like me can read that riddle to its end. At this moment Count Ambrosius knows that none of the tribes and their leaders will fully rally to him. His military caution offers them no glories, no plunder — only drills and exercises and, for the most part, the irksome rub of camp life. Warriors will not come to him, and those he has grow rebellious and many desert him. But if he lets Arturo run until all this country knows his name and the bards sing the renown of his victories . . . You do not see it? Then there is a rich tree in full bearing to be cut down for the fine ripe harvest of its fruit to be easily gathered. Aye . . . he will mourn Arturo and praise him — and then take his place for there will be no son to follow him. Believe me — Count Ambrosius will let no woman, be she wife or concubine, come to full term with any child seeded by him.' As he finished speaking he felt again in his wallet and pulled out a small alabaster amphora no larger than a pigeon's egg, its top thickly sealed with green wax, and handed it to Venutius. 'Guard it well, and when the right moment comes — which must be soon for the lady Daria is already, so 'tis said and so her belly shows, near six months gone — see that the liquid it holds goes into her wine or water beaker. It has neither taste nor true colour.'

'To kill the child but not the mother?'

For a moment the pedlar frowned, puzzled at what he took for the other's stupidity — or naivety. He said shortly, 'Why kill the foal and leave the mare to be served again? Both will die, but slowly so that it will have the look of nature.'

Venutius was silent, his lips tight. He had known that at any time he might have been ordered to assassinate Arturo and save himself as best as he could. A sharp coil of disgust tightened his guts at the thought of becoming poisoner of a mother and child.

He said, 'And this being done I will stay at Arturo's side?'

The pedlar, though he gave no sign of his thoughts, wondered at the innocence of Venutius's thinking, and doubted whether Count Ambrosius had made a good choice of this spy in the camp of the companions. He said, 'You would leave when she is dead and so sharpen all men's minds to the truth? No, Venutius, you are bound to Arturo for many a long year. You will become one of the noblest and most fearless of the companions. Aye, in truth you will come to love Arturo as a brother and when you kill him you will truly grieve him, but the tides of time will slowly wash away the stains of your dishonour. Believe me, it is so, for I have known many men, myself not least among them, who have passed through the sad vale of self-disgust and found high fortune or great command a quick balm to ease the raw bite of a troubled conscience.'

He raised a hand in parting and moved away into the heart of the crowded camp to join the other traders. Venutius slipped the amphora into his tunic breast and as the sick horse turned its head and nuzzled at his shoulder he put up a hand and gently stroked its muzzle, relishing the softness of its skin under his palm and the sweet body smell of

55

its sleek hide in his nostrils. So be it, he thought. Until this moment he had never truly known himself. But now the truth was locked firmly in his heart. He was a man whom the Fates had fingered. He prayed then that in the turbulent times ahead he might find honourable and gallant death in battle and so never know the shame of seeing the aureus of the Emperor Hadrian again.

Two weeks later he poured the liquid from the amphora into Daria's drink. The ease with which he was able to do it he felt might have been arranged by the dark gods. It was a night when he was guard commander, a night of sharp frost and a cloudless sky which blazed with bright stars. As he made his rounds in the late evening, he could hear the singing of some of the companions in the open hall which lay beyond the ridge of the plateau. He picked out the sweet voice of Durstan and the lusty bellow of Gelliga and, suddenly at some bawdy turn in the song, the high, neighing laughter of Lancelo. He knew and loved them all now, troopers and troop commanders, hard men, many of whom, since there were too few shelters to roof them all, wrapped themselves in their cloaks and slept in the open or huddled close packed under skin-covered lean-tos.

As he moved from post to post along the

perimeter he felt the soft rub of the leather pouch, hung by a thong around his neck, against his breast. In it was the small amphora. As he crossed the far neck of the plateau from high above him came the distant calling of geese and he looked up and saw the wedge-shaped skein of flying birds against the great stippling of stars. He moved on and spoke briefly to the guard who kept watch at the foot of the small rocky rise on which Arturo's quarters had been built.

The guard, a stocky tribesman, bow-legged from riding almost before he could walk, was from the country of the Ordovices far south of Segontium. Looking up at the geese he said, 'By morning, they could be harbouring on the flats of the Tisobis river where I have taken many of them with bow and arrow as they cropped the eel grass.'

Venutius smiled. 'You would you were there now?'

'Nay, my commander, not for my sake.' He grinned and leaned on his lance. 'But for my wife's, yes. A woman needs a man to keep her warm at nights. Cold nights try a woman's virtue hard.'

Venutius laughed and moved on. As he came to the front of Arturo's hut a figure, heavily cloaked, moved out of the doorway and he recognized the lady Daria.

He saluted her and said, 'You should be warmly asleep, my lady.'

Daria smiled and said, 'So I should, good Venutius, except for two things. There is too much noise from the men's hall and I have a raging thirst from the salt meat at table this night.' Her hand lifted to show him a bronze beaker. 'I go to the spring.'

Venutius reached out for the beaker and said, 'You stay here, my lady. This is no time, for you to be scrambling down the path.'

Without waiting for a reply, not wanting to see the starshine in her dark eyes, he turned away. As he stood at the thin overflow from the small well he pulled out his breast pouch and took from it the amphora. With his knife he cut off the wax stopper and then pierced the tough goatskin cover of the amphora's mouth. He filled the beaker and then poured the liquid from the amphora into it. He turned back to the path to the hut and felt his teeth clench tight and his face muscles stiffen as he drove from himself all thought.

Daria took the beaker from him and drank. She paused with the beaker half empty, gave a little sigh of contentment and said, 'You come from Glevum, don't you?'

'I do, my lady.'

She gave a soft chuckle. 'Once Arturo said to me that one day he would ride into

Glevum in triumph and I should ride beside him on a white mare wearing a cloak of scarlet with a lining of blue silk and about my waist a golden belt with a clasp of two singing birds, and that Count Ambrosius should come out to greet us and hand me a silver goblet full of new wine.' She raised the beaker and drank, finishing the water, and then went on, 'You warriors throw your promises about as lightly as you venture your lives.'

Venutuius shook his head. 'My lord Arturo breaks a given promise to no one. When the day comes you shall ride so beside him.'

Daria's white teeth shone in the starlight as she laughed and said, 'Aye, that I shall, my kind Venutius — for I shall remind him.'

Gone from her, Venutius finished his round of the camp sentries and then went back in the shelter of the little lean-to of hazel poles and bracken thatch he had long made for himself. He put the amphora between two cloths and with the heavy pummel of his sword smashed it into chips which he flung out into the night. He did all this as he had done everything from the moment he had taken the beaker to fill from Daria without thought or emotion, his heart and mind frozen.

That night as Arturo lay at Daria's side and her breath warmed the side of his face she took his hand and placed it below her breasts and said, 'Feel, the child moves.' Underneath his hand he felt the faint kick of his son. Aye . . . son it had to be for certain. Placing her hand over his Daria went on, teasingly, 'It will be another mouth to feed this winter but there shall be no lack for the babe for already I begin to grow as well-stored as the finest milch cow.'

'But lack there will be for all others, you think?'

'There must be. We are here without full corn bins or pits well stored with smoked fish or meat. The time will come and,' her voice changed to a serious note, 'I say this, my lord, because you will not say it to yourself — when horses will be put to the slaughter and men, before they will starve, will leave you for their homelands or to forage for themselves.'

Arturo stirred angrily and said, 'None shall starve and none shall so leave. We have come here under the gods who turned aside the spears of Melwas to name this our sanctuary. Tight belts we shall have, but for the rest the gods will provide. It is written.'

Daria said no more, but she smiled in the darkness to herself. It was written. The gods had spoken. Always it had been so with him and always would it be so, and his belief suddenly warmed her with a sweet flush of love so that she slid her hand about his neck and pressed her lips to his and made silent prayer to her own God that out of His charity the child she carried should be a son.

★ ★ ★

Two weeks later, when the sun rose to show the hilltop covered with a first and thin fall of early snow, Daria woke to find her body heavy with a lassitude which with the passing of the days was to grow to a weakness that finally held her to her couch and slowly began to waste her body. Within a month she was dead, passing away with her hand in Arturo's as the first owl-call of night echoed through the wood on the western slope of the hill. They cut a deep grave for her in a dell of the hillside, bowered by young beeches which still held their brown leaves against the winter gales. Pasco the priest spoke the burial rites of her own religion and old Ansold, her father, and Lancelo, her brother, filled the grave, and after them the companions piled stones and rocks to a cairn over her while all the time Arturo stood by with his face graven and speaking no word. When all was done Arturo turned and took the reins of the White One being held by Durstan. He mounted and rode slowly away down the hill, followed by Anga, armed but unprovisioned. None doubted that he would return, and a few like Pasco and old Ansold and some of the older companions moved with him in spirit for they knew that with the death of true love a man must move for a while into the wilderness and seek solitude before he can return to the world and live again.

# The Return to Isca

It was five days before Arturo returned. He came back leaner and with his beard grown matted and shaggy and with a hard, tempered look in his blue eyes which he was never to lose even when making merry with his companions, a look which, when he wished, seemed to throw an icy veil between himself and all others and, when it was there, make all men choose their words to him with care. Only when he laughed and played with children or spoke to the camp women did the look become remote. And on his return he began to organize the camp for the winter ahead with a grim and inflexible ordering of life on the hill which none questioned and none ever evaded. The daily mess issues were cut to a point where no porridge bowl was left until licked clean and no bone tossed to a hound until it had been picked bare and the marrow sucked from it. The dogs foraged for themselves and as the game around the hill grew scarcer so dogs and men foraged wider afield, the hunting parties often being away for days on end. Only the horses were treated with a more generous hand.

Every night before Arturo went to his bed in the hut on the rocky outcrop of the plateau he would walk with Anga to the head of the small dell which held Daria's grave. He would sit with Anga beside him and his eyes seldom left the rock-piled cairn. There was no inner rebellion in him against the bereavement which had been placed on him. He understood it and accepted it. The gods had gifted him and great things lay ahead of him. In return they had schooled him with this loss less there should have arisen in him any unwarranted arrogance or presumptuous pride to make him forget that he and all those he loved and cherished were mortal.

By the turn of the year the camp was a place of lean men, lean women and lean children and of rib-straked horses. Prayers and hopes for a mild winter went unfulfilled for the snows came early and stayed and the nights were either clear with iron frost or wild with the blanketing and drifting of snow. In the mornings crows and owls could be found dead and frozen stiff to their perches and the river Cam was quietened by a covering of thick ice. These were mornings when men, women and children found it no shame to gather the fresh dung in the horse lines and wrapping it in old cloths hugged it under their clothes to their bare bellies to give them heat and the false relief of food warmth in their guts. None, not even the hardiest, washed their bodies, and hair and beards were let grow long to protect faces and necks from the white patching of frost bite. Men and women in the sharp unending agony of cold and hunger called on their gods and goddesses for help, to Belenus and Dagda and Lug, the fair-haired one, to Nodens of the Silver Hand, to Taurus the bull, Epona the horse, to Artio the bear, to Cernunnos the stag and to Dis, the god of the underworld, from whom all mankind had descended — all those, that is, who were true to their country's gods. For the followers of Christos prayers were made to Him and His Father. And Pasco, the outcast priest of the divided heart and faith, called on them all for he knew that all were one and the same God.

In the middle of the first month of the new year when, in a night sky of pale ice-blue, the moon was passing to full and Orion's great belt hung high near the meridian, Lancelo came to Arturo's hut where he sat outside, cloak-wrapped, before retiring. It was near midnight and a bitter wind was sweeping across the hill, whirling spinning snow devils low across the ground, and now and again from the wooded slopes there came the clear cracking of some frost-split branch or tree trunk.

Lancelo, who next to Durstan could speak most informally to Arturo, said, 'I have just made the round of the sentry posts. Cuneda is dead. He was lying where he fell — struck through the heart by the cold.'

For a while Arturo said nothing. Cuneda had been one of the companions who had joined him at Pontes when he had been making his great progress to Londinium. He was from Lactodorum in the land of the Catuvellauni, a man of forty, built like an ox, black-bearded but without a hair on his head. Just as the winter's killing frost could rive the stoutest oak so had sturdy Cuneda been riven. That there would be others he had no doubt. The gods were testing him. Daria had been taken because they were jealous of his love for her, wanting him single-minded in his great resolve to restore freedom and greatness to this country. For him there would be no woman in his life until he had proved himself — and none ever that could truly take Daria's place in his heart. So would be the loss of any of the tried companions who stood with him now on this bitter, winter-plagued hill, these men of courage and similar vision to his own. Their going would mark his spirit with a grief which he could never know in same full

66

sorrow for any of those who would take their place and swell the ranks of the army to come. He said:

'Bury him in the beech dell.'

'The ground is iron and will not yield.'

'Take iron to iron. The gods have his spirit. The wolves and foxes shall not feast on his proud heart or bones.'

'It shall be so, my lord.' Lancelo was silent for a time and then went on, 'No man living can remember a winter like this. A man on his own or with wife and child would fare better in his homelands or tribal town.'

'Have they asked to leave?'

'No, my lord. They would die first. But if you gave the word . . . '

Arturo stern-faced said, 'The gods are with us and in the time of our greatest want they will provide. No battle is lost until the standard falls. When the moment of cruellest pinch-belly comes you will see . . . the gods will send us a winter harvest. But any who wishes is free to leave.'

Going back to the companions Lancelo said to them wryly, 'Without leave from you I have spoken to Arturo about our state here. He says two things. Any who asks is free to leave and seek warmth and food elsewhere. Against this the gods have told him that at our moment of greatest need they will turn winter want to summer bounty. The trees shall fruit, the corn shall grow and ripen overnight, the wild duck shall fly in and lay their eggs for us and then submit to killing and roasting. The gentle does shall climb the hill to be slaughtered and the white hares lollop to our cooking places and wait their turn to take the pot — '

Durstan gave a great roar of laughter. 'My mouth waters. And who would miss such a time? Have I not seen the spears of Melwas turned aside? Why then miss the sight of the sky clouded with quail and pigeon falling ready plucked and drawn to the waiting cauldrons?'

When the laughter died Lancelo said soberly, 'Who would ask to leave?'

Speaking for all of them black-bearded Gelliga from Lavobrinta in the country of the Ordovices said firmly, 'There is no leaving for any of us except by the hard road already taken by Cuneda.'

So the next morning they took mattock, pick and spade and before the early sunset reddened the sky above distant Ynyswitrin they buried Cuneda alongside Daria and raised a cairn of ice-coated rocks above him and Pasco who knew him for a Christos man commended his soul to the mercy of God.

Within the next three weeks a woman died

in childbirth, and another companion, wrapped in wolf skins and huddled deep in a bed of bracken under his lean-to shelter, died in his sleep. The same night, a roving lone wolf broke into camp and attacked the horse lines and, before it was killed by a spear thrust from Venutius, so badly mauled a bay stallion that the beast had to be killed and so provided meat for the pot for a handful of days. When the last of the horse meat was gone, the snows came again to lay a fresh mantle over the pocked and broken surface of the old snow and ice on the plataeau top. Venutius, thinking of the winter quarters of Ambrosius at Glevum with its glowing charcoal braziers and the hypocausts at full heat warming floor and wall ducts, knew that although all contentment was for ever denied him he was nearer to it here than he ever could be elsewhere. The gods had truly marked him and that day on which he gave death to Arturo — far ahead though it might be — would also bring him the dark comfort of death at his own hand. But in these days he was a true companion, eating and drinking less than his meagre share and giving all his care and concern to the horses.

After the snow the days were clear and bright as though the sword-sharp sweep of the frosty air had forever purged the skies of all cloud. Hunger and cold each day took toll of some living thing on the hill, a hound, a child, a woman, a camp servant and, twice, a companion. Although Arturo by word and manner held them firm and denied the death of hope and confidence, he hid the growing heaviness of spirit within himself until it could be borne no longer. There was no trial the gods could put on him which he would not accept. But the death and misery of others now defeated him.

He called Durstan and Lancelo to him and said, 'Tell the others that I go away for two or three days. When I return it will be with plenty for all.'

After a moment or two of surprise from them both, Lancelo said, 'You journey where, my lord?'

Arturo answered, 'To seek the charity of the gods. They have tried us hard and for my part, could try me harder. I take no shame in becoming supplicant to them for others.' He smiled and there was a swift glint of his old teasing spirit in his eyes so that Durstan at least knew that what was to follow would be no truth. 'Last night I dreamt that the gentle goddess Coventina spoke to me and said, 'Since great things are destined for you and your pride grows stiff and iron-bound I tell you for the sake of the others with you that

70

the gods wait for you to become a humble beggar. Before they grant you a kingdom you must come begging for a crust'.'

'You ride alone?' asked Lancelo.

'Yes.'

'And where?'

'I shall give the White One loose rein and the gods will govern her going.'

For a moment Durstan would have spoken. Always the nearest to Arturo he could read him in a way hidden from all the others. There would be no loose rein, he knew, for Arturo would head for Ynys-witrin and ask for charity from Melwas and the answer of Melwas no man could predict. He kept his own counsel. But one thing he knew, and knew, too, the cost to Arturo's spirit and pride, was that to go a-begging to either gods or men was to diminish his own manhood.

When the White One was saddled Arturo led her, slithering and slipping, down the steep hill path for none could dare it mounted, and with him went the now ageing Anga, gaunt-framed, and his coat staring with hunger-roughness.

At the bottom of the hill Arturo mounted and gave the mare slack rein so that she moved towards the river, but Arturo knew that soon the reins would come firmly into command of his hands for indeed he knew no other place to go nor other charity to seek than that of Melwas, and knew, too, that all the king's people would be on tight belly-strings for this winter had spared no one, and knew further that if the gods gave him any bounty there would never again be woman or child in any camp or army train of his. A man could gnaw the ice-cold ash bark in winter . . . *Aie,* and even take a handful of earth to his mouth and cud it for comfort, but women and children were gentler creatures. For each dead mother and child that lay on the hill he grieved because their death and misery before death came from his own arrogance in not forcibly sending them away in good time with their men. Light-headed a little from his own deprivation it seemed to him now that gentle Coventina had truly spoken to him in a dream for her heart had been moved where his had remained untouched . . .

As they reached the Cam, he took the reins firmly and turned the mare's head down-stream and he knew that all these troubles came from the sacking of the Villa of the Three Nymphs, where all could have lodged without lack this winter. One day Count Ambrosius should be given back in double score the misery and loss which he had heaped on the companions . . . And so he rode on towards Ynys-witrin knowing that he would get from Melwas not even a handful of oats enough to make a bowl of porridge. For this he could make no grudge against the king. A man must look after his own people when want held the land as hard and iron-fast as did the snow and frost.

A white-coated hare got up from the frost-rimed sedges at the river's edge and moved wearily away over the river's ice and Anga, seeing it, growled but gave no chase for the hound was wise in his weakness and knew that he could never overtake it.

For two hours Arturo travelled slowly, letting the White One pick her own gait. Man, mount and hound all harboured and conserved their little reserve of strength, and for Arturo the day passed into the substance of a dream. His eyes, narrowed against the blinding sunglare on the snow-covered earth, now and then played him tricks, creating the vision of things long forgotten and of desires long now unfed. A willow tree seemed suddenly to be loaded with a crop of fat yellow plums. A hollow in the ground ahead was a coolness to the eyes with a rich spread of now spring grass but as he rode down into it there was only the hard crunch of the frozen snow drifts under the White One's hooves. He talked to himself and also talked

73

as though there were others with him. The waters of the Cam were suddenly free of ice and he thought he saw a fish leap high in the ecstasy of a fast spring run from the sea, just as he had seen the salmon leap in the Tamesis river at Pontes on the day when Cuneda had joined him. But all the while there was a detached presence in him which understood all mirage and held firm to the burning truth of his real state. The gods, for their own purpose and his future greatness, were humiliating him, putting him to the trial of asking charity for himself and his people from a man who would give none. When that was done the story would run with him always. Arturo, the great one, the outlawed defier of Count Ambrosius and Prince Gerontius, went a-begging to a fish-reeking marsh king. *Aie* . . . the gods were demanding that so that in all the days of whatever greatness came to him it would be a never healing sore on his pride to remind him of his puniness below the gods.

It was then, as he sat his saddle, head drooping as the head of the White One drooped, that he heard Anga growl. He looked up and another mirage danced before his eyes and he watched it, wondering at the power of the mind to create fantasy from the weakness of his body and the loss of his pride.

A man, heavily cloaked and cowled, was riding towards him on a sturdy moorland pony, fat flanked and making light of the hard going. His robe was belted and from his right side hung a leather scabbarded sword. In the midst of his vision Arturo smiled weakly to himself, touched with the arbitrariness of the mirage which sent him a left-handed man. He lowered his head and shut out the hallucination, seeing only the White One's dipping head before him and hearing only now the slow bite of her hooves into the crisp snow crust.

Then clearly through the frost-purged air a man's voice said to him, 'You would pass without greeting one who holds you most dear?'

Arturo raised his head as the White One came to a stop to see that the horse and rider mirage now blocked his path. The man drew back the loose edges of his head cowl and Arturo knew then that the gods put further mockery on him. The other rider, lean-faced and his beard a rusty tan colour, was a man well in his forties with eyes the colour of ripe hazel nuts, and he was smiling with his face full of welcome. Arturo knew him, though he had not seen him for more than a year, and he knew too that this other lived only in his fancy as had done the ripe plums and the sweet meadow grass, and he marvelled at the truth of the mirage which had made this visionary man left-handed.

He said, 'If you were true man and not my brain's fancy I would give you the warm greeting of a son. Aye . . . and for all that you do not in flesh and truth smile at me from your pony I give you greeting and even hold my hand out as though to feel yours in mine and be warmed by the blood which we both share.'

As he spoke he held out his hand and the other took it and said, 'I am Baradoc, and I am flesh and blood and your father.' As their hands were clasped it was as though Arturo had been struck a sudden blow, for beyond all doubt of mirage or the mind's deceit, he knew his own flesh to be grasped by true flesh and blood and knew that his hard palm and calloused fingers were held by the like of his father's without shadow of doubt.

In that moment of truth before the gods gave him release from their trial they abased him with a final chastisement. He swayed in his saddle, his hand slipping from his father's, to topple to the ground in a fit of oblivion, and as he lay there Anga stood over him growling, the soft skin of his mouth drawn back to bare the ageing teeth and fangs. But when Baradoc dismounted and squatted on his hunkers alongside his son, he spoke gently to the hound in the speech which all men of the Enduring Crow used with their beasts and, slowly, the growling died in Anga's throat like the passing away of distant thunder.

★ ★ ★

There were his father and two other men whose ponies were heavily pack laden. He lay propped against the bole of a great oak close to the river. Above him the bare branches were hung with great daggers of icicles. They would have built a fire and made a meat and barley soup for him, but he refused for he knew now, though nothing had been said as yet by his father, that the days and weeks of starvation were over, and there was nothing which could make him fill his belly until he saw his own companions and camp people succoured first. He accepted only a pull at the mouth of a mead skin and the honey bite of it went through him like fire, a warmth that cleared his head and waked his weak body to the stir of new vigour. A little way from him the two men fed oats to the White One from an osier skep and Anga lay full length chewing at a piece of smoked deer meat.

Baradoc squatting at his side said, 'You

77

would have had nothing from King Melwas for he is not at Ynys-witrin. He has taken his people over the marshes to the hills where they live warm in the old lead workings but eat poor because the ice holds rivers and marshes hard bound and all the marsh fowl have gone south to Gaul or the open sea. If the gods sent you this way then it was to me. Half a day's march behind us comes a pony and sledge train with supplies for you from Isca.'

'Why should Prince Gerontius give me, whom he outlawed, such charity from his store?'

'He gives nothing. He is dead and now his son reigns, young Prince Geraint and I am made Pendragon of all the tribes of the Dumnonian lands and stand at his right side.'

'And knowing of our wants you begged for me?'

Baradoc laughed. 'Damp the fire of your pride a little. I begged nothing. Prince Geraint remembers you and was ever trying to persuade his father to pardon you. Now that he is Prince he has given the pardon himself — though since his writ does not run with Count Ambrosius at Glevum you are still outlaw under his mandate.'

'From Ambrosius I would accept nothing. Neither pardon nor provisions.'

Baradoc shrugged his shoulders. 'Time brings changes. But we live now and there is this winter lack on the camp hill which must be met. But Prince Geraint has more in his mind than present charity. He would meet and speak with you.'

'To what end?' As he spoke Arturo was remembering Geraint. He could give him a handful of years and there were many times when he had schooled and drilled the cavalry horses of Prince Gerontius when the boy had first watched and then ridden with him, a quiet youth with a pleasant manner who spoke little but clearly thought much of matters beyond his years for he sought seldom the company of those of his own age. And now he was Prince of all Dumnonia though in years he could scarce be yet twenty.

'That rests with him. As Pendragon I am his counsellor but I am far from knowing his true mind. But I know that he speaks fair and is a man of his word and favours you where his father knew only wrath for you. The pony train that follows us comes from him out of his good bounty, a charity which carries no threat to your liberty or your ambitions for this country.'

Arturo nodded. This news and the presence of his father already refreshed his body and spirit and he began to feel a new man and to know now with thankful conviction that his trial by the gods had always carried this fore-ordained end. He took another pull through his cracked lips at the mead skin and let its fire seep through him like a slow peat burn. 'How,' he asked, 'did Gerontius die? He was a man in good health.'

'He was trying a new mount that had been shipped from Gaul with other of its kind . . . an over mettlesome creature which threw him so that he struck his head on the ground. It seemed no more than a bruise a man would rub and forget but he was found dead on his couch the following morning.'

Pulling himself upright slowly Arturo said, 'For all those who love horses death is the distance between the saddle and the ground. May the gods keep him.'

As he began to move towards the White One with the clear intent of mounting Baradoc said, 'You ask not of your mother and the rest of your kin?'

Arturo paused with his hands on the reins, ready to mount, and he smiled. 'No harm can have touched them for the gods this day have done with trying me. But I take your scold with humility, and I ride now to take good news to my people on the hill of the Cam.

They have become my kin, tied to me by bonds as fast as any blood sharing.'

'You still dream your dream?'

'Aye, my father. A dream that was once yours. You once told me that you would turn the hill camp into a great fortress against the day the Saxons moved west. I see no signs of new work there.'

'My dream lives, but before I could assemble the workmen Gerontius and Melwas quarrelled and the marsh king closed his lands against our passage. Aye, the dream lives still but only as a sorrow in my heart.'

Mounting the White One Arturo said, 'The day will come when you shall do it.'

Baradoc laughed. 'A while ago you were a half-delirious and near to dead man, and now you talk like the arrogant son whose bare rumps I birch-marked often for insolence and waywardness. One would think it was the nectar of the gods I gave you to drink not the thin brew of an Iscan tavern keeper.'

Arturo shook his head. 'The mead was good, but my new strength comes from the far greater boon of seeing you and knowing the good fortune you bring. Come, my father — ride with me to give proof to my people of the great bounty the gods have sent.'

★ ★ ★

81

The baggage train arrived the next morning. There were twenty sturdy pack horses fully laden and two great sleds teamed by lank-shouldered, long-headed draught mules which Gerontius had bred from Gaulish imported he-asses on his moorland pony mares. The train brought food and stores in no great plenty but of a sufficiency to see the camp through the rest of the winter and early spring no matter how hard the weather should stand. Within a week starvation's marks began to pass from men, women and children and the horses and hounds, and where there had been little chatter and less laughter about the camp fires there came a singing and a gossiping and shouting which filled Arturo's heart with lightness except when he paid his nightly visit to the beech dell. Of Daria's death he had no need to tell his father for the news had reached Isca by one of the camp-visiting pedlars and Baradoc, knowing the nature of true grief, said no more than a few words about her going to Arturo and then talked no more of Daria.

Thin though the commons were they represented feasting to all. The hounds now had vigour to fight and quarrel and forage afield. Wet mash and oats began to put a new bloom on the horses. When Venutius walked the picket lines and pens at night and saw their eyes bright in the starlight and their breath pluming in the sharp air he knew a happiness which brought him for a time forgetfulness of Ambrosius and Glevum. The men of the provision train and mule sleds rode back to Isca, but Baradoc stayed to ride there later with Arturo and they spent much time together walking the old, broken, and overgrown ramparts and defences of the hill. Arturo — man to man now with his father and forging a bond which had never existed before — saw how, from a great warrior who had served south across the seas from Rome and knew all the lands from the Pillars of Hercules to far beyond Byzantium, Baradoc had by the loss of the full use of his right hand turned to new skills and had made himself a master of forts and defences and towers and knew from his own experience of them the art of making *ballistae* which could throw a flight of arrows or flaming iron bolts coated with tarred tow to flare through the air further than any spear could be thrown and knew, too, the setting up of large catapults — the *onagri* which the early Roman legions had used against Britain in the days of the great Queen Boudicca — that slung with ease large boulders to a distance far beyond any arrow flight.

Arturo knew that his father would have made this hill impregnable and many others like it to give a secure base from which the tribes and factions now holding the long spine length of this country could move forward to meet the Saxon's westward creep. But in his heart Arturo knew that the dream could never flower as his father saw it. When the Saxons came in sufficient numbers they would flow around each fortress like the tide round a standing rock. The true answer, he sensed, though the vision was far from clear with him, lay elsewhere. But a well protected winter base when none would move to fight he knew to be wise. Armies that gathered in spring, fought through the summer and then scattered, each man to his own holding and fireside during the winter, were no more than flocks of mad starlings who had lost all sense of due seasons. For himself he knew one thing with absolute conviction. The gods had sent him to this hill above the Cam. On this hill they had tried him and his people with the cruellest winter men could remember and, at the point of despair and disaster, had redeemed him. This hill was his and none should take it from him for already he began to see the glimmerings of the way he would use it. But first he had to bring Prince Geraint and King Melwas to his side.

In the first week of the month of the Roman god Mars, the great thaw came as a robust and warm westerly wind blew across the land. Every gully and rivulet ran high with water. The ice sheets that had covered the Cam melted and broke into floes which went racing downstream on a growing flood which in two days, as the winds became rain-laden, reached high over the banks and flooded the low-lying lands. All the country which had been a waste of whiteness now delighted the eye with the sweeps of green hillside and the lush growth of the first new grass. The thickets, woods and skies which had been bereft of all creatures now stirred with their return to renewed life. A stormcock sang with high melody each morning in the beech dell. Robins and sparrows and jackdaws and crows came back to the camp to forage for pickings about the cooking fires and middens, and kestrels, sparrow hawks and high-winging kites and buzzards and higher-pitched per-egrines took toll of the life below them or tore and gorged themselves at the thawed carcasses of hinds and hares and boar which winter starvation had claimed and the snow and ice had until now held locked fast under its iron pall.

The rain lasted three days and when it passed Arturo and Baradoc left the hill camp and set out for Isca. With him Arturo took one of the first of his camp servants at the Villa of the Three Nympths, Marcos whose dumb brother Timo had been killed in the fighting of the previous year. Marcos now was no servant but a fully trained and seasoned trooper. He left Durstan in command of the camp.

Some days later at noon they rode into Isca. They came along the old road westward from the Fosseway, a road which — now the winter had broken — was, the nearer they came to Isca, busy with the movement of pedlars and traders and drovers herding lean pigs and long-coated cattle towards the town. It was a road which long ago had known the steady tramp of cohorts of Roman auxiliaries beating out their twenty miles a day, their raised standard going before them, gilded and wreathed with their battle honours. They topped a long slope and Isca lay before them, its great Mount crowned with the partly ruined fortress where Prince Geraint had his seat. To the south below the hill lay the wide sprawl of the town itself, hearth-fire smoke wreathing lazily into the still air, and beyond it the curve and sweep of the river and the water meadows where Arturo had broken and trained new horses and learned the elements of his skill as a cavalryman. Seeing it a wry smile touched his lips as he remembered how he and Durstan had ridden from it on a night of storm to escape with their lives and be unjustly named as outlaws for the killing of two men who would have murdered them on the orders of the present Prince's father.

They rode through the town and up to the fortress over which flew the great scarlet Dumnonia standard with a green oak tree in its centre. Arturo and Marcos were shown to their quarters and Baradoc left them to go to the house of Master Ricat, the Prince's horsemaster, with whom Arturo had always been a favourite, though this had never saved him thrashings as a youth for wild conduct.

Before Baradoc left he said to Arturo with a smiling twist to his mouth. 'The Prince is young. Speak fairly to him. To be overbold will serve you nothing. So, keep well bridled — ' he grinned openly, ' — the arrogance you draw from the gods. At the moment you have more need of him than he of you — and so it is with me. I would see your camp well-fortified, and you need quickly more men and mounts than will come from other parts this spring.' He paused for a moment or two and then said straightly, 'Until now I have thought you a dreamer and a maker of your own myths — god-touched but in the way of men with disordered minds.

Now I know better, and now is the time for you to lay the strong foundations of your desire which is also mine — to turn the Saxons back to the sea and heal this country of its long sickness.'

Arturo nodded and said quietly, 'Have no fear, my father. This winter the gods have schooled me well.'

★　★　★

Later that afternoon Arturo was given audience by Prince Geraint. They spoke together in the large room where he had had his first meeting with Prince Gerontius when he had been a youth. Its floor was paved with black and red tiles. A long window flanked by wall niches looked out over the town and river, where the day was dying into the last red glow of sunset. A long couch held a tumbled cloak and a pile of papyrus reading rolls. On the marble floor was a vase full of the long sere stalks of mace reed, their heads split and curled with the bursting of ripening seed. An oak table held a great silver tray on which stood a glass flagon of wine and two drinking cups. At the head of this table sat the young Prince, not yet twenty, dressed in a surcoat of finely cured doeskin over a white linen shirt, and wearing red woollen trews whose bottoms were stained and still wet with mud from riding the water meadows.

He had his father's face and complexion, dark hair, and dark eyebrows that merged with one another over his high-bridged hawklike nose. But whereas the father's eyes had always seemed, under their heavy hoods, to be burgeoning with sleep or suspicion Geraint's eyes were warm and frank.

Ignoring all formal greeting the Prince put out a hand to warm it from the heat of a charcoal brazier which stood near his chair and said pleasantly, 'You remember me?'

Arturo nodded. 'Yes, my prince. The last time I saw you, you sat in a meadow puddle having been thrown there by a bay stallion moor pony that had far to go to be broken.'

'But in the end broken it was.' He nodded to the bench by the table. 'Sit — when I want formality you shall know it — and pour wine for us.'

As Arturo did this, he said, 'The whole land has known a cruel winter. I give you the thanks of all mine and myself for your bounty, my Prince.'

Geraint smiled, shrugged his shoulders, and took the wine cup which Arturo passed him, saying, 'Without it you would have held place. The gods would have sent ravens with meat and the corn would have pushed through the ice and snow to come to full ripening between dawn and dusk.' He drank a little of the wine, and went on, smiling broadly, 'Tell me, is it true that the spears of Melwas were turned aside from you in full flight?'

Arturo laughed and said, 'Is there any warrior when the mead flows who does not sing his leader's deeds in bold words, forsaking truth for fancy? No, my Prince. The spears were stayed by the command of King Melwas.'

'There are times when men, weary of the hard truth, look only for miracles. This is such a time. So now, tell me what is in your mind. I have freed you from outlawry where my writ runs, but you have made an enemy of Count Ambrosius and with a handful of men have given Hengist's red beard a more than gentle tweak. Where do you go now?'

'Where the gods lead, my Prince.'

The Prince shook his head and a hint of a frown marked his face. 'Let us now leave the gods from this for a while. They will stay or give their favours. Tell me in plain words what you have in mind.'

Arturo's hand tightened a little around his wine cup. For all his father's warning he found it hard to take the Prince's reprimand. Although he could only give him a handful of years they held all the difference between unfleshed youth and scarred warrior. Then, aware of his own arrogance and the great service the Prince had done him this winter, he said quietly, 'You shall have it plain, my Prince. I have dreamt a dream for this country and shall live in discontent until I have brought it to truth . . . '

So, while Geraint sipped his wine now and then and listened patiently, Arturo spoke his mind and clothed his dream in simple words of good sense, and the Prince heard him through without interruption. He heard him, too, without irritation because Arturo, who believed that he had been fingered by the gods, held now to facts, suppressing all fancies or god-predicted certainties. But though this was so there came into Arturo's mind as he spoke of practical things — of levies of men and garrisoning over winter, of stores and the weapons of war, and the need for armourers and smiths and the careful selection of good mounts and foot soldiers — the one prime argument which might hold this young Prince Geraint and all others like him as allies — and that thought he knew came from the gods.

He finished: 'This is a country now of great chiefs, princes and kings, many of whom although they fear the Saxon threat, fear more the loss of their own high states. They give no full levies to Count Ambrosius because in their hearts they know that by giving him victory they would be raising him high above them in full sovereignty. And this is true, for Count Ambrosius — ageing and waning as he is — sees himself as the coming Emperor and will never relinquish that dream.'

'And your dream?'

'I am of no royal blood. With victory in my hands no one has cause to fear tyranny from me. In anger I not long since underscored a message to Count Ambrosius calling myself *dux bellorum*. War duke of this country to give it freedom. When the victory is won and there is no more war then the title, like a morning mist under the rising summer sun, vanishes. I shall be content under my father or as chief myself to return to the people of the Enduring Crow to improve my lands and the lot of my people. You have been kind to me, my Prince. Be kinder. We are both of Dumnonia so it is fitting that you should be the first. And by your example in a few years others will follow.'

For a moment or two Geraint was silent, tapping his fingers against the side of his drinking cup. Then he smiled and said, 'You will find this hard to believe, but not long since I sat where you are and listened to my father speaking and he said much that you have said. More, too, he spoke of you and the things you have done this last year. Hearing you speak now I know that he had read much that was in your mind. Had he lived he would have soon pardoned you and called you to him. That is why you have your pardon and are here now. If this thing is to be done and achieved by you — then it is right that the first to aid you should be the Prince of your own country. Prove yourself in the coming years and the others will follow.'

'Even Count Ambrosius?'

Prince Geraint stood up to show that the audience was over, and said with a sly smile, 'Since the gods are so strongly on your side what need have you to over-concern yourself with him?'

That evening Arturo walked down to the house of Master Ricat, the Prince's horse-keeper, where his father was lodged. Here to his surprise, for his father had not mentioned her, he found also his mother, Tia. She rose from a couch by the glowing brazier that warmed the room and embraced him. Then stepping back but still holding his hands in hers she looked at him and said quietly, 'I loved Daria and know your grief. I say no more.'

93

Looking at her, a tall, handsome woman in her forties, her periwinkle eyes bright, her fair hair, caught with a braid of red silk, still untouched by any dull tint of time, he knew that she spoke from her own heartache during the long years when his father had been torn from her to serve as slave and then mercenary in distant lands.

He said, 'To you I can speak of her for you will know the truth in me. There is none ever that can take her place.' Then dropping her hands he said, looking beyond her, 'But who is this?'

On a stool, her lap full of simple embroidery work, sat a girl of about eight or nine years; a dark-haired, brown-skinned child with a solemn face.

The girl without bidding rose, her embroidery work spilling to the ground, and came to him holding out her hand in greeting as she said, 'I am your first sister, Gerta. Is it true that when King Melwas gave the order to spear you they were turned aside by the gods?'

Arturo laughed, his spirits lifting at the pleasure of being with his family, and said, 'Of course it's true, and to feed us on the hill during the snows the ravens brought meat each day.'

'Ah, then that, too, I shall work into my embroidery.'

'Enough,' said Baradoc. 'Once he starts his stories there is no knowing where truth begins or ends.' But when he brought a mead cup to Arturo there was a shine of pride in his eyes which Arturo had never known before.

★   ★   ★

That night when Arturo returned to the fortress he was summoned to Prince Geraint.

The Prince said, 'Not long since a trader who for years brought news for my father arrived. He travels freely in our lands and the Saxon shorelands because — ' he smiled, ' — he takes news to both sides though he would deny it to either. But he is a man of true news. He tells that Hengist is dead and that his son, Esc, rules all the lands south-east of Londinium in his place.'

Without thought of any irk it might give Geraint Arturo said, 'Then truly the gods begin to move. They stir you to forgiveness and bounty and now they take away the one man who held the first place over all the chiefs of the Saxon shores from the Ocelli point in the north to beyond Lemanis in the south. Each chief now will struggle and fight for leadership over the others since Esc is not the man his father was. Truly this is the time to begin to harry them. Aye, they will find a leader in time, my Prince, but long before then I shall have an army trained and battle-blooded by harassing them; an army which will, when in the years to come they find unity, meet and break them with bloody slaughter and drive them from our shores. The gods are with us!'

A spasm of irritation reaching near anger touched Geraint as Arturo spoke. The gods, the gods . . . always the gods. Aye, he had belief and faith in the gods, too, but was not blind as this Arto seemed to be that they worked their ends, shaping the destinies of men and nations, in a pattern that mortal eyes were slow to pick out. Then, oddly, he remembered the times when he had watched this Arturo school and break horses, had seen his love and care for them and the men in his command, and knew from Baradoc, too, the downing of pride that he had forced on himself to go seeking charity from King Melwas. In this moment he found a truth which he needed to keep countenance and temper with Arturo. He was not one man, but two, a dreamer and a warrior — and the one could not live without the other. So he now said evenly, 'Tomorrow we will talk more about this.'

# The Taunting of the Boar

A week later Arturo rode back to the hill camp with Marcos, but on the way he turned off and went to Ynys-witrin. As they rode to the settlement the flood waters lapped over the causeway still in places. He was escorted to King Melwas who with his people had now returned from their winter quarters in the old lead mines. The air was balmy with the first promise of spring and he found Melwas — who like all true marshmen was most at ease with the sky rather than a roof above — sitting in the courtyard of his palace, which was no more than a long hall built of timber and part stone quarried from the mount behind it.

Melwas, who was having the thick winter growth of his beard plucked and trimmed by one of his women, made him welcome. He sat at the rough plank table with him and a jug of crab-apple brew was set between them, and as they talked his men and women went about their business in the yard and the hall. Melwas was truly king but he had little love of ceremony or formalities.

As their beakers were filled and Melwas

waved away the woman tending his beard so that he could drink, he said, 'So you have charmed the young Prince — and now comes my turn?'

'News runs fast. But I have come to use no charms. Plain speaking serves us both best.'

Melwas laughed. 'Your tail is up. You begin to feel your oats after the winter fast. My answer is — nothing of charity will be found here.'

'Nor do I ask it. I need your leave to keep quarters on Cam Hill and to make the place secure. The need will be with me for many years.'

'You speak plain . . . aye, even a little rough for a beggar. Now, to your plain need add the golden tail.'

'One third of all loot we take. From this you pay the fighting men you bond to me.'

'First my land — and now my men! How many men?'

'Fifty.'

Melwas laughed. 'Young of course. And able — able to take bow and shoot the eye from a crow at fifty paces, and to throw a spear that will slit the throat of a bounding deer and so not spoil good carcase meat. This, too, at fifty paces?'

Arturo smiled. 'Is there any marshman who cannot do that?'

'No.' He scratched at his beard. 'But go on — the morning was dull until you came. Did Prince Geraint suffer your humour as pleasantly as I do?'

'He has seen how this country's needs must be served. He supplies horses and men and provisioning and asks nothing in return.'

'He is young and generous with his new inheritance. Even so you will have no great force.'

'Success will bring the growth I want. But I must have a safe stronghold for winter quarters for the next few years to come. This I ask you to provide, not from charity, but on fair terms. If I speak boldly it is because I know the gods will govern your heart.'

'You talk of the gods as though you supped with them on their feast days. People already sing the tale of my spears being turned from you.'

'And will sing it for a thousand years to come. Would your name live so long had not the gods brought us together? And longer still will it live when men sing of your wisdom and foresight in giving me Cam Hill for leaguer to begin the great progress against the Saxons.'

Melwas leaned back and roared with laughter and then thumping the rough table boards he said, 'There's a boldness in your begging which puts me on the edge so that I know not whether to smile and say yes — or shout to my men to throw you in the mere. Though, of course, should they do that the gods would see to it that you landed on your feet and walked the surface of the water.'

'Would you have me go elsewhere so that people in years to come will say that Melwas was — '

'Enough! You make my mind itch more than my winter beard does my face. I am a fool to like you and more fool to listen to you, but I have a son your age who shares your spirit and dreams and nags me like a gadfly to be allowed to take service with that old fool Ambrosius. You shall have what you want if he comes as leader of your bow and spearmen and all others of the same like who may join you in the days to come. He dreams of nothing but battle and wastes his days here in fishing, hunting and tupping the marsh maids.'

'He shall have command until the day he proves unworthy of it.'

'If that day comes he is no son of mine. Now go your way before the gods put it into your mind to ask further alms of me. Coroticus will bring his men to you within a few days and the hill is yours and your good father Baradoc can fortify it.'

'I give you thanks, and thank too the gods

who sent me to you.'

Melwas shook his head slowly and with a shy smile, his lips wet red through the tangle of his beard, said, 'So, so — but think me not deceived. You would have come gods or no gods.'

Coroticus arrived with his men five days later. He was of much the same age as Arturo, but with a marshman's small, lean figure. Dark-haired with a tightly trimmed beard, his face was grave and brooding and seldom showed any emotion, a dark pool of peat water showing nothing of the depths below. He spoke quietly and pleasantly except when he would be obeyed in exercise or command and then his voice could take on a rasp like the scything of a winter wind through the frozen sedges of his own marshlands. Pride went with him, too. Arturo saw, for all his men came dressed alike. They wore leather skullcaps, their hair bound tightly over the napes of their necks, and soft leather tunics belted over thick woollen shirts. On the left breasts of the tunics copper studs pricked out the rude shape of the Summerland and King Melwas's emblem of a hovering fish eagle. Below the tunics they wore leather aprons over short woollen trews and their legs and feet were bare each year from the first spring thaw until the first winter snow. Each man had a slung bow, a quiver full of arrows, a long knife in his belt and carried a heavy fighting spear. That the men were all dressed alike told Arturo much about Coroticus. Not only pride went with good appearance but the beginning of hard military discipline — and discipline was a rare virtue among the marshmen.

He said, 'You are welcome, Coroticus.'

Coroticus answered quietly, 'We are proud to come, my lord Arturo. There is no man with me not of his own free will. Show us some piece of this hilltop for our quarters and the rest we will do for ourselves. And so it will be on the march and in fighting camps.'

Arturo smiled. 'And will it be the same the day your fifty men become five hundred?'

Coroticus said, 'If I lead them then — yes, my lord. I wish only to serve you and fight against the Saxon men, and in all things to be obedient and faithful to you.'

From that day Coroticus and his men were as he had said they would be. And from that day there was a new beginning for all on the hill. They were days of drilling and exercises, days of training in battle and surprise attacks, when troops of horse went thundering down the long slopes of the neighbouring hills and valleys in mock attack and the marshmen came fast behind them to learn to take advantage of the confusion and panic in the ranks of imaginary Saxons. They were drilled for one long hard month in all the tactics and feints and battle moves which Arturo could devise, and there was not a man from Arturo down who came riding back from a day's training who, fatigued though he might be, did not still sit proud in the saddle or trot lightly, skin sweat-and-dust coated, with long spear at rest on his shoulder. The hill now was a company of men, for Arturo had sent all women and children back to their lands and settlements. He drove the men through all the lengthening daylight hours. When darkness came there was only rest in relay for those who came from guard and sentinel duties for they lived now as though they were camped in hostile country and attack could come at any time. No man grumbled, for it was clear to all that in these days the discipline was building habit and instinct on which their lives would rest when they moved away from Cam Hill to face the killing reality of bloody warfare. Their pride, too, blossomed in pace with the bursting sprays of blackthorn bloom on the hillside. They were Arturo's men, companions and fish eagles, the men of the west and all the other free lands.

One day only they rested — though not

from guard duties. This was the seventh day of the week. Then Pasco gave service and preached for those who were Christos men, and later for those who held to their country's gods did equal duty, though far fewer of these came to him because most of those who served the gods gave worship each in his own fashion before one or other of the many little rock-piled altars which had sprung up among the ancient, broken ramparts, altars that showed a bunch of primroses for Coventina, one of the first pale blue eggs of the shy dunnock for Morrigan, the Queen of Phantoms, for remembrance of the winter dead, a little carved warrior on horseback to Andraste, the goddess of victory, and plaited hair rings taken from the manes of the camp's mounts to Epona, the horse goddess.

At the end of the first month there came from Prince Geraint two troops of mounted cavalry volunteers and with them a fresh baggage train bringing supplies. The new horsemen were put to exercise and drills and within a handful of days ten of them were sent back to Isca (though their horses were kept) with the returning baggage train for under the eyes of Arturo and his troop commanders their worth was quickly weighed and found wanting.

Venutius said to Arturo, 'Returning these

men, my lord, could anger Prince Geraint.'

'Then angered he must be, Venutius. These are men of good enough nature but there is no true bottom to them. They came because they seek the excitements that come after victory . . . boasting and drinking and raping. Any bright lure of the flesh or appetite would draw them aside from duty.'

'How can you know this?'

'You forget that Durstan and I served with the Isca cavalry. We know these men . . . aye, and were friendly enough with them. But they are not what we want. No man rides or marches with me in this great beginning who looks to the spoils and lusts of victory before victory is won. How long would they last? We begin a struggle which will eat up many years. I need none who look no farther ahead than a summer's span.'

Hardly daring, but unable to hold back, Venutius said, 'You can say that of the marshmen, my lord?'

Arturo laughed. 'Not I. But go study Coroticus. He would have none who were other than he.' He paused and then with a smile asked, 'You think me hard?'

'No, my lord. Determined.'

'Then take this for comfort — to each man I have sent back I spoke the truth of his going. You shall see that a half of them will

105

return to find us when they have chewed the cud of their rejection.'

Before the end of April Baradoc arrived at the camp with more provisions and a party of workmen to begin putting the hill defences in order and to raise new ones. The carts and horses he brought were taken over by Arturo to add to his own to make the baggage train for his force. Army it could not be called, nor did he see it as such. This first year, he knew, could only be a probing, proving campaign. The baggage train would travel well in their rear. He was seeking for swiftness and suddenness. Every man would carry with him — in saddle pack or back sack — that which would keep him for a week, dried meat, hard biscuit and, if pack or sack hampered him in fighting, it would be abandoned until the fight was over and then sought afterwards.

That the news of his hill camp and his campaigning intentions must have spread far abroad, he knew. *Aie* . . . the very swallows and returning birds would be crying it from south to north of the land, as were the pedlars and traders that visited the hill. But none knew the way of his going or his coming. This he kept to himself for he was determined that for the Saxons the first sight of the companions should be the streaming of the White Horse standard coming over down slope or breaking from wood or rearing above the river mist as dawn broke. No, he told himself, no army yet. But that would come and when it did — remembering his talk with Venutius — he knew that he would draw men of doubt and opportunity and must take them; but none should ever wear the scarlet and white cavalry scarves of the companions or the copper-studded marsh eagle unless they were proved heart- and battle-worthy.

At the beginning of May, two days after the feast of Beltine, and the night before Arturo's men were to move from the fortress of Cam Hill, he walked in the half gloaming to the beech grove where Daria lay. As he sat there a nightingale began to sing from the nearby thickets of elder and was answered by another from the valley of the Cam. The gods he knew held all men and women in the hollow of their hands, and they had taken Daria from him to make the long passage to the Blessed Isles cradled in the Western sea where Cronus slept his long sleep. For himself he knew the years would be long before he followed her, and knew too that this was the ordering of the gods for they had reft him of the full joy of human love so that the seed should spring and flourish of another love far more demanding of his devotion.

* ★ ★

As he sat there in the beech dell there was one who at the same moment had Arturo much in his thoughts, and this was Count Ambrosius.

He sat in his command tent at the Sabrina camp outside Corinium. A fair breeze coming over the distant river from the Cymrian hills lifted and flapped the blue folds of the tent cloth above him and set flickering the flames of the two oil lamps that stood in tall holders at each end of his table, the smeech of their burning wicks strong in his nostrils. Standing before him, waiting for his attention while he studied a map drawn on fine parchment, was his Praefectus Castrorum.

Without looking up Ambrosius waved a hand to a chair and said to the Camp Prefect, 'Sit — and take some wine.'

Grinning briefly to himself since Ambrosius was not looking at him, the Prefect sat and helped himself to wine from the flagon and glass on the table. Both flagon and glass were old and each held an engraving of the god Bacchus. The old man, he thought, must be in a good mood, for except on feast days he seldom touched wine.

As though Ambrosius had read his thoughts, he now pushed the map aside and with a thin-lipped smile reached for the flagon and poured wine for himself, and said, 'We make no great campaign this year. Such levies that have arrived can be sent back.'

'There will be no grumbling from them, my commander. They are a poor lot and all forced men. But it will be hard for our regular troops to sit in idleness.'

'There will be no idleness. We go first west through Cymru to show our strength to these hill chiefs and then north to Luguvalium on the Wall.' He sipped his wine and added pleasantly, 'You think we waste a year's campaigning now that Hengist is dead?'

The Camp Prefect shrugged his shoulders. 'Esc is young and not the man his father was. He can never hold the other Saxon warlords together for now they will fight among themselves. Still, I should have thought, my commander, that — '

Ambrosius cut him off with a wave of his hand. 'That this was the time to march against them? No. That would serve us badly. To hunt summer wolves who have all broken pack would gain us little. And neither is there need — for our young Arturo will do that for us.'

'True, my commander. And in so doing will draw more men to himself and new glory to his name.'

'Which serves us well, though he may be long in seeing it. He shall make an army and a name for himself, and in a few years we shall shake the fruit of his growing into our basket. I would have the Saxons finish their quarrelling with the rise of a new leader — be it Esc or some other — and then we shall have again a head and heart to strike at.'

'And Arturo and his army?'

Ambrosius flicked a finger nail against the rim of his glass so that it rang, the high note trembling and then dying. He said quietly, 'At heart he's a raw western savage, full of courage and bloodthirsty, but his brains are in his backside and only work when he sits a horse. I have handled his kind many times, chiefs of the Brigantes, the Ordovices and the Dobunni in our own country here. They think only of the glory of fighting and the triumphs of victory. The building of a great state and the craft and judgement which that demands is beyond them. When they meet their limits they come to hand like broken horses. It is for this that I have called you here. You will send an envoy to him to say that he is outlaw no longer and more, that I give him free right of passage for his army throughout the land. A handful of sweet oats to feed his pride.' He paused for a moment and pulled from his hand one of the rings he wore, and slid it across the table to the Camp Prefect. 'Let this go to him with the pardon.'

Outside the tent the Camp Prefect weighted the ring in his palm. It was gold, a signet ring with the seal worked into an intaglio of Ambrosius's head, laurel wreathed. For a moment or two he wondered whether the Count practised some wisdom beyond his seeing. Arturo was more likely to throw pardon and ring back in the face of Ambrosius. But maybe the Count knew that and wanted it to happen so that a sharp edge should be honed to Arturo's strong contempt for him . . . a goad to prick him forward to higher and bolder deeds which could be used by the Count to shape his own destiny. Aye, perhaps so, for his master could be as patient and cunning as a serpent, and knew well how to make others work for him without their being aware of it. Well, so be it until time made it plain. But on one score his commander was right. There was no gain in marching against the Saxons this year for they would never come out to fight in full strength until they had another leader who could call and gather them to full battle unity.

Some days later a Sabrina cavalry troop leader with an escort of two of his men arrived at Cam Hill. Olipon, the troop leader,

111

left his two men at the foot of the hill and rode the path to the battlements alone to show his peaceful coming. The sight that met his eyes surprised him. Work was going ahead on the great ring of fortifications and inside them was a well-ordered camp, full of bustle, and preparation for the coming campaign. The horses were sleek and well-fed, every fighting man moved with a spring and alertness which showed growing zest for the fighting days ahead. Here was no rabble of disorganized tribesmen under an impetuous, plunder-hungry chief. Things moved here with almost as much order as they did in the Sabrina Wing at Corinium. And why not, he thought, since as he was led to Arturo he saw many a former Sabrina man among them? Aye, and was called to and jested with by men who had been his friends and companions in arms so that it was hard for him not to wonder whether they had moved to a wisdom and understanding of this Arturo which escaped him. Momentarily the urge took him to deliver his message and then ask to be allowed to join this company, for nothing but a long dull summer of parades and show-of-strength marches lay ahead of the Count's army.

He was led to Arturo's hut, over which flew the White Horse standard. Outside on guard stood a short, dark-haired, dark-skinned marshman, resting on his spear, the copper studs of his fish eagle insignia burnished to catch the sunlight. Arturo came out to him and he was at once less and more than he had expected: a young man wearing a loose linen shirt belted over his leather trews, smiling, fair brown hair and blue-eyed, his beard tightly trimmed, who could have passed without notice on the Corinium drill grounds until at second look the force of the young face and the depth of the blue eyes suddenly spoke of some tight-bridled passion. It was all there to see if a man had the eyes and wit to see it. There was iron in this man and an age beyond his years.

Olipon raised his right arm in the old Roman salute, announced himself and gave his message and then handed Ambrosius's ring to Arturo. Arturo nodded, his face unchanging as he weighed the ring absently in his hand after giving it no more than a glance, and then said, 'How many days are you from Corinium?'

'Three, my lord.'

'Hard riding. You would stay the night to rest yourself, your men and your horses?'

'You are kind, my lord — but no. I give my commander's message and return with your . . . your — ' Olipon broke off.

'My thanks, you think, to Count Ambrosius?' Arturo smiled.

Recovering himself, Olipon said, 'I shall speak, my lord, as you shall command me.'

'Then say this to Count Ambrosius. When I and my good companion Durstan were first outlawed by Count Ambrosius I swore a promise that men now call Arto's Promise . . . aye, they still call it so to mark any idle boast.' His smile was frank and good-natured. 'Tell your commander that promise was made under the gods and still holds faith with me. I come only to Count Ambrosius when, as equal to equal, he sues me for help. On that day I will ride to Glevum and be with him in good faith to serve this our country.' He handed the ring to Olipon. 'Take back this, too. He wears the laurels of victory well ahead of due season, but to spare you his anger you need not give him those words.'

Riding down the hill to rejoin his men there was a moment when Olipon was half-tempted to turn back and ask leave to join the companions. Then his good sense prevailed. Plenty of chiefs had gone their own way before and made fight against the Saxons, refusing to league with Count Ambrosius. Few still lived and those that did held to their wild homelands and sent the Count their spare levies with bad grace.

114

When Olipon was ushered into the Count's presence some days later to speak Arturo's words and return the ring — though he said nothing of his wearing the laurels ahead of season — Ambrosius merely nodded and showed no emotion. But when Olipon had gone he slipped the ring back on his finger and smiled broadly to himself. Many a warband like Arturo he had seen come with promise and go chastened after a few fighting seasons back into the obscurity of their bogs and mountains. But now the Fates, it seemed, were truly sending him the man he needed. Had Arturo accepted the pardon gratefully then he would have known that there was no hard lasting in him. But last this western hothead and dreamer would until the day when he should decide on his going and with no mark of infamy on him gather up his victories and his army for himself. So . . . in due time he would sue Arturo for help and let him come riding to Glevum in triumph, and in further time, when he gave the word for Arturo's death, then the full harvest of his victories and the full strength of his army would fall to him and he would make himself master of this land and bring it back to the greatness which it had once known under those other proud wearers of the laurels and the purple.

* ★ ★

On a May morning with the high soaring
downland larks filling the bright air with their
song the Companions of the White Horse left
Cam Hill and began their long march
eastwards. They numbered three troops of
thirty-two horse each. The first ranking troop
was commanded by Durstan, who had for
second-in-command Garwain. The second
was headed by Gelliga with Borio at his side,
and the third by Netio, the right side of his
face puckered with an old sword scar, with
Marcos to second him. In reserve, behind the
two baggage trains, was the reserve troop
— mostly men and mounts from Prince
Geraint — commanded by Venutius in the
place of the dead Cuneda, and served as next
in command by an Iscan trooper called
Branta. Holding the flanks, split into two
detachments, were the marshmen of Coroticus. In the baggage train, ridden by the camp
servants, were twenty remounts. In all there
were close on one hundred and fifty horse
and cavalry men — for no servant rode a
remount unless he could turn fighting man
too — and fifty spear and bowmen.

At their head rode Arturo, and Lancelo
carrying the White Horse standard. Anga, the
ageing hound, kept pace at Arturo's side. It

116

had been in Arturo's mind to leave the hound behind for the days ahead would be long and hard, but if death were to come to Anga, he decided, then it should not be pining on the hill top. He should die on the march or in battle.

They rode out, red-and-white scarfed and fish eagle studded, all weapons and fighting gear true, the rising Spring-lust in them for action and triumph; and with them went Pasco on a moorland pony, Pasco who had wearied them with a too long sermon and blessing before they left the hill.

Watching them go, Baradoc, stiff-faced with pride in his son, swallowing the gall of his own envy to be fighting fit and to go with them, remembered the day when he and Tia had landed on Caer Sibli where Arturo was to be born, remembered too what the hermit, Merlin, had written of him, scratched on the face of a rock:

Cronus in the dream spoke thus
Name him for all men and all time
His glory an everlasting flower
He throws no seed

Glory, Baradoc thought, kneading his crippled right arm, was coming to him for over the days he had spent here he had found a new Arturo and, though he tried to deny it in himself at first, had come to accept that he had fathered a man who was to be marked out among other men. Then thinking of Daria lying in the beech dell he wondered if the gods would deny Arturo the common gift of a man's love for a woman because they would keep him bound indivisibly to them for the full length of his days . . . *Aie*, Arturo was close to the gods. He accepted that now. But there was always for such men some great tribute to be paid. He raised his eyes to the far down slopes and saw the cavalcade strung out and spread across it and the red and white scarves and banners burned like a slow flame over the new grasses.

★   ★   ★

In the following days the Companions rode down the old road to Sorviodunum and on to Venta through peaceful country, the news of their coming running fast ahead of them. In Sorviodunum — where the citizens were slowly rebuilding their town, which had been sacked in a raid by sea pirates some years before — they were welcomed and freely provisioned during their stay. At Venta the same greeting met them. They then at Arturo's orders — and none knew what they would be beyond the day's march ahead — turned south-east towards the coast and rode two days to Noviomagus. Here was a strong community of Christos people and also the seat of the bishop of the diocese, an ancient, not fully witted man who believed that the rule of the Great Empire still ran through the southern lands. He gave Arturo and his chief companions lodgings in his palace. Hearing from the priest Pasco that Arturo had been baptized in the Faith before his marriage to Daria, though not that he had done so because he held all gods in reverence and some, because of their greater powers, in more reverence than others, the bishop came out at their departure and gave his Christian blessing to the little army. He also presented Arturo with a rich scarlet sleeveless surcoat embroidered with the blue-robed figure of the Virgin Mary, the halo about her head formed by clusters of small seed pearls cropped from the oysters that flourished in the nearby sea creeks and tidal flats. Arturo wore it until they were out of the bishop's domain. After that it was put with his spare gear on one of the baggage carts.

As they went eastwards between the shore and the rising slopes of the great forest of Anderida to the north, Durstan dropped back to ride with Arturo. After a while he said, 'We ride gently, as though in triumph, all victories won. This way what shall we meet but a handful of raiding sea pirates now that the good season makes fair passage and landing for their keels? The true Saxons from the Cantiaci lands seldom come south through the forest.'

Arturo nodded. 'You speak the truth. This way we ride gently — but far slower than the news of our coming. The forest is full of eyes. The word goes swiftly from charcoal burners' stands to swineherds' huts, and to the boothies of fish- and bird-trappers and so by smoke signal and fast runners to Durobrivae and Durovernum to find Esc and his warriors. Last year we were a warband, no more than a thorn in the side of Saxon pride. Now we come as an army, a sword thrust which must be met. Though it draws not Esc himself, he will send men to meet it. If he would hold his father's inheritance this is no moment for him to lose the smallest part of his valour. The eyes of his people mark him to see whether he is worthy son and successor to his father.'

Two days later, when they were almost on the borders of the lands of Eleutherus, who held the fortified British town of Anderida and called himself King, but stayed in power because he had compounded an uneasy pact

120

with Hengist, they turned northwards up the valley of a sluggish river which cut through the thick forest. Three days later they broke free of the trees and thickets on to the stream-laced high land of the river's watershed. Here, as they marched in battle order, with outriders ahead and on their flanks patrols of Coroticus's men, a horn sounded loud and clear from the front, giving the warning for the sighting of the enemy.

Riding ahead to the leading troop, Arturo saw that the Saxons had placed themselves well. The land fell away into the narrow mouth of a steeply cut valley. Three lines of Saxons held the valley bottom and its steep sides. No cavalry charge could take the steep valley sides for no horse at speed could safely assault them from the front. The Saxon lines at the valley bottom were equally well protected, for any charge down the sharp slope — if the Saxons opened ranks to let it through — would take men and horses into the marshy quagmire which was the nurturing ground of the stream that flowed north down the valley. The soft ground would hold a man with ease. But horse and man would sink and flounder in the quaking bogland to become easy victims to the long sabre-curved scramaseax swords of the Saxons.

Looking down at the enemy Arturo saw

that they were no hurriedly gathered band of undisciplined settlers and townsmen. Although few of them wore any body armour, being clothed in short leather trews and tough skin and pelt surcoats belted tight to carry axes and the sharp, deadly seax knives with which to cut the throats of a fallen enemy, they stood proudly, many of them leather helmeted and all carrying small round shields which they struck into the face of an opponent while their swords went into his guts below. More than a few, he noticed, carried a spear instead of a scramaseax and he guessed that they were local men, no true warriors, pressed into service to swell the ranks. He realized, too, that behind this confrontation, lay the warcraft, if not of Esc himself, then one of his trusted commanders, warcraft which was designed to tempt him to disaster or give him the humiliating choice of turning aside from them. But to turn aside from them would be all the victory Esc needed for the news would run like a summer heath fire and his name would be shamed before the gods and all men.

With Lancelo at his side, the White One moving a little restlessly under him so that Anga stayed away from her, Arturo ran his eyes over the Saxon lines — the warriors unnaturally silent for usually they shouted taunts and abuse — and knew that the gods were putting him under trial. And, under the gods, he knew too that there was no choice for him, nor did he seek it. Now was the time when the long days of drills and exercises back at Cam Hill must be shown to serve them all in bloody reality.

He turned to Lancelo and said, 'Give the call of the Taunted Boar.'

Lancelo put the horn to his lips and sounded the call. It was one among many that had been born of their training days, and all of them were named . . . the Taunted Boar, the Coiling Snake, the Wolf Circle . . . and there was not a fighting man or a baggage man who did not know as the notes rang out exactly what was demanded of him. The horn wailed, high and screaming, changed to a quick succession of sharp blasts and then was suddenly silent as its echoes rolled down the valley still.

Curbing the restless white mare, Arturo watched the pattern of his men and horses move and swirl and heard the shouts of the baggage train handlers as the end of the column closed up and the reserve troop rimmed it in a double-rowed crescent.

The two forward troops went wide on each flank, well above the valley head, and held their mounts champing and restless in double lines, the forenoon breeze teasing their red and white scarves and helmet crests, the sun striking points of fire from the scabbard-freed swords of each front rank and sparking the lance tips of the second lines.

Then into the forefront of the battle formation came Coroticus and his men, spears slung behind their backs, their bows drawn and arrowed and each man holding three arrows crossways in his mouth. They trotted down the slope in two lines abreast and when they were within easy bowshot of the ranks of Saxons Coroticus called an order. The first line of marshmen dropped to one knee and the second line stood two paces behind.

For a moment or two there was no movement save that of restless horses, no sounds save those of the high chorusing larks. Not even from the Saxon ranks came taunt or shout for they were meeting now a move which puzzled them for they had expected an onrush of cavalry to cut through them and throw them into disorder while the marsh-men followed up behind with their spears.

Coroticus, who assumed no commander's privilege in fighting itself and knelt at the right end of the first line of bowmen, gave a low curlew's whistle and, flexing his arrow-charged bow, took aim at the throat of a man on the right flank of the centre line of the Saxon warriors in the valley bottom. The arrow sped true to take the man in the gullet and with a high choking scream he toppled backwards. As he did so the marshman on Coroticus's left sent his arrow through the left eye of another warrior. And then the next marshman, unhurried, following the well-learnt drill, fired another arrow, the goose-feathered shaft sinking deep into a Saxon's left breast. Deliberately, without hurry, a few moments between each shot, the marshmen picked their targets and fired, and not until twenty of their men were down did the Saxons stir and break their silence. The taunting of the boar had begun and Arturo, watching, knew that the Saxons barring the marshy ground would not long hold themselves in check for it was the nature of these men to go to meet the enemy eagerly, filling the air with their battle cries.

So it proved. As man after man went down, now from the middle ranks and now from the valley-side flanking ranks, the cries came and grew louder and angrier, and those Saxons with spears flung them at the marshmen. But Coroticus had gauged his front well and they all fell short. Then suddenly like the onrush of a tidal wave, in a great burst of noise, the three ranks of Saxons, on the steep hill sides and valley bottom, enraged that they should stand like sheep to wait the arrow which would send them to Valhalla, broke ranks and surged forward shields high, scramaseaxes swinging, eager to come to grips with their foes.

Arturo at Lancelo's side smiled as he saw their coming. Thus was the taunted boar goaded to break cover and offer itself to slaughter. He nodded to Lancelo and the horn called, echoing down the narrow valley.

Coroticus's men, as the Saxons rushed for them, turned and ran back and as Coroticus passed Arturo he looked up. There was a gleam in his dark eyes and — seldom seen in a marshman except in drink — a broad grin on his face and the faces of all his men.

As the Saxons raced after them, leaving their boggy ground far behind, Gelliga's flanking troop came galloping down upon them, the heavy swords of the first rank swinging and slashing and cutting into the enemy, killing and maiming. Behind them came the second line of lances to bring death to those wounded warriors who from the ground on their knees or backs tried to hack and stab at the legs and bellies of the horses. Then, after the passing of Gelliga's troop, there came down from the opposite flank, charging through their already blooded companions, the troop of Durstan to hack and hew and carry their killing lances through the shouting rabble of Saxon warriors.

Arturo watched as the two troops wheeled, reformed and charged again. This time the Saxons broke and ran hard for the safety of the lower soft ground from which they had been tempted and kept running even as Lancelo's horn sounded behind them the call to break action. Watching them go Arturo knew that this was a beginning, a good and god-given beginning, a gift from Badb, the god of battle, and an offering to Andraste, the goddess of victory, and proof that — great fighters though the Saxons were when they saw victory coming to their grasp — they were no men to stand and die in defeat if any loophole of escape still offered itself to them.

Close to a hundred men lay dead or dying, their arms to be plundered, and their small wealth of rings and torques, brooches and armlets which they wore into battle to be taken into the war chest of the Companions against the wants of the long campaigning days ahead. The news of this first clash would run fast and far and wide. Looking up, Arturo saw in the clear afternoon sky the beginning of the first circling of the prey birds, kites, eagles, the diamond-tailed ravens and the already bickering crows mobbing the stately circling buzzards to ease their impatience to arrive at the waiting feast below.

That night, as Arturo made his round of the sentry posts with Lancelo, he heard from the downland hollow where his men sat around their camp fires the voice of Durstan singing:

The boar in the east does not call
No more in his bracken lodge does he
    sleep
The hornet flight of the arrows of
    Coroticus
Have taunted him to rage
And the swords of Arturo
Have stayed the strength of his red
    anger

Under the moonlight his saffron tusks
Make perches for the ravens who feed
    on his eyes
And on the dead pine branches
The eagles sit heavy from feasting

128

# Girl with a Harp

For the rest of that spring and summer they sat nowhere in camp for long. For the first part they stayed south of the river Tamesis, moving, sometimes in small bands and sometimes in full strength, along the borders of the Saxon lands, harrying and destroying the outlying settlements, of which there were many; for the Saxons were no lovers of town life. They lived mostly in family and kinship groups in the clearings they had made in the forests or on the slopes of the gentle river valleys.

They came and went with no pattern of movement or settled strength which the Saxons could anticipate. They were a wolf pack, marauding now in force and now in small groups. They leaguered their baggage train well to their west and then for a week the cavalry troops of the Companions would disappear to the east with Coroticus's men to attack at dawn or as last daylight faded, until the time came when they mounted a strong assault on the heavily settled outskirts of Durobrivae, the next largest town after Durovernum. They came at night and set fire

129

to the hovels and round huts and squalid log cabins along the river so that the flames turned its waters to blood. When daylight came — for the Saxons had no taste for night marching — and the warriors had gathered in the dawn to pursue them they had melted away, splitting into small parties of eight or ten horse and a few marshmen, each group going its own way back to the baggage train. Then, when at last Esc — who had other matters on his mind — finally gathered a force to overmatch them and marched westwards they were nowhere to be found on the borders of his land for they had gone north around Londinium — which the aftermath of plague had turned into a ghost city, though even without such a scourge there were now few who chose to live and trade there — and were sitting openly and in force on the road to Durolipons which bordered the land of the Trinovantes held by the East Saxons.

Now, too, though Arturo never gave explanation of his overall strategy, the shape of the design that lay in his mind began to come clear to most of his leading Companions, and — since he had served under Ambrosius as a staff officer — abidingly clear to Venutius. This year and for a few more years the pattern would be fixed. Harry and raid and go. They would stand and fight when the battle was fairly matched, but not otherwise. A man or horse lost in a useless foray or an overmatched confrontation gained Arturo nothing. This was the first sowing of a rich crop to come and the sowing would be not of one year but many. Already fighting men were coming to them, seeking them out and to all of them the answer of Arturo was the same: to ride to Cam Hill, come the autumn, where a welcome would await them. None joined him now who did not know the ways of the Companions and had not their training and discipline. No man could fight with them until he had learnt their ways, their discipline and proved himself, and Venutius saw readily the virtue of this demand. One man accepted by Arturo would be worth ten reluctant levied men. He saw too — perhaps more than any other Companion — that patience was now yoked with Arturo's warlike, eager spirit. The dream he dreamt was not to be accomplished in a few years. Already he was looking ten, twenty, thirty years ahead. Ambrosius had dreamt and schemed like that, did so still, but time was now against him unless he let Arturo enrich his fame and his power and then, with no sign of villainy, gather them to himself. Venutius tried often to shut the thought of that moment from his mind, but each day it was with him inescapably for he knew that he was trapped. When Ambrosius's messenger came with the nicked golden aureus of the Emperor Hadrian he would have no choice. If he let Arturo live then Ambrosius would make it known that he had poisoned Daria and, no matter the esteem Arturo might have for him through his service as a Companion, he would be killed . . .

Against the East Saxons that year they pursued the same tactics as they had done with the South Saxons. Then as summer began to pass they moved farther north through Causennae to Lindum, where the news of their coming had run ahead fast of them. Here, where the city and surrounding country were precariously held by the Coritani, they were welcomed warmly by the townsfolk and the bishop. The Companions made camp on the gently rising ground to the south of the town, but the bishop insisted that Arturo should take quarters in his own palace, and on his first evening they supped together.

The bishop, a small, spare man of fifty, a sparrow of a man, with a dark, cheerful glint in his eyes, entertained him alone, and was full of eagerness to hear of his progress along the borders of the Saxon lands.

He said as they ate a dish of stuffed carp, 'I shall be in bad grace with Count Ambrosius for making you welcome but 'tis long since he was here and may be longer before he comes again. But who am I to deny hospitality to one who brings a gleam of hope for this wretched land — and one, too, who is a Christian. Is that not so, my son?'

'It is, your grace.'

The bishop smiled. 'But have, too, I am told, a great respect for this country's old gods.'

Arturo, who liked the man, and had measured quickly his nature, said, 'This is my country. Without its gods it would be nothing. For love of my dead wife I became a Christos man. For love of my country I also worship my country's gods. A warrior, your grace, needs all the help he can get.'

'I will not argue that point with you. Time will make a better argument than I can.' He sipped wine from his silver mounted glass and went on, 'It is a pity that there is bad blood between you and Count Ambrosius. God knows you are welcome here for we live dangerously and are raided often by the fen Saxons beyond the great Car dyke.'

Arturo shrugged his shoulders. 'The Count is a dreamer of dusty dreams. As dusty as the old ways of Rome to which he clings. He waits for a miracle. I work for an end and, if the gods spare me, will come to it. While the South Saxons are all in disarray he should have gone against them, but I hear that he holds back because he thinks they will not come out against him, lacking a strong leader. Why wait? If I had two thousand men this summer I could have swept through the Cantiaci lands and driven them into the sea from Tanatus round to Lemanis, could have smoked them out of their holes like rats. But the day is coming when I will have those men, and this summer I have made a beginning under the gods . . . ' he paused for a moment, and then added, ' . . . and under the banner of Christos.'

The bishop nodded, his mouth pursed with a wry smile, and said, 'You have an interesting approach to theology — but a very direct and admirable one to the great matter of this country. In a man who loves his country so ardently many things can be forgiven.' He sighed. 'Ah, me, yes. The good Lord works in a fashion not always easily understood. But we grow too serious. We shall have music to sweeten the rest of the evening.'

He spoke to the servant who was attending them who left the room to come back a few moments later with a young girl who carried a small harp. Sitting herself on a bench by the open window she began to play and sing for them in a sweet, though not oversure voice at first, as though she were nervous. But after a little while she grew confident.

Leaning back in his chair Arturo listened to her as his eyes marked the evening hawking outside of the young swallows who were beginning to flock together for their southerly passage. Already the swifts had gone. Soon the geese and the migrating peregrines would go and the host of small warblers and finches. Summer was fast deferring to autumn and his first campaign was almost done. The stone had been thrown into the still pond and the ripples were spreading. How many summers, how many campaigns before . . . ? He sighed, touched for a time by a sudden sense of weariness. In that moment, seeing his return to Cam Hill, he knew a brief and bitter flare of sorrow for the one love who could give him no greeting.

Through that moment of rare self-pity the young girl's voice came to him, clear and sweet. She was singing an old song which he knew well; a song the Companions sang around their camp fires. Daria lay in the beech dell. Ten of his Companions and as many of Coroticus's marshmen would see no return to Cam Hill.

I have a hut in the wood
None knows it but my love
An ash tree this side
A hazel on the other
A little hidden lowly hut
Where waits my flame-haired love . . .

For the first time Arturo looked closely at her. She was a girl of twelve or thirteen years, her young breasts scarce challenging the soft material of the short white linen robe she wore. Her bare legs were sun-browned and on her feet were red sandals of soft doe skin. Sensing that the two men were now listening to her song, she raised her head, her fair hair caught with a ribbon of the same colour as her sandals, and smiled at them. For a moment the pink tip of her tongue ran like some small soft animal between her teeth and there was a momentary widening of her blue eyes. Deep, dark blue, Arturo saw, like the flash on a jay's covert feathers.

The black cock calls from the high
    heather
We eat sweet apples under summer's
    mantle
Her lips the red of the ripe bog-ber-
    ries . . .

136

A child still, thought Arturo as he sipped his wine, but with already something of boldness in her eyes. In five or six years' time she would turn the heads of young men and many would sigh for love of her.

When she had finished the song the bishop said to her, 'It is a song fit for a resting warrior. Play once more for us, child, and then away to your couch.'

On the word 'child' Arturo saw the flick of her eyebrows, momentary as the beat of a bird's wing, mark a fast passing frown and remembered the childhood years when, feeling himself more, he had bridled at the same word.

She lowered her head over the harp, her face hidden from them and touched the strings strongly so that the notes came boldly and arrogantly —

The boar in the east does not call
No more in his bracken lodge does he
    sleep . . .

Beside him the bishop began to chuckle with pleasure and looked at Arturo for approval.

Arturo smiled too as she played on and when she had finished he said, 'From where do you get such a song?'

Without shyness she said, 'From your men, my lord, who walk the city. I would have liked to have been there to see the taunting of the boar.'

Arturo laughed. 'It was no fit place for a girl.' Then seeing the brief tightening of her face, he went on, 'But you sing sweetly enough to shame the nightingale at dusk and when the words are of war you have all the music of the dark torrent.'

She laughed then and said, 'You tease me, my lord.'

'And I tease you more straightly,' said the bishop, smiling. 'Get you to your couch and be glad you will become a woman and have no part in wars. Away with you.'

The girl rose from her chair, bowed to them and went to the doorway. There, her face full now of mischief and spirit, she drew her fingers across the harp to sound a full, loud run of chords, bowed and went out.

Both men laughed and then Arturo asked, 'Who is she, your grace?'

'She is from far north of Eburacum. Her father, one Loth, is a good friend of mine. She visits here with her mother, who is my sister, for there is some talk of placing her with the nuns here, though . . . ' he sighed a little, 'I doubt that it will serve her much. She is high spirited and wayward when she chooses. But also full of womanly charms and guile when she needs. I have my own minstrels here, but tonight she cajoled me — no difficult task with a doting uncle — to be allowed to play and sing for you. So you see, your fame begins to run fast before you. Arturo of the White Horse and his Companions are more to her liking than the sparrow chatter and spartan life of a nunnery.'

'And her name?'

'It is Gwennifer.'

That night as he lay on his bed Arturo was long in finding sleep. In a few more days the Companions would turn and take the road south to find Cam Hill. There were many good welcomes to await a returning warrior, but none sweeter than the woman of his heart. If the gods blessed him with long life and with victories and the true shaping of his dreams for this country they had already taken their toll in return for his triumphs to come. Daria slept in the beech dell with Cuneda to guard her. True heart and true friend. Without these a man's life was barren. Thinking this he dropped a hand over the side of the bed and his fingers found the hoary head of Anga sleeping alongside him. He remembered the day of his fourteenth birthday in Isca when his mother had given him the hound puppy as a present to take the

139

place of old Lerg; remembered, too, his grief when the old hound had died. Some griefs passed so that memory ran without pain but others endured, their season unending. An owl called and the rising moon began to limn the room with pale light. As sleep began to touch him he remembered his first meeting on the Dumnonian moors with Daria who travelled north with her father, old Ansold, and her brother, now his good companion, Lancelo, and how she had said that they travelled to this town — though they never reached it — where . . . Her voice rang clear in his memory. *To hear my father tell it — where every other spring flows wine instead of water, where the birds on the trees have golden wings, and the cattle grass grows knee-high and lush through winter.* And he had replied — *One day I will come to Lindum and seek you out . . . I shall come and woo you and we shall lie in the long grass, listen to the golden birds sing, and drink the new wine.*

He slept and the memories slept with him.

Two mornings later he woke to hear the lowing of heifers being driven up the street below, the cries of their drovers and the ringing of the high towered bell of the nunnery, a bell which rang the alarm when over the green marshes and low willow thickets to the east beyond the great Car Dyke the lookouts marked the approach of raiding Saxon bands. This morning they served as a farewell to Anga for the old hound had died in his sleep during the night. Arturo took him, wrapped in his cloak, and buried him under a mulberry tree in the bishop's garden. Three days later the small army left Lindum marching south-west down the old Imperial road of the legions, a road broken, neglected, but still serviceable that ran in a long diagonal across the land through Crococalana to Ratae to Corinium and from Corinium to Aquae Sulis and then through Lindinis to Isca Dumnoniorum.

Not long after they had left Lindum there were cries and shouts from the rear troop and the baggage trains. Slewing round in his saddle at the head of the long column, Arturo looked back. Coming down the road was a youth on a small skewbald pony galloping fast, and laughter broke through the bright morning air as now and then he was forced by baggage cart or troop formation to veer to the side and take to the rougher going of the roadside vallum.

Arturo, signalling to Lancelo to keep the long strung column moving, pulled aside free of the road to a bank where already the tall spikes of sweet balsam were being harvested by the bees and wasps. The youth rode up to him, his face flushed with sweat and dust He wore a loose cloak that reached to the knees of his short leather trews and a red scarf wrapped like a turban about his head to trap all but a few loose curls of his fair hair.

Arturo smiling, knowing that the deceit of habit was not meant for him but to fool — though it scarce could have done — the gate sentries of Lindum, said jokingly, 'We seek no recruits who are not of age — especially one who rides so awkwardly.' There was no mistaking the deep, dark blue eyes and the fair hair and poppy bright lips of Gwennifer.

The girl was silent for a moment, catching her breath. Then dropping her reins she pulled the scarf from her head and her hair fell in a tangle which the breeze teased so that it was a moving web of gold threads under the sun, and she said solemnly, 'My lord Arturo, I ride not to join you, but to bring you that which may ease a little the sorrow in your heart.'

Then, urging the pony forward a little so that she was at the side of the White One, she fumbled beneath her drawn cloak and drew out a brindle and white-throated puppy which squealed as she held it from her and from fright piddled a little so that the liquid sprayed one of her bare legs. She said urgingly, 'Take him, my lord. He is of the best blood and will be a good hound. The bishop would have none other in his kennels.'

Touched by the gesture, Arturo covered the quick emotion rising in him, and said chaffingly, 'The bishop will give you no thanks for pillaging his kennels and I would not see you in trouble for your kindness.'

Gwennifer frowned and said firmly, 'But he is mine to give. My uncle made present of him to me when I came here with my mother. Take him, my lord.'

Arturo hesitated for a moment, then reached out and took the puppy — which could scarce have had three months since its whelping. Its belly was warm against the palm of his hand, and the sweet hound smell strong from its pelt. He said, 'I take him and give you thanks. What is he called?'

'Cabal, my lord, and he will be a hound above all hounds for the gods have told me so in a dream.'

Cocking an eye in open doubt, Arturo asked, 'The gods speak to you in your dreams?'

'Sometimes. They have shown me many things that will happen. Some I like and some I like not, but then . . . ' she shrugged her shoulders lightly, ' . . . there is no changing the fall of the dice they have shaken.'

'You talk old for one so young. The Christos nuns will have their hands full with you.'

She shook her head and laughed. 'I shall make them such trouble, my lord, that they will cry out to be rid of me.' Then eyeing him boldly, she said, 'Why wish them that trouble? I can keep these clothes and come with you to Cam Hill to serve you as well as any other. I can do — '

'Enough.' Arturo shook his head and his lips tightened severely. 'I thank you for your gift and for the gentleness of thought that provoked it. But now you go back to Lindum to your mother and the good bishop. And to make sure you do I send two men with you. Back to Lindum. This I command.'

'Then I shall go — for such I would have done anyway since I came only to lodge Cabal with you. But this I say, my lord, and further risk your anger. One day I shall ride into Cam Hill and you will welcome me since in a dream — '

' — the gods have shown you this,' finished Arturo for her.

'Aye, my lord and more.'

'Then I believe you. Now ride for Lindum.'

He turned from her back on to the road and called for Marcos to give her escorts and handed him Cabal to find place for on one of the baggage carts. Then he rode to take his place at the head of the main column — for one troop of horse rode well ahead even in this peaceful country — alongside Lancelo.

Lancelo grinned when Arturo told him what had happened and said, 'All Lindum and Eburacum, it is said, knows her for her wildness and, although she is a girl, her father has taken the birch to her for some of her doings.'

Lightly Arturo said, 'Some women are born with the hearts of men, and some men with the hearts of women and for the making of trouble there is no choosing between them.' He said no more but as he rode and looked down to where Anga had for so long padded alongside him, he knew gratitude for the gift she had brought. The gods had sent him another hound. Let their gifts to her be always so good . . .

★ ★ ★

They marched that day to the outskirts of Ratae where they made camp. That evening as Arturo sat outside his small tent Durstan came and joined him, bringing a bowl of goat's milk for the hound puppy. As they watched the puppy drink Durstan said, 'You

145

mean to keep this road for the full march?'

'I do.'

'We march through Corinium?'

'We do. The more we are seen the more will men come to us this winter.'

'And what of the Sabrina Wing? We are no match for them as yet.'

'There is only a small holding force at Corinium. Count Ambrosius is still making his progress, so the bishop told me, and is at Deva.'

'He is well informed.'

'You do not stay bishop long otherwise. I learnt much from him. He is with us, and will make and find friends for us among the chiefs north of Eburacum.' He picked up Cabal and stroked his white throat. 'We are only at the beginning of things. We need the friendship and the help of his kind over the years to come. The Christos bishops and their people grow stronger in this country. The more a country suffers . . . aye, and they with it, the more their strength grows and we have chance to turn it to our advantage.'

Durstan plucked a tall grass stalk, chewed its end for a moment or two and then, even he not knowing what reception his words might provoke, said quietly, 'But you are no true Christos man, Arturo. They will come to know this.'

Arturo frowned. 'I am as true a Christos man as any for he is a god with other gods. When you are with fever you do not pray to Epona. You send your prayers to Nodens of the Silver Hand. In battle you cry on Badb not Lug who blesses the seed of man in woman. But when a whole nation suffers then you call on all the gods. I would think it no shame or treason to put on the surcoat given me by the bishop at Noviomagus and go into battle wearing the image of the blessed mother of Christos.'

Durstan said nothing. There were times when the reasoning of Arturo escaped him. He prodded the flank of Cabal and the puppy turned and began to worry at the hard leather of his campaign boot.

The silence between them was broken by the first evening churring of a nightjar and the flames of the bivouac fires from the camp spread around them on the sandy heath they had chosen for the night were cut by the black shapes of the sentries who patrolled the limits of their resting place.

Arturo said quietly, 'What has to be done will be many years in the making. Only if Cronus woke from his great sleep could he speed the years so that they seemed but weeks to bring us to end of the long labours which lie ahead. We are mortal and so must

147

live and fight and build to the measure of our own breathing.'

Four days later they marched through Corinium. The small holding party which Ambrosius had left at the Sabrina Wing camp had advance news of their coming. When the dust of their marching showed the commander called his men to arms and two troops of cavalry were deployed in battle formation along the eastern front of the camp which was flanked by the Ratae-Corinium road. Ambrosius had left him without orders for this happening. But he was a man of good sense and not without admiration for Arturo. When the long snaking column of Arturo's Companions came into view with Coroticus's men and mounted scouts guarding its flanks, he put his horse to the trot and, leaving his men, made to the place in the long column where the White Horse standard flew in the soft breeze.

Seeing him coming Arturo rode away from the road and across the bare, hoof-packed training grounds to meet him.

Reining-in the White One, Arturo said, 'We come in peace. We fight the same battle and follow the same cause as Count Ambrosius.'

The commander's mouth twisted to a wry smile and he said, 'Aye, that is true, my lord Arturo. Then pass peacefully. I can give you no provisioning or quartering here for under the writ of Count Ambrosius you are outlaw still.' He shrugged his shoulders, and with a firm hand gentled his restless horse. 'A pity . . . for otherwise we could have shared wine, and I would have had pleasure in good talk with many of my old friends whom I now see among your ranks.'

Smiling Arturo said, 'A pity, true — but if you feel their loss so much you could join us.'

The commander shook his head. 'Not me, my lord. I am one of the old Ambrosiaci. When you were a boy I fought with the Count in the days of the great raidings of the South coasts. We were young then and fought at Anderida and Noviomagus to tame the sea raiders. My battle scars were suffered under him. I carry them with honour and — though he grows old now like me and, in truth, less venturesome — I am his man. So, pass in peace, my lord. Break it and we shall come against you.'

'We pass in peace, and may the gods give you honour for your loyalty.'

So Arturo and his men passed in peace, over the clear waters of the river that curved gently around the north-eastern side of the city, a river where the trout grew fat on the jettisoned offal from the market slaughter-houses, and the citizens opened the newly built portals of the Verulamium gate. A great crowd lined the streetway that led through the city's heart to the far Aquae Sulis gate and Arturo — now at the head of the column — smiled to himself as they passed the Forum on their left where, on a rainy day now seeming far into the past, he had scrawled with a piece of charcoal, words of defiance at Ambrosius when he had first been outlawed. Over the heads of the crowd he could pick out the very pillar of the Basilica colonnade on which he had written . . . *Between the empty promise of Arto and the sloth of Ambrosius where shall a warrior blood his lance?* Bold words, but seeded with truth, a truth which this last year had seen grow and flourish, and there was no hollow ring to his youthful promise now. The gods had set him on his way and he knew that he was in their hands for the rest of his years.

They came to Cam Hill on a day when an early and sharp frost had set the leaves of the riverside willows and the ash trees on the camp slopes falling. His father, Baradoc, was there to greet him, and had been there with his workmen for all the spring and summer months. Work on the plateau fortifications was running fast; a great hall, troop quarters and stables had been built of wood and roofed with reed and hazel-bough faggots and there was now a small set of private quarters for Arturo. New ground had been broken in the valleys, crops sown and harvested, and hay gathered and stacked for the horses against the winter so that they would have to make no great call on Prince Geraint and King Melwas for provisioning. Ansold had set up a smithy and forge for the repair of arms and armour and stores of charcoal had been bartered for with the cutters and burners in the woods to the west. But most pleasing to Arturo was the sight in the valley to the south of a camp where was quartered a force of near a hundred men and horses . . . free men and trained cavalry men and their mounts, and two men — sons of a chief of the Durotriges — who had come, provisioned and armed, to beg leave to join the Companions. As the good name and the renown of the Companions ran wider Arturo knew that there would be many a glory-impatient son of a tribal chief pestering or bullying a father for leave to take men and mounts to come and join him.

The following night a great feast was set to celebrate their return. The chief companions filled the long table in the new hall and all the other men sat at rough tables or squatted around the fires that ringed the hall and whose blaze could be seen afar on Ynys-witrin

151

top and the sea-dominating knoll of Brant. They roasted three heifers, two pigs and long spitfuls of trussed wildfowl taken from the Cam river marshes. Six goatskins of new mead and apple ale matched their thirst, and flat cakes of fine-querned corn flour were spread with sweet thyme-and-marjoram tanged honey which had been brought as a gift by the two sons of the chief of the Durotriges.

Before the feast Pasco said a common grace, calling on the names of Christos and His Father and others from the crowded pantheon of the country's true gods. He then called for the first filling of cup and beaker and horn and leather tankard with wine and mead to drink to the memory of their fallen comrades and to make plea for their high cherishing in the halls of the gods. The great shout which went up after each beaker and cup was drained at a single draught sent the harbouring starlings into wild night flight from their roosts in the trees so that their high calling sounded like a matching paean of praise. This done, all set to, eating and drinking without stint, heedless of the morning which would bring them thundering wine-pounded heads and the sharp belly cramps of gluttony which could sear a man's guts as cruelly as winter famine.

Much later when the men still held to the

long hall tables and the lowering fires, laughing and singing and over-gilding the tales and exploits of their campaigning days, Arturo left them and with Baradoc at his side sat outside his own private quarters, teasing the ears of the sleeping Cabal in his lap.

Baradoc said. 'My son, you have begun what I would have done when I was your age if the gods had been kind.'

'I know, my father. But the gods have marked you for as great a work. There are other hills like this which need your art and provisioning. To campaign is one thing, but when Latis weeps and the rains come and the snow denies passage to man and mount then we must have harbour to hold us through the winter. Although the men sing of our triumph, I know that it has been but a little thing to give me understanding. We must have such places set from south to north across the country, from Lindum down to Noviomagus so that men and arms can at all times bar passage to the Middle, East and West Saxons. We must hold them to the lands they have and strike if they try to break through. When the time comes that they weaken because few come now across the seas to join them because there is no true promise of new land to settle or easy raiding for plunder and slaves . . . *aie*, then we shall press against them and send them into the sea and to their long keels.'

'You talk of many years ahead.'

'Aye. Of a full life time. But it will be granted me for the gods have promised it. Next year, if Prince Geraint give you leave, we must find such a place set back from the front between Lindum and Londinium from which in winter and all seasons the Middle Saxons can be held, and then between Londinium and the Gaulish sea to hold the others. And Londinium — still little more than a desert, shunned by traders and not looked to as market place for the Tamesis settlers — must be held and garrisoned to bar all land passages between Esc and the Saxon shoremen to his north. Aye, the thing is a loose tangle in my mind still but with patience and years the yarn shall be spun and the good cloth woven . . . '

Listening, Baradoc felt the force of the passion that worked in his son and without harsh regret he knew that the dream he had dreamt at Arturo's age had been put into the hands of this fair-haired, lean-faced warrior of his own seeding to accomplish, and that the gods to aid him had given him the gift of foresight so that, as a golden eagle soars high to take the full span of a country in sight, Arturo saw not the year ahead, saw not five or ten years but held in view the years of a lifetime. For the first time then, piercing him so that he felt the hair-prick of awe touch the back of his head like a chilling wind, he gave surrender to the full and new truth that indeed the gods had marked him.

He rose and, touching Arturo on the shoulder, gave him goodnight and walked away, rubbing gently at the stiffness of his injured right arm. As he went laughter and shouting ceased from the long hall and through the sharpening air of the night came the voice of Durstan singing to the clear, vibrant notes of a harp.

The knife has gone into the meat
And the good wine fills the horn
In Arturo's hall . . .
Here is food for your hound
And corn for your horse
In Arturo's hall . . .
But none there shall enter unless he be
Swift with a sword and comrade to
all . . .

Long after his father had gone but while the singing and playing still made bird and beast uneasy over the hill top and slopes, Arturo rose and, holding Cabal warm under his cloak, went down to the beech dell where Daria lay.

He sat still and brooding for a long time, so still that once a disturbed hare came lolloping past him within spitting distance. The gods had taken Daria from him and the taking had place in the pattern of the life they had marked for him. On the march and in skirmishing and forays a man had no thoughts of women. But when the winter came and there was all to refurbish and peaceful nights to lie abed in warmth a warrior's manhood called for companionship and close harbouring under the warm furs and thick woven covers. Even as he thought this it was as though the mood of his companions matched his own for the sweet voice of Gelliga came clear to him.

Take my true greeting to the girl of
   thick tresses
The sweetheart I lay with in the glen of
   green willows . . .

He sat listening as Gelliga sang on of the hot yearning that not even battle and the chance of death waiting at the opening door of each fighting day could smother. To tumble a willing girl in the high quakegrass, its falling pollen sweetening all kisses, to slake the blood's hot fever in the arms of some milk-breasted matron . . . *Aie*, these the gods would permit him. He had paid the full barter price in the loss of Daria. To take another wife and worship her, though her flesh and warmth could never cloud the memory of Daria, would be no affront to the gods now nor stir their jealousy. They had marked him for their own and could justly claim they had given him the only love he needed, constant and life-abiding . . . the love of his country. With the passing of years would come the great consummation of that love — freedom from tyranny for all men.

Cabal stirred within his cloak and then the hound's head was thrust free from the folds that cradled him. Cabal yawned, then whimpered and struggled free to the ground. Yawning still, Cabal piddled against a mole hill.

The next morning early Coroticus came to Arturo to take his leave and return with his men to Yyns-witrin. His men were drawn up in line on the plateau grass land and with them were two ponies laden with the share of plunder spoil that went with Coroticus for his father Arturo walked with Coroticus down the double line of men and there was pleasure in him at their appearance. Pride they had always had for few marshmen were born without it, but now they had added to it a sense of brotherhood and a spirit of discipline which he knew would mark them out from all other marshmen and fire more men to join them in the years to come. The past campaign had brought them losses, a sad price that had to be paid for the discovery of an abiding purpose in the seasons of fighting to come. Although their dress was marked, as were their bodies, with the scars and rubs of fighting, they stood proudly, the sun flashing on the copper studdings of their fish eagle emblems. Standing back from them with Coroticus at his side, he spoke to them, giving them his thanks and warming their pride with a fair eulogy of their prowess. When he had finished Coroticus called on them for the marshmens' salute and — all of them moving as one man — they drew their bows, notched their goose and heron feather flighted arrows and with a great shout sent them high into the air above their heads, the song of their flight a great keening through the morning brightness. Then the arrows turned at the top of their flight and came hissing back to earth to form a circle of trembling, feather-plumed wands about Arturo and Coroticus.

Coroticus stepped forward and pulled one of the arrows from the ground and with a quick movement snapped it in half across a raised knee. He handed the feather-tipped

half to Arturo and said, 'My lord Arturo —
you are the first man not a marshman to be
given the royal salute of the House of
Melwas. With that broken shaft in hand you
are free of the Summerlands and marshes for
all time and wherever you show it my people
will know it and give you welcome and safe
passage for all the years of your life.'

He touched his forehead in salute and then
moving to the head of his men led the
company of marsh warriors, the proud
wearers of the fish eagle, away. Arturo stood
and watched them go until the last man had
disappeared down the wooded slope of Cam
Hill.

# The Woman of the High Rocks

For near six years Arturo campaigned, building slowly to the great plan which now lay clear in his mind, to hold the Saxons behind the line that ran from Lindum in the north down to Londinium and thence south-west to the fringes of the great forest of Anderida. Behind this line the Middle and East Saxons — denied any leaguing with Esc — and the South Saxons of Esc himself sat and stirred themselves only occasionally to make token forays. It was as though a great sleep had overcome them from which now and then they waked and, petulant at the disturbance, made a brief show of strength. But Arturo — though he was content over the years to see his forces grow and new camps organized by his father — knew that the day would come when Esc or some leader of the Middle and East Saxons would take the field to try and break him. Nothing could stop this happening because their own kind still came over the seas to them, though in smaller numbers since eastern Gaul and the great prizes lying to the south and beyond the Alps drew most of the land- and plunder-hungry

160

warriors. The Saxon enclaves in the land were like leather water skins which were slowly filling to overflowing point.

During these years Count Ambrosius kept strict intelligence of all he did, and of the growth of his forces to which more and more men flocked. To avoid conflict with him — since Arturo was serving him without knowing it — he limited his own campaigns to the country well north of Eburacum and to the western and southern parts of Cymru where now the Scotti raids and encroachments had to be met and contained. There were times, too, when he acknowledged that the young Arturo, now near his thirtieth year, for all his passion and lust for war, carried a wise head on his shoulders and schooled himself with a patience beyond his years. Where there were small peaceful Saxon outlying settlements to the west of his line he left them untouched and forced tribute and stores from them. If unwisely they took to arms and raiding he rode down on them and there was a burning and a slaughter to signal a flaming and bloody warning to their fellows. But the passing of the years now began to build an impatience in Ambrosius. His years were limited and the past of his beginnings when he had stood against the Saxons at Noviomagus was a misted memory. Each day now the itch for the great triumph, the lust for the day when he could ride, laurel-wreathed and wearing the purple toga, to the full inheritance he claimed in this land, bit and worried him, denying him sleep and forcing upon him an impatience which ate into him with each passing day.

On an autumn evening as he walked in the rose garden of his headquarters at Glevum and his feet sank deep in the first frost-fall of leaves from the great walnut tree which some long forgotten Roman commander had brought from mid-Gaul, his Camp Prefect came to him with the news that Arturo, instead of returning to Cam Hill, was staying with a small army to winter in Lindum. Walking stiffly, aware of the rheumatic ache in his legs which had come over the years from hard lying and campaigning, and from that awareness conscious with a sudden pang of bitterness and anxiety that his years might be fewer than he thought, that the gods even might be tiring of the slow game he played and would turn against him, he decided that the time had come to make the throw which would win him the game which he had played for so long with patience ... aye, and suffering, for he had taken the arrogance and open contempt of Arturo with a softness which hid his true feelings.

A week later, as Venutius sat in his lodgings in Durobrivae where he had come with Arturo to make an inspection of the small force of cavalry and foot soldiers who were to garrison it for the winter, a travelling horse dealer came to him to make an offer for some of the foals which had been dropped by the mares of the Companions but had been rejected by him as horsemaster as unworthy of their winter keep. When the bargain was struck the man, a pleasant-faced, affable fellow, took a coin from his belt pouch and dropped it on the table before Venutius, saying, 'This is payment and more for the foals.'

On the table between them lay the nicked golden aureus of the Emperor Hadrian. Venutius looked without emotion at the coin for he had known for some time now that its coming could not long be delayed. The mind and the emotions of Count Ambrosius were nothing strange or unreadable to him He said, 'Say what you have been told to say and say it quickly.' Just for a moment the spark of hope burned in him that the man's words would not be the final ones from Ambrosius.

'It is to be done, and done quickly and with no loss of honour to your reputation or forfeiting of your standing with the Companions. The room that Arturo's going makes is to be filled by you under the Count. You have proved yourself with the Companions. There is none among them more fitting to take his place than you.'

He spoke the truth for over the years Venutius had slowly come to stand closer to Arturo — not in friendship, but in military worth and the ordering of large commands of men — than any of the Companions who claimed his warmest friendship, and stood now acknowledged as Arturo's right-hand man. He could turn them to Ambrosius and with that done Ambrosius would move Prince Geraint, King Melwas and the ever growing ranks of tribal chiefs and overlords to acknowledge him while doing honour to Arturo's memory and greatness.

He picked up the coin and said, 'Tell Count Ambrosius it will be done.'

After the man had gone he sat on and, pouring himself a beaker of wine, drank absently, his eyes looking into the future which the gods had set for him. There had never been any escape for him from the day when, in all ignorance of Arturo, his loyalty to Ambrosius had sent him on his way to Cam Hill. Nothing now remained to him but that loyalty and its rewards and the slow, enduring stain of his own self-disgust that there was not the courage in him now to fling the golden aureus from him, take his side dagger from his belt, and make an end to his already crippled life. But the power that stayed his hand from the dagger was beyond his changing for it had true place in his nature. Raising his head as he drank more wine he saw that outside the first heavy snowflakes of the onsetting winter had begun to fall.

The snow fell all that night and in the morning lay deep on the ground. Since the road from Durobrivae to Lindum was safe and picketed by winter quartered patrols of Arturo's men, Arturo and Venutius rode it alone with the hound Cabal, now grown to prime, at their heels. No Saxon band ventured westwards to raid the road in winter. A few hours after leaving Durobrivae the snow thickened and with this came a strengthening wind which swept it into growing drifts and white-pelted their tight-drawn riding cloaks. Horses, riders and the great hound moved through it with their heads lowered. After a couple of hours' slow going both men knew that they would be hard put that day to do more than reach Causennae, a small town little more than half-way to Lindum.

Drawing up to breathe their mounts Arturo looked across at Venutius and laughing said, 'Where is road, and where is sky, and where the good earth? We move through the biggest goose-plucking ever made in the halls of the gods on high. They must make some great feast tonight.'

Venutius said, 'We must keep moving. The wind blows from the north and that way lies Causennae. And where is Cabal?'

Arturo looked around and then shrugged his shoulders. 'He will find us. The snow balls up on his pads and he sits to chew and worry them free, but even in this his nose will bring him up to us in time. I would the gods had chosen another day for their feasting.' He stirred the White One to a walk and moved ahead.

Following him Venutius knew that the gods had chosen this day for more than feasting. Although they headed into the wind, they were soon lost to the road. The snow was so thick falling now that there were times when it was hard to make out the shape of Arturo and the White One ahead of him. The thought came to him that a man alone on his horse on such a day could be thrown by a stumble, crack his head against tree or rock and lie unconscious while the snow covered him and froze him to death. That Arturo's death should look natural he had always known. No suspicion must touch him or Ambrosius's treachery would be clear and then not even the meanest camp follower among the Companions would turn to him. Truly the gods were setting to his hand the time and the season for his work. No man would doubt his word that in the blizzard they had become separated.

Ahead of him Arturo pulled up to rest the White One. The snowdrifts now were almost to their mounts' knees. To their right Venutius caught a glimpse now and then of a tall craggy rock face, the wind sweeping the bare falls and slabs free of snow. He rode up behind Arturo, who was leaning forward sweeping the matted snow from the ears and long nose of the white mare. He pulled his sword from its scabbard and raising it struck hard with the flat of the blade at the back of Arturo's head. Arturo cried aloud, made to turn and then fell sideways from his mount. He lay still on the ground face downwards.

Venutius eased his horse into the shelter of the rocks and dismounted. He moved to Arturo and squatted by him and there was a coldness in his mind far greater than the icy bite of the blizzard wind. The only small crumb of grace granted to him was that Arturo's face was pressed into the snow so that he could not see it. Within an hour the freezing wind would have leached all warmth from his body and within the next hour all

167

life would have gone from him. Any who found him would know that his horse had stumbled and when he had fallen to the ground the startled mount had kicked him . . . the gods had given him the day and he had done the deed. But at this moment Arturo stirred and, from shame that even for a few moments Arturo should turn his face and see him, he raised his sword and struck with the flat of his blade again. Arturo groaned and lay still and in that moment the gods, needing sport and cruel jest before they feasted, brought savage irony into play.

Limping in the lee of the rocks came Cabal to see the sword blow. Silently the great hound came across the snow and leapt at Venutius to take him by the neck with his strong jaws. Venutius screamed and fell sideways and the scream was fast choked as Cabal clamped his great teeth through his throat, worrying and shaking as though he were holding down an overrun stag. The sword lost from his grasp in the first assault, Venutius beat with his fists at the hound and twisted and rolled to find freedom, but Cabal held him, his life blood running from the hound's ironfast jaws to carmine the snow while the two horses, frightened at the screams from Venutius, stampeded and disappeared into the blizzard.

Growling low now, his jaws set fast, his weight holding down the now weakening struggles of Venutius, Cabal stayed bound to his prey until all movement died in the man. Then he rose and went to Arturo, sniffed at his head and body, nudged him now and again with his iron grey muzzle and then, with a low whining, couched himself down alongside his master, pressing close to him. They lay together as the light went fast from the day and the snow laid a mantle over them and the red stains of Venutius's life blood.

From a cleft at the foot of the rocks a woman watched them, as she had watched from the time the White One had first whinnied on reaching the rock face. But for the hound she would have shown herself long before, but she feared the animal. Now as she watched, Cabal, who had long scented her and knew her presence, slowly rose from Arturo's body and came towards her. She would have turned and gone back into the rock shelter but Cabal stopped a little way from her and lowering his head whimpered softly. Hardly knowing she did it the woman spoke softly to him and Cabal came forward, whimpered again and swung his tail in friendship. He raised his muzzle to her hand and, taking heart, she stroked his head and spoke to him with soft words. Cabal turned and moved back towards Arturo, stopped and looked over his shoulder and then moved on.

No fear in her now, the woman moved out into the deep snow. Under her belted greasy furs her body was strong and full, and her bare arms and legs were weather-tanned. Her long black hair flared in the strong wind as she came to Arturo. Kneeling by him she turned him over. His eyes were shut, his face grey with cold and his dull copper-coloured beard matted with snow. She knew him and had recognized him and the White One when he had first ridden into the lee of the rocks. She put her hands under his armpits and dragged him across the snow into the narrow cave which was her home. A small peat fire burnt dismally at the back of the cave, the smoke wreathing up through a fissure in the roof. Close to the fire, on a low bed of rough boards, was a thin mattress stuffed with dead bracken that spilled loosely from a slit in its side. At the foot of the bed rested an untidy bundle of hides and furs. She pulled him to the bed and then rolled him on to it with ease for she was strong and hardy. Many a man among those who visited her she had rolled, limp with drunkenness, on to the bed.

Talking to herself and to Cabal who had couched himself by the fire, she stripped Arturo to his under shirt and wondered whether he would live for, apart from the blows to his head, the freezing cold was set into his body, and when she put her ear to his mouth there was no moving touch of warmth from breathing. And this, she thought, was my lord Arturo who rode the White One and had made this part of the country safe for men to travel in peace, and whose name rang through the land like the calling of a great brazen bell. The gods had served him badly this day, but they had set her in his path . . . a worthless woman, trapped long ago by her own wildness and beauty . . . beauty of which only the coarse mockery now remained. Yet woman she was and her body was a fire which could fight off the killing clamp of the death cold which was taking him.

She went to a rock ledge and found a hard corn cake which she threw to Cabal who nosed it but refused to eat, his eyes on Arturo. She dropped the leather curtain over the rock face opening. Then, in the darkness shot only by the dull red eye of the peat fire, she stripped the furs from herself and lay down on the bed with Arturo. She pulled the furs and hides over them and took him into her arms, shivering herself at the first touch of his ice cold flesh and then conquering it with the fierce animal heat of her own naked body and limbs.

She lay awake all that night while the snow fell and the wind screamed and howled and there were times when she knew that she lay with a corpse, cold and stiff, and she mourned the passing of one who above all others would be most mourned in this country. But as dawn put grey fingers through the rented and torn hide curtain and she held him tight, feeling his coldness now begin to overcome the warmth of her own body and legs, her chill cheek was touched by the feathered brushing of his faint breath as he returned slowly from the limbo to which the gods out of their unfathomable reasoning had sent him.

And while that night passed the White One, separated from Venutius's mount, ploughed the drift and found shelter in the open-fronted shed of a reed-cutter. But wolves found the other horse and killed it, and towards dawn they came to the high rocks and, while Cabal growled and stood guard at the opening curtain, they found easy prey in the body of Venutius, dragging it away, fighting and quarrelling over it as the blizzard matted their pelts, so that what had been the shape and shame of a man was no more than a butchered, bleeding hideousness, and the golden coin of the Emperor Hadrian, falling from his fang-ripped belt pouch, sank into the trodden snow to find lodging when the thaws came in the moss and reeds of a swamp.

★ ★ ★

The snow lasted three days. On the fourth the skies cleared and, as though the gods still feasting needed yet another jest to tease men with, a warm thaw set in which filled the air with the running of snow water and swelled the streams and meres with flood while the sun shone with the heat of summer and the birds found song again.

Those days were a dream through which Arturo lived and of which he was never to have clear memory. He knew the warmth of the woman that brought him back to life and sustained his growing strength. Warm broth and porridge made from the black peas of vetch were fed to him and then the mists of delirium passed and clearness came slowly to his mind as strength grew in his body.

He sat now on the edge of the wide bed, wearing his shirt and long leather cavalry trews, and chewed on a corn cake spread with honey while the woman squatted by the fire broiling dried fish in herb-spiced mead. The beauty which had once been hers was clear to him, and he knew that it was her body and

173

warmth which had brought him back to life — but he knew little else.

He said, 'What do people call you?'

She smiled. 'Genara — and much else besides at times, my lord Arturo. My husband is long dead, but I would lie if I said I lack men to comfort me.'

'For saving my life you shall have reward which will take you from this place.'

'No, my lord. I need nothing but your thanks and the truth of knowing that the gods put me here for a purpose. I rest happy here and seldom lack company. You have no need to do me great favours.'

Putting a hand to the rags which wrapped his wounded head Arturo said, 'Then let me call on you for a favour.'

'If it is in my power, my lord.'

'These things you tell me you saw. The way of my wounding and the death by Cabal of my friend Venutius — you would do me favour if you keep silent about them always.'

'That I will, my lord. But what do I say, and you, my lord, about your wounding and being here?'

Arturo smiled. 'That I fell from my horse in the storm and wounded my head and you found me close by. As for Venutius — you never saw him or his death by Cabal. I shall say that we were separated by the blizzard,

174

and the wolves found him.'

'Which they did, my lord — on my threshold.' She stood up and came and took his eating bowl and smiled down at him with a sudden boldness. 'You will go this day, my lord? Causennae is close by.'

'Aye, I go this day.'

'Is one day more lost of great account even to my lord Arturo?'

Arturo laughed and standing began to pull on his long overshirt. 'No. The days are ours to squander, but I would not cap these last days in which you have served me better than you can ever know with a final one which would not be god-touched. But remember this — ' he picked up his riding cloak from the bed ' — if you should ever want ought that I can fairly give you in the future you shall come and ask and it will be given.'

Genara, her dark eyes bright with teasing, came to him and drawing the cloak close across his shoulders fastened the holding brooch. 'Maybe my lord in these last days you have already given me the gift I ask and I would but know it again before you leave.'

Arturo took her hand and kissed it. 'It could be, but if it were so then it was of the gods' doing not mine.'

'The gods were kind to you in sending you here. Maybe they were also kind to me. But let it rest so. I will walk with you to the Causennae road. You are still a sick man and should have company at hand.'

And Arturo was still a sick man. A few hours after reaching Lindum and being installed in the bishop's palace he was taken by fever and passed into a delirium which lasted for seven days. When he woke, his head clear but his body still weak, on the morning of the eighth day it was to find Lancelo standing at the room window and to hear the steady fall of rain from outside.

Hearing him stir, Lancelo turned and came to him. He grinned and said, 'Welcome back, my lord. And to give you more heart I tell you that the White One was found four days ago and is now in the bishop's stables.'

'I give thanks for that.' He sat up, shaking his head to stop Lancelo's offered help. 'I've been too long a-dreaming. But in my dreams the gods have spoken to me and now there is work to be done.'

Lancelo shook his head. 'The season is too far gone for campaigning.'

'There are some campaigns served better by pen and parchment than men and horses. Get me the stuff for writing and I would have Durstan and a troop ready to ride at noon for Glevum.'

Knowing all Arturo's moods Lancelo

recognized this one as not to be crossed.

When the writing materials were brought Arturo sat up in bed and wrote with the fine goose quill in the Roman language which had been beaten into him by his tutor at Isca, the drunken Druid priest Leric. When he had finished Lancelo brought him braid and wax for its sealing and then wrapped it in a sealskin pouch for protection against the weather.

'Durstan will ride with the white flag of peaceful passage, but fully armed, to Glevum and will himself see the message into the hands of Count Ambrosius and await his reply. If mishap falls on the road and there is danger of the loss of the writing he is to destroy it without looking at it. And now have sent in to me a jug of wine and bread and goat's cheese. I have been absent from this world too long and return with sharp set appetite.'

A little later there came into the room a young woman in her early twenties, fair-haired and tall, wearing a red gown caught about the waist with a silver linked belt, each link fashioned in the shape of some running animal . . . hare, wolf, horse and charging boar. She set a large wooden platter of wine and cheese on the table at Arturo's side.

Stepping back, she said, 'If you need ought

else, my lord, you have but to call. I am within earshot.' She smiled. 'It is good to see your old force returning to you at last. The priests and nuns of the bishop have prayed for you without let — and to their prayers have been added mine.'

'Then I thank you and them, mistress — ' He paused, and then added, 'What do they call you?' He reached for the wine jug, but his hand was stilled as the young woman gave a laugh.

'My lord Arturo, you ask my name? Am I so changed in six years or so?'

For the first time Arturo looked at her with attention. Then, shaking his head, he said pleasantly, 'You ride a few lengths ahead of me.'

'Then I am set down. Why even in your fever sleep you called my name, though there again your memory faulted you a little, but I do not grumble for in these last years there have been many things to crowd your mind. I am Gwennifer, though your swollen tongue could do no better than Genara. Yes, my lord Arturo, I am that pony-riding Gwennifer who brought you Cabal — ' she nodded to the window where the hound lay full stretch ' — and I am that Gwennifer-Genara who combed and trimmed your rust-red beard while you slept and fed you broth. And when

178

you complained of the cold in your fever and called me I brought you more wraps to heat your body.'

Arturo laughed suddenly and shook his head. 'Of course . . . Ah, mistress Gwennifer you have my apologies and my thanks. The good nuns trained you well in the care of the sick.'

'They trained me in nothing, my lord, for I did not stay long with them.'

'Then what do you do here now?' As he spoke he was thinking that she had grown in beauty but nothing of her spirit had changed. Behind the self-possessed young woman was still the tom-boy, restless and wayward, waiting chance to show.

'My mother is dead these two years and my father stays little at Eburacum for he winters and fights in the north against the Picts to hold the land he owns there. So I am here to run my uncle's household. And rare tedious work it has been until you came. When you leave you should make me master of your household and I will doff these — ' her hands plucked at the folds of her gown ' — for trews and tunic and serve you well.'

Smiling Arturo shook his head. 'I can find no such service for you. Our ways are rough and the sermon the bishop would preach me for harbouring you rougher.'

'Maybe . . . then marry me and all will be proper — '

Arturo laughed, cutting her short, and the wine in his cup spilled to the bed coverings. 'You talk wild and wilfully and frank — the nuns were well saved from you.'

'Nay — you put me off. Maybe you called not me but some other named Genara in truth, one who claims your love.'

Arturo eyed her in silence for a moment and then said firmly, 'There is no living woman that I love and call for.' Then shaking his head, a smile touching his lips, he went on, 'Where do you find this bold way you think and speak?'

'My lord, that is easily answered. What I feel I show. What I think I speak. So the gods made me, and I have no quarrel with them.' Before he could move she bent over and kissed his forehead lightly and then, laughing, moved from the room.

★　★　★

The room was warm with an even steady heat for the old hypocaust system had been repaired and was fired now with seacoal that came upriver from the mouth of the Sabrina. The wall sconces gave a steady light and on the table in a bronze holder burned a fat tallow candle which threw its full glow on the parchment which held Arturo's letter to Count Ambrosius.

Munching a russet apple which he took every evening with his wine before retiring, Ambrosius, flattening the stubborn creases of the parchment, began to go again through the message from the Dumnonian warrior. In places it was tedious and his eyes skipped the passages of no real intent. The young Arturo wrote as he lived and fought . . . often with an undue waste of effort. But the truth of the overall matter lacked nothing in good sense . . .

. . . and this Venutius, being your man, served you well and, but for the protection of the gods, would have faithfully worked your purpose. Dead he is now, and no stain against his name for none but I, and now you, know the dark truth . . .

Ambrosius sipped his wine. Aye, lost in a blizzard and torn to death by wolves and now, he touched his greying hair and smiled wryly; the young Arturo standing on the advantage of his growing popularity and increase in forces could make the truth known to spread through the country to raise a cry like the howling of wolves against his name and bring an even shorter fall in the raising of levies and a jibing at and cursing of his name. Maybe the old gods truly worked for him. He knew now, too, how to seize his advantage with the smooth shuttle of changing policy.

I will come to you as long ago I said I would when you sue me for return. This done I will serve you faithfully as *dux bellorum* and acknowledge you as *Comes Brittanicus* for I have no wish for king or overlordship of this country — only to fight and win its true liberty under the gods and then return to my people . . .

Ambrosius smiled and picked an apple pip from his teeth. Aye, likely so. But the truth in a man of thirty was only one season. In twenty years success would bring on a different fruiting. Still, by then his own seasons would have wintered in to death's unending keep. He smoothed the parchment and reread the fine hand. The man was no barbarian. He wrote with the smoothness and polish that few now brought to the Roman tongue; and, writing, asked now for that which was to feed the young pride in him.

This is how I would ride to join you at Glevum and this is the manner of your greeting and none shall know that it is other than the true courtesy of a father welcoming a son, none other than the measure due to a well-serving War Duke come to be honoured by his noble Commander..

Though in truth it was much other . . . Aye, but why not so? Few in this country would fail to follow Arturo, where many now grew tired of him and withheld their men and loyalty. Leagued with Arturo he would still hold supreme power. Many Caesars when young had fought in the field and many, when age and success came, had been content to leave the war grounds and work for the peace and prosperity that followed victories. Of one thing he had no doubt. For this country both he and Arturo wished and lived for the same thing, that it should rise to freedom and greatness again. And truth it was that his ageing bones and body found no joy in hard lying and the eating of hard tack, and the supping of cold ale or spring water on the black and windy nights of mountains and bare heathland.

With sudden pleasure and a curt dismissal of all irony he freely gave ground to the run of time and chance. The promise of Arto should be made good. He pulled his purple cloak to proper set over his long sleeved white toga and beat twice on the gong which stood on the table. His Praefectus Castrorum came in, the man Olipon who had once visited

Arturo on Cam Hill. He said, 'Send to me Arturo's man.'

When Durstan entered and was alone with him, he said, 'You are the man Durstan?'

Durstan nodded. 'Aye, my lord.'

'Who was outlawed by me with Arturo?'

'That is so, my lord.'

'You are no longer so.'

'I am so, my lord, so long as the writ runs against my lord Arturo.'

For a moment Ambrosius would have been angry. Then he laughed and said easily, 'Aye, you are a stubborn lot, you Arto men. But you have no need to be now. The writ against Arturo no longer runs. There is peace between us.'

'Then I thank you, my lord.'

'Return to your lord Arturo and say from me that all shall be as he wishes and that he shall find true and warm greeting from me.'

When Durstan had gone Ambrosius took the parchment — which could have been washed and scraped clean for further use — and reluctantly burned it in the flame of the big candle, the smell of its burning acrid in his nostrils.

So it was that in the year of Christ four hundred and eighty on a morning when the hawthorn bushes showed scarce green with yet to open buds, and the past year's leaves of

184

the beech were burnished copper and gold on their branches defying the new growth, and the first swallows and martins were yet to come, Arturo made good his promise to his dead wife Daria to ride in triumph with her to Glevum. He came riding the White One, his war cap red and white plumed and wearing — in honour of his wife who had been a true believer — the rich scarlet surcoat with the blue robed figure of the Virgin Mary given to him by the Bishop of Noviomagus, his sword sheathed, his lance raised high and his small red and white battle buckler slung on his back. Behind him in mounted troops came five hundred Companions, red and white plumes and scarves flaring in the robust breeze, and five hundred marshmen with Coroticus at their head, their spears over their shoulders, the fish eagle device on their breasts, their bows slung on their backs and their quivers showing blood-red dyed goose feathers as flights for their arrows. There was no man among them not tried and proved by battle. Behind them on the rising slopes to the south the rest of the army, save for those who still kept winter stations along the far east line, lay in camp and cursed the draw by lot which kept them from place in the proud company on this day that the great War Duke Arturo made good his Arto promise.

185

But none, except those closest and dearest to Arturo of his first small band of Companions, knew the meaning of the great white mare that, riderless, her hide gleaming like polished ivory, kept place alongside and made pair with the White One. Across the mare's back was laid a cloak of scarlet with a sky blue lining caught about the waist with a golden belt with a clasp of two singing birds and from it hung a soft leather pouch which held three locks of Daria's dark hair which Arturo had taken from her before her burial.

As Arturo rode at the head of the column to the East gate, where Count Ambrosius with a guard of honour waited to greet him, in his memory coursed clearly the words he had long ago spoken to Daria in Corinium while yet his bold promise was a thing of wind and angry boast. *It is written that on the day of my triumph you shall come riding into Glevum with me on a white mare, wearing a cloak of scarlet with a lining of blue silk and about your waist a golden belt with a clasp of two singing birds. And when Count Ambrosius comes out to meet us he shall hand to you a silver goblet full of new wine . . .* And then, curbing the smile that touched his lips, came memory of her reply. *And then and then will be the day when the pigs shall be flying and the salmon coming up the Sabrina*

186

*shall wriggle ashore, their mouths full of sea pearls to lay at my feet . . .*

Before him now, a spear's throw away, stood Ambrosius not knowing or caring to know the reason for the coming ritual, knowing only that it was small price to pay for this alliance and that the wagging of tongues in the years to come would give it meaning or myth for this stalwart warrior knew the power of riddle and mystery from the god-touched side of his nature.

Ambrosius waited, helmeted and cloaked, his ancient well-burnished cuirass shining in the sun, purple-cloaked and leather-belted and highly honed heavy legionary marching boots on his feet, studded and unchanged in design from the boots worn by the fighting men of the Twentieth and then the Second Augusta Legions who had first built and held Glevum, *the colonia Nerviana Glevensium,* under the governorship of Julius Frontinius when the Son of the Virgin that Arturo wore on his surcoat had been dead little more than seventy years. And now, mused Ambrosius, here comes one who served willingly any and all gods and was mad — or shrewd? — enough to make his own rituals though there was no denying the sense in him which understood and used the power of mystery to carry his name through the land and bring

187

men to him and enslave the affections and loyalties of those who looked and longed for greatness to return to this country.

As Arturo drew up a few paces from him and the long column halted behind him, Ambrosius went forward with his bodyguard while at his side came, too, his Camp Prefect carrying a great withy-plaited tray on which rested a fresh-run Sabrina cock salmon, its partly open jaws stuffed and overflowing with sea pearls. Beside it couched on its belly, its hide smooth scrubbed, lay a young dead pig with a pair of dove's wings fixed wide-spread to its back and a goblet of wine held between its fore trotters.

The two men gave greetings to one another and then Arturo leaned forward and took the goblet from the tray, half turned and poured in libation some of the wine over the scarlet cloak on the mare at his side and then spilled the rest to the ground.

Arturo raised his right arm high and from the long column of warriors behind him came a great shouting and chanting — 'Ambrosius . . . Ambrosius . . . Great Count of Britain!'

Erect, shoulders tight-drawn in pride, Ambrosius smiled and drawing his short, broad-bladed, double-edged legionary sword from its wood and bronze scabbard raised it

188

high to return the salute. As he did so he knew that the gods had served him well in sending Venutius's treachery and his own awry, and knew too that in Arturo he had found the first warrior ever in this land who read his mind and guessed his dreams and had the spirit to bury other men's evils if in that way lay true service to his country. Whatever the future held their names would live and for once — touched by a rare humility — he knew that he cared not which name would prove the greater.

# Elegy for a Warrior

Arturo and his men stayed ten days at Glevum, and in that time he became convinced that not only had the gods intended this alliance, but that it was meant to show him how much still he had to learn and to understand about the art of warfare which lay behind the straightforward marshalling of men into fighting positions when the enemy, in large or small bands, was sighted. His respect for Count Ambrosius increased when he realized that not only did the man share his dreams for the future of the country but he faced the task with an industry that covered every least aspect of the enemy. He gathered news of the Saxons from a discreetly organized network of pedlars, traders, disaffected Saxon warriors, and from their own countrymen who lived as slaves or worked, barely tolerated, in the Saxon lands.

Sitting in Ambrosius's room until late in the night the Count brought out for him maps and reports which for the first time gave him a picture of his own country to which he had almost been blind before. Seeing and understanding this Ambrosius smiled and said, 'Before the first sword is drawn or spear thrown if an army leader has done his work well then the battle should be half won. Would you waste time besieging a Saxon hilltop knowing that they hold stores and water for a month? No. Pass them by and then they must follow you and somewhere come to equal terms. You know why Esc lets you parade along his borders and only a few glory-hungry bands of his young men come out to find honour or a welcome in Valhalla by swarming like hornets around you? I tell you — because he sits content knowing you have not the force to come to him. So, he farms and harvests his lands and waits to make the move on the playing board which will surprise and defeat you.'

'What move?'

'Of that later, my Arturo. But remember this, Esc is the true son of his father, and like his father he makes others work for him — as did now dead Vortigern.' He smiled and sipped his wine. 'Now — for he will have had the news — that we are drawn together he will know that time is short for him and the move he would make must soon be played.'

A little roused, Arturo asked firmly, 'Why should I not know of this move now? Tell me so that I can prepare to meet it.'

'And find that nought waits for you to

meet? Esc has his men here as I have mine with him. If I seem unduly secretive unfitting our new friendship it is because I wait for more news to be sure of Esc's mind. For now take one half of the men you have with you and go to Cam Hill. Send the others east to Lindum. Draw such extra men as you can from Prince Geraint and — if things move as they should — my Camp Prefect, Olipon, whom you know, will be with you within a few weeks to tell you my mind.' He paused for a moment, watching Arturo's face, and then went on gently, 'So soon after my treachery and our new accord you take this caution well. But — though it give some shame — who is to know that there is not among your men . . . aye, and mine . . . some new Venutius. All great commanders dwell on a peak of loneliness. Until the day comes to march trust no one for there is no man living who has not his price.'

Arturo's mouth tightened as he held down the momentary anger at this cynicism and the shame it held for him to withhold trust in any of his near Companions. But remembering Venutius, he saw the wisdom of it. Nevertheless he said, 'Under the gods then there is no true trusting between man and man?'

'Nor between man and woman — when the man has been marked by the gods for his work. You are now in truth and all honour Dux Bellorum of this country. You will find the wind blows chill on your high peak. When I was your age I had all to learn and none of true wisdom to help me.' He smiled, scratching the tip of his beaked nose. 'Now you have me, and with our coming together a force far larger than I ever had. And more will come. In time we shall be victorious and this country will stay as it is now, the last part of the great Roman Empire never to be overrun by the barbarians.'

'And then you will call yourself what? King? Emperor?'

Ambrosius shrugged his shoulders. 'What matters the name? King or Emperor? It is the power that counts. Since my remaining years are few I may not live to make the choice. That will fall into your hands.'

'I seek no such titles. The work done I would go back to my lands and live in peace.'

Ambrosius shook his head. 'So you think now. The thought does you honour, but you will find that the years you have to spend on that cold high peak will change you. To warm your loneliness you will have need to wrap yourself in the cloak of majesty. There will be no escape for all men will demand it of you. The gods are on your side. Your legend begins and you are already sacrificed to them.'

Arturo rode back to Cam Hill with his men and for a month he sat waiting for word from Count Ambrosius. In that time he drew fresh men from Prince Geraint and put them into training and schooling to the ways of the Companions.

Towards the end of that month Prince Geraint rode into the camp with a bodyguard. Talking to Arturo as they ate together in Arturo's small dwelling, he said, 'I stay with you, my lord Arturo, to march with you and my men.'

Wiping grease off his lower lip from the chewing on a roast wild duck leg, Arturo was silent for a while, studying the man. He was now in his late twenties. He grew each year more like his father, dark-haired, dark-browed, a smouldering warmth in his eyes and a restlessness in his body as though he held down deep impatience.

Quietly Arturo asked, 'Why so, my Prince?'

'For two reasons. One — you wait the coming of the Prefect Olipon. The second — I am young and have sat at Isca too long without true taste of battle.'

'I wait for Olipon, it is true — but how could you know this?'

'Because by direction of Count Ambrosius I come in his place. Olipon we shall join in good time where he waits for us. For now I speak for him.'

194

Straight-faced, thoughtful, Arturo said, 'It was to me that Olipon would come, and for me to wait for him by command of Count Ambrosius. I trust and honour you, but — '

Prince Geraint laughed. 'You raise your hackles? There is no need.' He put his hand in his belt pouch and laid a gold ring on the table between them. Arturo knew the ring for Olipon had once brought it to him from Ambrosius and he had in defiance handed it back to him. 'This is from the Count to show that I truly speak for him. Matters have moved fast and Olipon was needed else-where. Now will you hear me?'

Arturo nodded, his face easing into a smile, but even so he felt the bite of the truth which Ambrosius had so recently spoken to him. The high peak was lonely. Never would he have believed that he would have spoken so to his own Prince. And in far Glevum Ambrosius had read his mind and sent the ring to ease his caution. Reaching over he refilled the Prince's cup with ale and said, 'You could have given me the rough of your tongue first and the ring after. The ways of the field and fighting I know. Now I begin to learn new arts and observances.'

'It is forgotten. Now listen to the words of Ambrosius.'

For more years than most men could

remember, around Noviomagus and to the lands south and close up to Venta and along the shores of the Vectis sea and on the island of Vectis itself, explained Geraint, there had long been settled sporadically small Saxon settlements that gave little trouble and an uneasy truce ran through all these parts. More trouble came from the pirate raiders from the Gaulish seas once the seasons turned fair. At this time there was as leader of this straggling, ever-changing territory a leader called Cerdic, still a young man, whose birth lines were unknown but variously described. His name was clearly British, and British he might have truly been, or as truly — as many claimed — either the son of a Saxon born in or out of marriage with a British woman, or — and his name was strong argument for this — the son of a Briton got with a Saxon woman. Whatever his birth his ambitions had grown with the coming of manhood and his loyalties and ties were all with the Saxons. This man, so Ambrosius's intelligence ran, had been chosen by Esc to lead the first of his moves against Arturo and Count Ambrosius. As soon as the spring brought the right weather Cerdic — who was already secretly marshalling the local Saxon settlers into a fighting force — would be joined by the arrival of a seaborne band of Saxon warriors, five or six hundred strong, all adventurers eager for plunder and land who would sail into the Vectis sea and make a landing somewhere between Noviomagus and Clausentium, on the long broken coastline full of deep inlets and creeks. All this Prince Geraint explained, and finished:

'These sea Saxons will come on the first good wind and tide as the season betters. That cannot be more than a few weeks distant. If Cerdic is successful then Noviomagus and all the lands right up to Venta and the western limits of the Anderida forest will be his. Then will come a linking up with the South Saxons who under Aelle now hold Anderida itself. With the creation of this new territory of West Saxons the whole right flank of this country is open and the way clear right up through Calleva to Corinium. Would you be happy to fight or even hold the line you have now, knowing that Esc would move out against you while Cerdic can march north and take your rear?'

Arturo who had been toying with the bare-picked duck leg frowned and tossed it to Cabal at his feet . . . The hound rose and went out into the night with it and the sound came clear of his teeth crushing the fragile bone. So this, he thought, was one more lesson among the many to be learned, the lesson of the value of foreknowledge which gave a commander long sight to prepare his moves. So far, although he had done much and made the country ring with and rise to his name, he had, compared to Ambrosius and his secret gathering of news, been no more than like some lucky, impetuous, feckless raiding son of a tribal chief adventuring the good seasons away to cure the itches of an idle winter.

He said, 'Only a fool would wait for the dagger thrust in his side as he crosses swords with the enemy. Where is Olipon now?'

'He sits with a small party well north of Venta, a handful of men that will cause no tongues to wag and word to run to Cerdic. We go to join him at the full of the moon and march by day through Sorviodunum and take the Calleva road as though making for Londinium, there to move north to Lindum or south to the borders of the Cantiaci lands which Esc holds.'

'Which all men would expect of me.' Arturo said it wryly, though not without a sense of amusement for he was truly being taught a new lesson in the craft of warfare and with it a light touch of the switch from Count Ambrosius to his high mettle by making all this plain to him through another and so — to which he had good and acknowledged right — reminding him that he served a master. He scratched gently at his beard and went on, 'And when we meet with Olipon? Am I still to be under instruction?'

Prince Geraint laughed. 'No. You will hear what Olipon says, take the news of his gleaning about Cerdic and make your own decisions. I come with you from here on my own will. I have two sons now, the elder, Cato, now in his sixth year so the Dumnonian line is secure should aught happen to me. If the gods take me then your father becomes his ward until he is of age and if anything happens to your father before then you will take his place. But I pray the gods spare me for I have that still to do in Dumnonia which one day you shall see and for which you shall give me thanks.'

'You talk a riddle, my Prince.'

'Aye, a riddle of time and blood.' He rose to take his leave and as they walked out into the night for him to go to his own quarters, he put a hand on Arturo's shoulder and said, 'Prince I am but from now on I march with you and take your commands without question as you would those of Count Ambrosius.'

As he walked away in the moonlight Arturo watched him, moving with the ground mist

199

knee high about him, and he knew then that the fashion of all his future days was to be changed. He had come from boasting outlaw to make his Arto promise good, riding in the favour of the gods, and now if he would keep their favour and his ambition for this land bright he had new and hard lessons to learn . . . *aie,* and would learn them fast and use them with the years better than any other before him.

He looked up at the moon and an owl called from the trees. The moon was just moving out of its first quarter, the month of Mars and Badb, the gods of war, was with them. In eight days it would be at the full. Calleva was three days unhurried march, and unhurried they would march as though going back to their old lines to relieve the winter stations — for now, although he might never know them, there were eyes that watched him and tongues that would send words running to the ears of Esc and this Cerdic if the pattern of these last years should show change. Unhurried for sleep he made the rounds of the new turf and timber-revetted parapets his father had begun and which were still yet fully to make and, since it was the marshmen's night of duty, met Coroticus coming from his round.

He greeted him and then went on, 'Good

200

Coroticus, you people of the Summerlands know the true coming of the weather — is that so?'

'Some of us, my lord.'

'You?'

'Aye, my lord. All the royal house — ' he grinned, ' — for they need it most.'

'How will this month of the war gods be?'

Coroticus bit his lower lip gently for a moment and then looked up at the sky and the moon and said, 'Tomorrow a change comes and we shall have wind and rain until the full of the moon. As the moon dies so will the bad weather. The last days of the month will find the wind in the south and the land early ready for sowing.'

'This you will promise?'

Coroticus laughed softly. 'Aye, but it will be a marshman's promise — not one on which he would stake his life. But that it will rain until the full moon is true for neither water ousel nor wild duck have moved to nestmaking, knowing there is flooding to come yet to the rivers.'

★ ★ ★

The weather until the full moon was as Coroticus had predicted. The rivers ran bank high and the meres and lakes rose until only the tips of the rushes and reeds showed above water. The short turf of the downlands was sodden so that the passage of men and horses turned it into quagmires and even the amadou tinder a man carried safe wrapped in his pouch for fire-making became useless as it breathed and caught the dampness from the air.

Three days after the full of the moon, the rains now ceased, Arturo moved out with his company to meet Olipon. He had with him two hundred mounted Companions, nearly the same number of Coroticus's marshmen and eighty mounted Dumnonian men under Prince Geraint who had yet to prove themselves as Companions. They met Olipon ten miles north of Venta on the Calleva road close to the headwaters of the river which ran south through Venta to find the sea at Clausentium. Olipon had with him a company of sixty odd men, all tried footsoldiers, which was split — for Ambrosius still clung to the old Roman divisions — into self-contained parties of eight men who shared a tent or made their own from brushwood and ash poles, managed their own cooking and provisions and had a horse to pack their gear. They carried heavy spear and either a short broad-bladed gladius sword or the longer spatha and wore mostly heavy leather helmets, surcoats and short trews. A few boasted ancient pieces of chain and scale mail and counted themselves fortunate for their were few armourers left in the land.

That first evening in camp Olipon gave Arturo his report. Cerdic had mustered nearly three hundred footsoldiers from the local settlements and these were lodged halfway between Noviomagus and Clausentium, split into small parties and hidden away in the marshes and along the creek sides, waiting the arrival of the long boats. As he spoke he drew with a stick in the heath sand the dispositions of Cerdic's men. On the high ground north of the Noviomagus-Clausentium road he had placed lookouts to light a smoke fire at the sighting of the long boats and another party on the downland to the east of Venta to make smoke fire when the first signals were seen. When he had given all this information, he looked with a tight-lipped smile at Arturo and added, 'We join forces now, my lord Arturo, and I think that the gods have made it so with clear intent. It was to the east of Clausentium that I fought with Count Ambrosius long years ago when he first began his war. His body grows old but his mind is still blade sharp. The gods have given him you and have chosen this place for your trial.'

'There shall be no failing. How many warriors will there be to a long boat?'

'Since they come as warriors and not as settlers with wives and family there could be fifty to sixty a long keel. With at the most six boats — say, three hundred and sixty men. With Cerdic's army you have rising seven hundred men against you and you have well less than six hundred.'

'It is enough.'

Olipon said nothing, but he knew that the words were not made in boast.

That night Arturo lay long awake. The whole stretch of country from Venta to the sea lay open in his mind, and beyond that picture he could see the long boats coming in on the growing tide so that they could reach and beach their craft at the head of the creeks. The gods were testing him where they had first tested Ambrosius. To meet the keels as they grounded would be a child's folly for Cerdic would long have known his coming and there might be no landing. Even if there were, then he would be fighting with only half his force for the creeklands and marshes were no place for his mounted men. This — no matter what the future held — was his first real testing by the gods. If he were to fail them then they would turn to place their favours elsewhere. Anger flared in him at the thought. Then with its passing he knew that now he faced in truth the real understanding of many of Ambrosius's words to him. The winning of battles must be shaped long before the first spear was flung or the first troop of horse thundered into action.

The next morning he called Olipon to him and said, 'Send word to your smoke fire parties. They are to keep place after the landing and send fresh signals when Cerdic's men and the sea warriors have crossed the Clausentium-Noviomagus road and are well set on their march to Venta.'

Olipon nodded and there was now no tight-lipped smile on his weathered face, but a frank grin as he said, 'You learn fast, my lord, to pick your own ground.' He looked up at the sky which was pocked with the drift of a few light clouds, moving before a southerly wind.

Two days later the first smoke signal billowed and plumed into the air south-east of Venta. The next morning the smoke came again, rising high and flaring away like the streaming of a horse's tail in the wind.

That evening Arturo marched southwards. By the time they were below Venta the sun had long set and they had the light of the dying moon. Coroticus's marshmen went ahead in a wide crescent-shaped screen.

None could move faster or with more ease and quiet than a marshman at night. Behind came the troops of cavalry while Olipon's footmen were split to march on their flanks.

Before dawn while the first bird had yet to sing the coming daylight and the last of the beetle and root-grubbing badgers had returned to their holts, they saw below them the dying night fires of the Cerdic forces and, with the first pale wash of light in the eastern sky, could pick out the stir of the Saxons as they rose and began to prepare themselves for the coming day.

That day was one of triumph and bitter sorrow for Arturo. Without the cry of battle horn or wild shouting Arturo led the cavalry of the Companions. They came down with the gathering dawn like a horde of wolves and were on the camp before most of the Saxons could buckle on their sword belts or reach for their scramaseax. Those that were armed stood and fought and made time for their fellows to seek their weapons.

The Companions streamed through them, killing and maiming and, once through them, turned and splitting into two rode back around the flanks of the camp to re-form on the higher ground as the marshmen ran forward and from a safe distance poured a swarming flight of arrows into the camp.

When their quivers were empty the battle horn of Prince Geraint blew and the marshmen drew aside as his company of Dumnonians rode down and carried sword and lance to the Saxons. But by now the Saxons were past their first surprise. They formed a ring about the camp and faced their foe, shouting and crying, their swords finding many a trooper's groin, their seax knives quick to cut the throat of any who fell. The bright morning air was full of the screaming of maimed horses and the last calls and shouts of dying men.

As Prince Geraint's troopers spent themselves and turned away to reform, Arturo led his Companions to the attack again, closely followed by Olipon and his foot men and Coroticus's spear-carrying marshmen.

On this attack, their lances tossed aside for they were of little use now, Arturo's men took the fight to the Saxons with their swords and with their small round bucklers held low to protect their groins. Riding hard, knowing that the surprised Saxons must soon break and run, the air full of the bitter tang of sweating men and horses and sharp with the bite of dust and blood, Arturo saw beyond the camp the first of the enemy to run and knew they would be Cerdic's men, the tolerated settlers who had no real heart for battle.

Again the Companions broke the Saxon ring and rode it through while the footsoldiers came hard behind them. As he fought and hewed with his sword, Arturo knew again what he already knew that, once the fight was joined, a man could see nothing but confusion and know nothing but the shock of iron and flesh, but knew *now* that which had been beyond him before, that each man and trooper in this battle held to his place and to his duty under his commander knowing that the design of battle scratched out in the bare dust and loose sand the day before must be followed and, because they took pride in their training and their god-filled duty, would follow it to death. And many there were who found death, and many more among them who lay open to it and were saved by their comrades. Among these Arturo took company for as he cut and slashed his way free from the heart of the camp a wounded Saxon, lying on the ground, half raised himself and thrust with his heavy spear at the breast of the White One. The mare screamed and reared high, throwing Arturo to the ground where one of the White One's flailing hooves struck him on the side of the head and sent him into oblivion. Lancelo and Durstan jumped from their mounts and stood over him. They were joined by four others of the

Companions, tight pressed, fighting off the crowding Saxons, and stood fighting them off until Prince Geraint and his countrymen came again at the charge and broke a great passage through the ring into which Olipon and Coroticus led their men.

They fought while the prey birds began to gather above, spiralling on the soft southerly wind. They fought while Prince Geraint and his men re-formed and charged again, and they fought on when they saw the Prince go down as a great axe broke the left foreleg of his mount. He fell to take a spear thrust through his throat and then, as his dying cry burst from him, the Saxons broke and ran. Those who were Cerdic's men ran, throwing arms and war gear from them, to seek the safety of their marsh huts and wood boothies, and those who were sea warriors ran for their long keels and prayed to Woden that the news of their defeat would not outstrip them and give courage to the country's natives to come out and burn their craft.

Seeing them go, Olipon, who now stood in command, gave orders for the marshmen to gather their arrows and harry the enemy to the coast. The rest of the army re-formed and stayed where they were to make camp, to collect their dead and mourn and bury them, and to shelter their wounded and care for them. As darkness came the cooking pots simmered over the wood fires, the guards were mounted and the horses hobbled and fed and watered, and those that lived blessed their God or gods but, having little stomach for food, took the pack train ale and drank to those who would drink no more on the sweet turf or in the shady thickets of their green land. And Borio who, beneath a warrior's sweat and blood soiled shirt, carried the heart of a bard gave rein to the spirit in him and sang of the day and its triumphs and its sorrows.

His voice was the first which Arturo heard as he came out of the blackness of coma where he lay under a canopy of laced willow boughs with Olipon sitting outside watching the dance of men's shadows around the camp fires. Arturo, his head throbbing, lay still, and Borio's voice coming to him told him of the day's victory and its grim losses.

At the battle of the men of the Long
    Boats, I saw
Arto's men who flinched not from
    spears
Under the thighs of the Companions,
    swift chargers
Long their legs, wheat their fodder,
    swooping like eagles

Men in terror, bloody their heads
At the battle of the men of the Long
  Boats, I saw
Great Geraint, Lord of the land of the
  West
Before Geraint, the enemy's scourge
Loud the clash of swords, bitter the war
  cries
Lovely to behold, the glory of the West
When Geraint was born, the gods
  touched him
At the battle of the men of the Long
  Boats, I saw
Geraint slain and Heaven's gate open
The gods give him welcome, the Bright
  One
Lovely to behold, the glory of Britain

Arturo closed his eyes and to stiffen himself against the sorrow in him, ground his teeth. The gods gave and the gods took and there was no tracing the pattern of their ways. They gave men friendships and broke them by death and, since the pattern of his days was clear to him, he knew that grief must be a silent thing for there were no words to speak its truth.

Olipon came into him and Arturo sat up. Before Olipon could speak, he said, 'I have heard Borio singing of Geraint. I saw the spear go into my White One.'

'She is dead, my lord, and buried deep where no vermin can touch her.'

'And now tell me the rest.' His voice was level and his hand unshaking as he took a beaker of water which Olipon carried for him.

'Coroticus's men followed to the long boats. Men from Noviomagus had set fire to two of them. Three got away with less than a hundred to crew them . . . ' He went on, telling the run of the day and the toll of losses, and finished, 'You have done what Count Ambrosius wanted done. Esc will squat like a broody hen for a long while yet.'

'Cerdic?'

'He was not among the dead. He will lie safe for a long while. The story of this day will run for more years than any child of living man will ever see. I leave for Glevum tomorrow, my lord, with your permission, to give a full account to Count Ambrosius.'

Arturo nodded and sliding his legs from the bed stood up, massaging the back of his head with his palm, saying, 'And I for the East.'

He moved out of the shelter and saw the thin slip of the passing moon above. Borio's voice came again clearly to him.

At the battle of the men of the Long
    Boats, I saw
Men who did not flinch from spears

212

Great Arto's men who now drink wine
with the gods . . .

Cabal walked at his side and he dropped
his hand to the hound's head. Anga was gone,
and now the White One. The White One it
had been who had brought Daria to him
when, running wild and free in the forest, he
had caught and broken it and brought it to
her for betrothal gift. True love, though it was
mortal, raised a man near to the gods. But it
was a once-given gift. All love that followed
was no more than the broken reflection on
the face of troubled waters of joys past.

★　★　★

That year Arturo took his men north to
Lindum and on to Eburacum along the
borders of the northern Saxon enclaves. Few
came out to meet them. Twice he rode to
Corinium to meet Count Ambrosius. At
Glevum and Corinium men now came
flocking to join the army of Arturo, the great
Dux Bellorum, the flame of his name and
exploits drawing them from their craggy tribal
lands in Cymru and north as far as
Luguvalium on the great Wall of Hadrian.
By the end of the good season the men
were trained and sent to increase and

213

strengthen the growing line of armed camps and stockades that formed the long stretched frontier against the Saxon East, leaving Arturo free to withdraw the bulk of his cavalry to Cam Hill and the west for the winter so that with the coming of the next war-season he could turn to the clearing of the wild lands of the Tamesis river valley to school or destroy the Saxon outcasts and adventurers from the lands of Esc. These were men who called no man leader and lived by raiding to take crops, plunder and — highly prized — slaves to trade with their fellows in the east. But beyond this clearing which would safely open the approaches to Londinium he knew, for he learnt fast the craft and foresight of an army commander, that when the day came for Esc and his fellow chiefs to break out, the main force must move westwards along the Tamesis for it led to the heartland of Britain.

A week before he and the Companions were to leave for Cam Hill Arturo with Lancelo and Durstan rode into Lindum to take their farewell of the bishop. In the place of the White One Arturo was now mounted on a black stallion which was a gift to him from Count Ambrosius, a beast with a fiery war temper and a wilfulness at times which brought hard bridling from Arturo, and often made him long for the smooth understanding needing no words, no hard mastery, only the pressure of knee or foot to know his will, of the White One.

As they entered the palace courtyard the bells from the monastery and nunnery rang for them and the bishop came forward with his household to greet them. Arturo dismounted and embraced the bishop. After their greetings were made Arturo was shown to the room which stood always ready for him in the palace. A bowl of warm water, scented with the oil of honeysuckle, was brought to him for his washing. As he stood alone, combing his beard after washing, he heard the door open behind him, and he smiled to himself for by now he knew the ways of the Lady Gwennifer.

Without turning, he said, 'I had been told that you had gone north to your father.'

'I did, my lord. On two matters of importance. But now I am here and you grant me only a view of your dusty tunic back. How could you know it was me?'

Arturo turned slowly. 'When I hear the scolding of a wren in the wild clematis, the sweet plaint of the nightingale in the hazels, or the complaint of the chiff-chaff on the poplar top — do I have to see them to know them? When you move the silver bells of your

215

bracelet ring — and more, there is none in this town but you would pass through my door without knocking.' He gave her a little obeisance of his head. 'You should be schooled to small courtesies.'

'It is of a schooling already done that I come to you.'

The sun through the window burnished the long sweep of her fair hair, and the blue eyes which seemed to shade or brighten with her moods now had the depth of the wood-bowered columbine. She stood proudly, of good height to match his own, the long white gown close collared about her neck, its folds caught smooth across her breasts with a crossing of red silk ribbons, its looseness below her waist moulded in the draught from the open window to caress the run of her legs. She had a beauty which had been in his mind often this campaigning season. Seeing his eyes on her, she was caught in a rare moment of uncertainty and raised her right hand to touch the side of her sunbrowned face so that the bells of her bracelet broke again into soft, sweet sound.

With a sudden gruffness that served to cover a rare stir of desire in him, Arturo said, 'I am in no mood to tease myself with your riddles.'

She laughed quickly, knowing her power to

216

move him, and came forward and took his hand. 'Then come, and an end to riddles. Please come ... humour me, in this, my lord.'

They went down the flights of curving stone steps and she led him through the bishop's herb garden and into the stable yards. Standing in the middle of the yard was a white mare, bridled and carrying a red leather saddle and strong braided girths of the same colour. At its head stood her personal manservant, Lacus, a dark-haired, bow-legged, middle-aged man whose right eye sat askew from the healing of a dagger cut underneath it.

Her hand still in his Gwennifer said, 'My lord should always ride the White One for all men know him as Arturo of the White One. My father bred her in the lands below the Wall and would neither sell nor make gift of her to anyone. Mount her, my lord, and see how well she has been schooled. She moves to the whisper of a voice between her ears. The scratch of a finger nail on her proud neck will tell her your mood and her mouth is as soft as the inside of the nest your wren makes in the wild clematis.' Her eyes shone with teasing and excitement.

Arturo went to the White One, holding down the choking in his throat as he thought of the day of the battle of the Long Boats. She stood like a queen and her eyes were pools of peatstained mountain water, and the curve of her arching nostrils marked her spirit and her pride. He put a hand on her withers and felt the pulse and strength of her body and he caressed her bowed neck as a lover might smooth the white flesh of his beloved, and he spoke to her in the soft language that came from birth to all the Epona-blessed and she tossed her noble head and curled her lips back from her strong teeth and neighed softly.

He took the reins and Lacus knelt and made a cradle of his hands for him to mount. He walked her round the yard and felt the movement in all her muscles which he had known with the White One, and he was thinking how Gwennifer had brought him Cabal to take the place of Anga, and now brought him this god-fired beast to take the place of the White One. Because all good fortune came by threes there was no escaping the impulse that took his eyes to Gwennifer as she stood watching man and mount move over the great flags of the yard.

He rode back to Lacus and dismounted, handing the reins to the groom who said quietly, 'My lord Loth, the lady Gwennifer's father, says her lines go back to the great horses of the Syrians who served on the Walls three hundred years ago.'

'Can history be told so true over so many years?'

Lacus grinned so that his right eye closed. 'History with my lord Loth is known by its horses. Her sires have borne Caesars and now, my lord, she will bear another.'

Laughing Arturo went back to Gwennifer and taking her hand kissed it. 'First Cabal and now the White One. I thank you but there are no words fitting to mark your bounty. But one gift deserves another. Come.'

He took her hand and led her back through the herb garden and up to his room. She went with him without words for she had none to command against the beat of the strong pulse in her neck as her heart raced.

In his room he sat her down and poured wine for them both and asked, 'Who schooled the mare?'

'I did, my lord.'

'And the matters of importance you had with your father?' As he spoke he went to his saddle pack.

From behind him Gwennifer said, 'The first was of the White One. Of the second I cannot yet speak without immodesty.'

Smiling he came to her and laid across her lap the scarlet belt with the clasps of two golden singing birds which had ridden with him to his triumph at Glevum. 'Your present calls for this return. It was my wife's. Now it is yours.'

'I thank you, my lord.'

He raised his wine cup and drank to her and Gwennifer drank too, lowering her head. This, she sensed, was the time when she stood waiting the sweet or sharp turn of her destiny and must keep her eyes from him so that no shadow of change on his face should give her forewarning of his words to come.

Arturo poured the wine which was still in his cup to the ground. 'The wine is spilled and now so freely runs my desire. Two things greatly loved you have given back to me. There is a third still in your gift. If it is in your heart to grant me that gift then there is no need of words. Share your wine with me and I know that the gift is to be given.'

Gwennifer looked up at him then and her eyes were bright now with the clear blue of the flax flower and she stood proud and radiant before him and slowly held out the wine cup.

'Drink, my beloved lord Arturo.'

Arturo took the wine and drank. Making no move to her, his eyes narrowing with gentle mischief, he asked, 'And now tell me — what was the second matter of importance you had with your father.'

She was silent for a moment, then throwing her head back a little she laughed, and said, 'It was to ask him that if you should speak for me in marriage that he would give his leave.'

'And his answer?'

'That the likeliness was as remote as pigs flying, but if it should happen then he would be proud of the honour done to both of us.'

'You are both wrong. The honour is done to me.'

He reached out and took her hand and drew her gently to him and embraced her. As they kissed, Cabal, who lay by the window, rose, stretched his long body and gave a half-yawn half-whine and then thumped back to the floor and beat his tail against the boards.

★　★　★

The return to Cam Hill was delayed for two weeks.

They were married by the Bishop of Lindum and, to do the God of the Christians honour, Arturo wore the surcoat given him by the Bishop of Noviomagus and a ceremonial sword sent him as gift from Count Ambrosius. At his side Gwennifer wore a white silk robe with a saffron coloured cloak and saffron coloured shoes. Above her hair was a circlet of bay leaves and she stood at Arturo's side as the bishop joined them in marriage and her lips were dark red as the hawthorn berries that grew on the great dike which rimmed the city on the east. Watching them old Pasco, the priest, held down a smile at the sight of the surcoat which Arturo wore. Arto was no man to dedicate himself solely to one god. The more who watched over him the better — but he never lacked a fitting sense of any serious occasion. And the lady Gwennifer . . . all had known that in her fixed way she had chased him and lured him with the sparkle of her blue eyes and thrown a net about him in capture as golden and finely spun as her own corn-gleaming hair. She was — he sighed a little to himself at the frailty and fleetingness of human moods — a woman of all weathers, changing like the wayward days from sun to cloud, from the balms of spring to the coldness of winter. It would be long before the beauty with which she blinded Arturo passed.

The night of their wedding Arturo and Gwennifer withdrew early from the feasting and as they lay abed, she full woman now and he no longer lacking manhood's joys, the soft breeze of the warm late autumn day which had favoured them stirred the window

222

drapings through whose opening the full moon, hanging low over Lindum, silvered the floor and tipped the grizzled pelt of Cabal with ivory points. Clear to them as they lay in each other's arms came the singing from the feasting hall and Gwennifer kissed the hard muscle of his shoulder as the words came to them.

> Set your strawberry coloured mouth
> against my lips
> O skin like foam; stretch your lime-
> white arms around me . . .

And later, when Arturo slept but Gwennifer lay awake and the singing still lingered:

> She's the white flower of the blackberry
> She's the sweet flower of the raspberry
> She's the best herb in excellence —
> For the sight of my eyes

Lying there she knew she had gained that which she had wanted from the first time of setting eyes on Arturo as she had played her harp to him. Her need for him was passionate and absolute. Sensing the glory that with the protection of his gods must come to him she desired no more than to bear his sons and one day be his queen. No woman in the land should have claim on him or issue from him but her. Thinking this there came back to her the stable talk and camp stories freely spread of the woman Genara whose ill-fame was known in Causennae who claimed birth of her son from the fathering of Arturo when she had spread her body over him to drive the killing cold from his heart . . .

Thinking this she stretched her love-eased limbs in the great bed knowing that no woman or child should live to lay claim to the smallest part of Arturo's coming glory or prove blood claim for any male child. She yawned with pleasure and the joy of long-sought possession.

★  ★  ★

Three days after Arturo rode out of Lindum on the White One with Gwennifer at his side and the Companions raising the dust behind them, Lacus went at night to drink with Genara of the cave. The boy babe whose age was yet to be numbered by years slept under cloths in an old corn pannier. Lacus was good to the woman, drank and ate with her and praised the babe whom she had called Anir. Because there was a mustard-sized grain of compassion in him he waited until dawn while mother and child slept, the one in

224

drunken stupor and the other in innocence, and cut their throats with less noise and little more thought than he would have given to the butchering of pigs.

# The Horses of the Gods

They returned to Cam Hill for the winter where now on the plateau top there were stout log-built quarters for men and horses, and the store huts and barns were well stocked with fodder and provisions to take them through to spring. On the low land around the hill the ground had been turned to long ploughed strips and the winter corn sown. Northwards towards Aquae Sulis two more fortified camps were almost completed and here — since the growing army of Companions could not be held at its full strength on Cam Hill — were lodged garrisons of four troops of cavalry each under the separate commands of black-bearded Gelliga and Tarius of the sword-scarred face. To the south-east not far from Vindocladia another camp — under the command of Garwain — had been fortified with the help of the Durotrige people who, thankful for the victory at the battle of the Long Boats, now acknowledged the overlordship of the Prince of Dumnonia.

That Prince was now the six-year-old Cato for whom Baradoc stood ward in Isca. To Isca at the turn of the year Arturo rode with Gwennifer and a small band of his men to be welcomed and lodged in the old fortress. Here Arturo found Baradoc and his mother Tia and his eldest sister, Gerta. Gerta, now seventeen, was six months married to Adipo, the son of the chief of the Durotriges, and in this Arturo saw the hand of the dead Prince Geraint and his father, Baradoc. Blood bonds were the stoutest ties between tribes. But looking at the tall, slim, dark-haired Gerta, seeing the happiness in her face — and the slight burgeoning of her body beneath her green gown that spoke of a child to come — and the pride of young Adipo beside her he knew that matching the diplomatic union was that of love given and love returned.

His mother, nearing her fiftieth year, proud of Baradoc's position and her son's fame, held the beauty now no longer of a woman's summer, but the fullness of ripe autumn. Her golden hair was touched with the silvering tints of time, but there was still a defiance of her years in her bright cornflower blue eyes and in the bold vigour of her body. Baradoc had aged and looked more than his years. The hard, weathered face held sometimes a weariness at odds with the vigour of his speech and his actions and his troubled right arm had grown stiffer — but the keenness of his fertile mind and the unslaked passion he held for his country's future and his hatred of the Saxons ran unabated in him.

That first night when Arturo and Gwennifer retired to their chamber, Gwennifer said, 'In your father I see you. And more I see. Your fame is a great joy and a slow bitterness to him. You are doing what he dreamt of doing. Am I right?'

'You are. But there is one thing you do not see. Without him I could never have been what I am. In the long years to come though men may remember my name and forget his there will be no forgetting in the hall of the gods for they know that the victory that comes with the breaking wave crest of a cavalry charge could never be without the abiding strength of the sea behind it.'

Gwennifer laughed. 'Prettily said. You never lack for words.'

'At this moment I lack for sleep and would have the warmth of your body to make it come fast.'

Lying awake beside him as he later slept Gwennifer thought of the beginning of proudness in Gerta's belly and her hands smoothed the flatness of her own. Maybe, she thought, the ache of longing to be full with his child by its own force delayed the fruiting of the wish. If the love of the gods held, king

Arto would be of this country and she his queen and she would bear him children so that his blood and glory should live forever. Tight-lipped with sudden impatience she knew that sleep would be long coming.

The next morning as Arturo came down to the fortress courtyard, the jackdaws calling and quarrelling on its ivy-covered walls, it was to find his father and Master Ricat — the horsemaster of the Princes of Dumnonia, now greying and, though crabbed by age, still sitting horse as though he and beast were one — mounted and waiting for him while old Ansold, the swordsmith father of Daria, held the White One already saddled for him.

Without ceremony Baradoc said, 'Mount and ride. We have things to show you.'

For a moment Arturo eyed them all, then knowing his father's humour, mounted the White One. They rode off with Ansold following, his lean legs flapping loose over the back of a moorland pony. Horses Ansold loved, but for their mettle he had no time, preferring a docile mare or a plodding pony.

They rode out of the fortress and down the southern hill slope through the old town and took a path that led seawards along the river Isca. Herons stood among the sere reeds fishing. A pair of otters cruising upstream, whiskered faces and bright eyes turned towards them, left a widening wake behind them. The late salmon were running and they were well-fed and bold. The sky was a pale blue-grey wash with the sun carrying a filmy cloud halo. Nostalgia touched Arturo. Here, in this Isca and on its water meadows, he had come as little more than boy to serve Prince Gerontius and to pass from stable lad duties to trooper and cavalry training. Here, south down this river, he had seen his father make his return after long years to be reunited with his mother, Tia, a father taken by sea raiders first to slavery and then to war service in the lands above the middle seas when Rome was bleeding to death from the wounds of the Goths and the Vandals.

Following a turn in the river he saw now that which had never been here in his time. A small meadow held in the river's bend had been palisaded around with a high stockade fence. Guard platforms marked its perimeter, all manned, and at its only gate, spanned by a log-faced watch tower, other guards stood on duty.

The gates opened as they rode up. Inside the great enclosure was lined about with stalls, stables and storehouses. Piped water ran into the drinking troughs from a small aqueduct that tapped a stream coming down the slope to the east of the stockade. In the centre, shut off by barred rails, was a large tan-bark ring.

At the entrance of the ring they halted. Baradoc, who, Arturo knew well, lacked no sense of the dramatic, nodded to Master Ricat who put two fingers to his mouth and whistled shrilly.

From the far stalls there came then twelve stable servants each leading a horse. They filed into the tan yard, the servants straining back against the leading bridles to curb those mounts touched by mettle.

The prick of surprise and wonder needled Arturo's cheeks as he watched. Roan, black, grey, chestnut, bay, piebald and skewbald, mares and stallions . . . these he knew were the horses of the gods. Now and again he had seen great horses and the White One he rode could match them, but here were twelve and over the half stable and stall doors around the enclosure he could see the heads of others. In all, his quick glancing eye told him, there were no less than a hundred of these animals.

He turned to Master Ricat, under whom he had served as youth, a man who had used birch and the flat of his hand to him for misdoing, and he said, 'Master Ricat . . . this is the dream of Prince Gerontius come true.'

Master Ricat, lips pursed, nodded his head, and then said, 'Thank the gods he lived to see it. For years he worked at this. Aye, and the secret of it has been well-kept. Until this year the horses were lodged in a well-guarded valley near Nemetostatio. Whenever there came news of a great horse in this country, it was sought out and bought. And not in this country alone. Some of the sires and dams of these you see were shipped from Gaul, bought in the great horse fairs of Hispania. Bred they have been, and mercilessly weeded, for their size and strength and courage. It was horses like these that served in the legions that Caesar brought to this country — the Second and Twentieth Augusta from Argentoratum and Novaesium, the Ninth Hispania from Pannonia and the Twenty-Fourth Gemina from Moguntiacum and — ' he stopped suddenly and smiled. 'I can see that your mind is less on history than the beasts before you.'

Arturo grinned. 'My mind is on history to be made, not that which is dead. These are the horses of the gods. How many is the tally?'

With the precision characteristic of him Master Ricat said, 'One hundred and seven of age and ready for battle, and eighty-five that run from yearlings to four- and six-year-olds. No big increase, but Prince Geraint, like his father, would have none to live not truly thrown to his standard. Of brood mares that have stood to stallions this autumn there are thirty-one.' He sighed a little wearily. 'And sore hard have been the loads for feeding and care and the guarding against robbery.'

'With horses like this one charge against the standing Saxons would be as the fall of a cliff to crush them,' said Arturo softly.

'There is more,' said Baradoc. 'Now, when you charge, you have your lance or spear which you must thrust into your enemy by your own strength and that finely gauged so that the shock does not unseat you from the saddle and with always the thought in your mind that a thrust does not come to your groin if you lower not your buckler. When you abandon or lose your lance and take to your sword with how much of your full strength can you use your blade edge or point since you must clamp knees and legs to your beast to keep your seat? The full vigour of your sword arm must be tempered to the firmness of your seat. Sit astride a thick tree branch and throw a stone. Stand on the ground and throw a stone. Which goes the farther?'

'From the ground to be sure, my father.'

'On the back of the White One now, you are as on a branch. But need be no longer. Ansold with others has made for you that which will turn the White One's back from branch to ground.'

He called to the groom who held a chestnut stallion in the middle of the line. As the man began to lead the stallion to them, Baradoc went on, 'I show you something now that I remembered from my lost days soldiering along the southern and eastern shores of the Middle Sea. Lost, too, from my memory it was until you and your Companions began to grow to strength and triumph.'

The groom halted the stallion before them and Arturo saw that the saddle on its back was of thick leather, plentifully padded on its underside and that fore and aft it rose into a wide high pommel or saddle bow which would cover a man's groin before and the base of his spine behind and thus give protection from the thrust or swing of sword or scramaseax. He saw, too, that hanging from each side of the saddle in line with the girth bands hung thick leather straps to the ends of which were looped heavy iron rings with their lower rims flattened out to fit flush to the sole of a man's boot. At once he understood all and marvelled at the simple good sense of these devices and marvelled more at the blindness that the gods could put on men to stay their fashioning of such devices.

He would have spoken but Master Ricat said, 'Watch, my lord Arturo, and you shall

234

see the power given to a man who rides with his feet on the ground. The man who rides the bay mare wears leathers and stirrup rings. The other rides his saddle with his feet free even as you do now.'

Ricat called to the line of horses and two men carrying heavy swords mounted their horses, one a grey and the other a bay which bore the new saddle and stirrups. They trotted to the far end of the enclosure and then turned. Putting their mounts to a gallop, each man holding his sword free, they came thundering down towards two stout ash posts which had been set firmly and deeply into the ground in front of Arturo and his party. As they swept by each man struck at his post and circled away. The force of the sword blow by the man riding the grey cut deep and sent a great chip flying into the air. The sword blow of the bay's rider swung into his pole and sliced clean through it.

Before the horses could rejoin the lines on parade Arturo, his face stiff with pleasure in him at the vision of power to come, said sharply, 'How many of these new saddles with their hanging irons do we have?'

Baradoc said, 'Ansold and the other craftsmen have made eighty-four.'

'I want one hundred and fifty before the feast of Beltine and as many each month after that as can be fashioned. The increase of the great horses comes slow at Epona's pace, but even the horses we have now will with these saddles give a man double the strength in his sword arm.' As he began impetuously to wheel away, he called, 'The gods give you glory, my father and Master Ricat — for this day, too, they have given the promise of triumph to our arms!'

They watched him as he cantered out of the stockade and Master Ricat turned and looked ruefully at Baradoc. 'I would have told him . . . aye, in a pretty speech, that all, horses and new gear, was a gift from Prince Geraint, sworn before he left here to join him.'

Baradoc laughed. 'How many times did you flog him as a youth for impatience and heeding naught but his own desires? You shall see him fret this winter away, eating his heart out for the moment to ride against the Saxons again. I know him. He rides now alone down the river and, maybe, prays to the gods to turn winter to spring in a day. Aye, and though he must wait like all mortals the due change of the seasons he will live this winter with a fury in him to leave only small part of his mind to others.'

Master Ricat shrugged his shoulders and said sourly, 'It seems that those whom the gods touch make poor company for their fellows.'

Baradoc said nothing, but he knew the truth of the words. His son, Arturo, was fated to live apart from other men, for, like a man on a bare, high hill top, his view spread wider and farther than that of those who hugged the comforts and shelter of the valleys.

Later, on the afternoon of that day, when Gwennifer came into their chamber it was to find Arturo seated in a chair with his feet up on the broad ledge of the window opening, brooding and staring out at the great curve of the Isca river far below. She came up behind him and kissed him gently on the neck and he absently reached up a hand and caressed the side of her cheek.

She went and sat at a small table which caught the light from the window and, loosening the braids from her hair so that it fell loose about her shoulders, began to comb it, studying her face in a large polished bronze mirror that stood on the table.

'I have heard, my lord, about the great horses. Some rumour of these had reached my father . . . '

Arturo grunted, his thoughts far away. Knowing his remoteness and its reason, Gwennifer smiled and began to pluck at her eyebrows with a pair of silver tweezers,

237

studying her face closely in the mirror and taking pleasure in her beauty. Now, it was only when she rode with him or they made long progress from one camp to another that she dressed as a man in long trews and tight-belted surcoat. Leaning forward she touched the skin under one of her eyes. It was rough and the lower rim of her eye was a little inflamed and swollen, a common complaint when one rode much and wind and dust blew in one's face. She reached for a silver goblet which she had filled with scented salve and, dipping a finger tip into it, smoothed the ointment close under her eye. A man, she thought, would scarce heed the beauty of a woman's face or body when his mind was full of affairs and dreams of the future. And clearly this was the way with Arturo now. But when the need rose in him like a returning tide for the joy of his beloved and the pleasures of sweet congress, then he marked all of beauty or blemish with the eye of a peregrine falcon. To tease him from his mood, the turn of the new-minted words coming easily from her and making her long for her harp to enrich them, she sang, half-turning to catch his response:

Proud on the meadow, great horses
Grey of the winter mists

Black of the raven god Lugus
Brown as the new-turned ploughland
Epona's children, Badb's delight
Great horses for the Chosen One
Great horses of all the gods

To her delight the words reached through Arturo's mood and he turned, smiling at her, and rising came towards her. But, as he was poised to bend to kiss her, he halted and a frown darkened his forehead, a cloud over the sun of his smile.

His voice sharp, he said, 'From where did you get that goblet?'

Surprised at his curtness, she looked at the silver goblet in her hand, and then confused said, 'I did my duty to you, my lord, by unpacking your campaign chest and found it. Look — ' she smiled, hoping to overcome the anger in his face, ' — I have cleaned it for you with fuller's earth and the polishing of my own warm breath.'

'Take the ointment from it,' said Arturo curtly. 'It is not a chalice to be used for any ordinary service. Clean it and put it back in my chest.'

Without another look at her Arturo walked to the door and she, stung by his uncouth manner which rode her high mettle hard, called after him angrily as he went from the chamber, 'Command me to anything, my lord — but not in the voice of master to servant!' She raised the chalice high and flung it after him. It hit the long curtain over the door opening as it fell back on his going and dropped without sound into the softness of trailing folds on the ground.

She sat, hearing the sound of his footfalls on the stone stairs fade away, and then with a shrug of her shoulders, anger quickly gone from her, she got up and retrieved the chalice. She held it, the spilled salve sticky against her fingers, and wondered why Arturo had been so moved because of her found use for it. It was the size of a drinking goblet with handles each side, curved and worked in the form of rams' horns. One of the horns was badly bent and the bowl itself was pocked here and there with dents. Around the outside rim ran a continuous Greek key pattern and on one side of the bowl, worked in relief, was a large round boss in the shape of an almost circular wreath of bay leaves enclosing the simple outline of a human eye.

That night after Gwennifer had retired to her bed, Arturo stayed long below talking with his father and Master Ricat. There was no sleep for her as she lay watching the long shadows cast across the chamber by the tall

240

candles whose flames swayed in the draughts like yellow crocuses in a spring breeze. When at last Arturo came to bed she pretended sleep. But as he lay alongside her he was not deceived. After a time, without touching her, he said, 'I have offended you and rightly you give me no welcome. For this I ask your forgiveness. I was harsh to you who are gentler than the soft-breasted dove on the red rowan trees, but that only because the chalice you used for your salve has a holiness that comes from the blood of the Son of the Great Father in the heavens whom the Christos followers worship. When He was crucified it was this bowl which caught the blood that dripped from the spear wound in his left side — so the story runs from my mother who was given the chalice in return for her goodness by a hermit. It is said that if it is filled with water and held by one marked for greatness the water flushes to the colour of the Christos blood. Twice this has happened to me. First when I was a babe without understanding, and again when I was newly in manhood and near dying from an arrow wound of an enemy. I am the offending lover. Between us lies the winter of hasty speech. Turn then and speed the seasons to the clover-scented warmth of summer.'

In the darkness Gwennifer smiled to

herself. When he chose his tongue could drip honey. Hasty he had been and would be again, but that came from the loneliness in him and was no more than the kingfisher play of summer lightning. She turned and put her arms around him and her lips to his.

★   ★   ★

The following fighting season, during which Arturo began the clearing of the valley of the lower Tamesis to make the approaches to Londinium secure, he made no use of the heavy horses. The Saxons about the river, he knew, would never come out in sufficient force to warrant their use — and, additionally, he was in no hurry to apprise Esc of their existence. The time would come when the Saxons made a real show of strength. Enough horses were drawn from Isca and taken to Cam Hill to form two troops and left under the command of Gelliga, with young Borio and enough men to mount them and to begin their training while Ansold, with other smiths and leather workers, made saddles and stirrup irons to accoutre them.

Nearing the end of the summer the approaches to Londinium were secured and the city — which had long recovered from the plague — was lightly garrisoned by local

242

recruitment. But, as the Romans in the long past years had seen, it was no place to be heavily fortified and manned to stand as a strong point. For the time being it was slowly coming back to its old position as a trading centre and port which even the Saxons of Esc used through the offices of merchants and craftsmen who put commerce higher than patriotism. Nevertheless Arturo left it strongly enough held to stop any movement by land between the Saxons of the South and those of the East and Middle lands reaching up to Lindum. At the end of the season he left a troop of cavalry there under the command of Netio, hawk-nosed, face sword-scarred, who had been one of the first of the Companions to join him from the Sabrina Wing at Corinium.

He rode back in the autumn to Cam Hill and then to Isca where he found that, of his mother's three other children, Gerta, his eldest sister, had given birth to a boy whom she had named Mordreth, that his young brother, Gareth, had died of the summer fever, and that his younger sister, Amla, was fast moving from childhood to girlhood and growing in looks more like her mother every day. His mother's hair was greyer and there was a calm and serenity about her face through which her true feelings seldom showed. Baradoc was alert and vigorous when anyone was near him and still improving the Cam Hill defences and those of the other hill sites running north to Aquae Sulis. But caught when he felt that none observed him the weariness in him and the growing pain of his right arm seemed to mark his face and body with far more years than he could claim. His time, Arturo sensed, was running out too fast for his spirit and there was an honourable disappointment in him that the dreams he had cherished as a young man would stay dreams to be shaped by the hands of himself to true life. That this should be so was the god-sworn duty of Arturo.

For Gwennifer, his wife, there was only wonder in Arturo. The blaze of her beauty and the warmth of her love for him were like the light and heat of a never-setting sun. Her laughter and high spirits, marking her great appetite for life, enchanted him so that he could refuse her nothing and, since he could never find the love in him for her which he had held for Daria but at times wished he could, he sought to humour and grant all her indulgences and wishes. And her wish — which was his, too — for a son, he humbly prayed to the gods to be granted. A son he needed as much as she did for the day would come when all that he should create would, at his going, need his own flesh and blood to take from his hands and build to even greater glory. For this he prayed to the gods, and not always with modest patience.

And Gwennifer prayed too, and while that autumn, as though the march of the seasons had been stayed, ate well into the last months of the year she watched for the signs of the springing of his seed within her and sometimes, in moments of disappointment, alone in her chamber at Isca or in the now comfortable lodge at the top of Cam Hill when none could see or hear her, she would vent her impatience in strong action or words, striking her fists against the top of her toilet table, sometimes smashing unguent or salve pot, and once deep denting her polished bronze hand mirror while she swore with the words and fury of any trooper amongst the Companions. Arturo would be king of this country and where was there king who did not yearn for a man child to carry his memory and greatness forward into the future?

But the day came when this passion of frustration passed from her. Going from their chamber one late afternoon to the eating hall of the Isca fortress she passed the door of the room in which Baradoc and Tia were lodged. The door was ajar but covered on the inside by the long hanging doeskin draught curtain which was also partly drawn. Clearly to her came the voice of Baradoc and his words made her halt.

He said, 'There is a recklessness in the Lady Gwennifer which Arturo should curb.'

'Why so?' The voice of Tia was a little absent as though her mind were on her toilet or needlework.

'She took one of the great horses yesterday and insisted on riding it in battle drill with the troop. *Aie* . . . and in wildness and indiscipline left them all trailing, riding like one of the Furies.'

'She is high spirited, true. But she rides as well as any man.'

'This I know. But the time could come — or may have come now without her knowing — when she could be with child, and by her wildness lose it. Arturo needs a son, for himself and for this country. Arturo will say nothing to her, even if I ask him — but you could speak to her and she would listen for there must be in her as in us a longing for a man child.'

There was silence for a while and then the quiet, firm voice of Tia said, 'Have you forgotten the words that Merlin wrote on the cliff rock the day we came to Caer Sibli?'

'What words?'

Tia laughed gently. 'You know well, but do

not wish to remember. He wrote of Arturo, even yet to be born but carried within me —

> Cronus in the dream spoke thus
> Name him for all men and all time
> His glory an everlasting flower
> He throws no seed

— so there will be no child, no son, no daughter. It is the price which our Arturo has already without his knowing paid to the gods for his coming greatness.'

Baradoc grunted intolerantly. 'Who believes Merlin and his nonsense?'

Tia said quietly, 'You should for he warned you, as you have since told me, that you should not put your boat to water to leave the island until the first swallow had come north. But you did — and were gone from me for many a long year. There will be no child of Arturo born to Gwennifer and my heart aches for her.'

Stiff-faced from the sharp turn of emotion in her, Gwennifer moved on down the stone steps.

★ ★ ★

The year lingered, mild and unseasonable. There was still thin growth in the pasture grass, the great geese that came always from the eastern lands which had been the cradle of the Goths were still to arrive, and the peregrines of the Dumnonian cliffs and the mountains of Cymru still lingered, and the holly trees were almost barren of berries as though they knew the birds would have no need of winter feeding. On a morning when Baradoc's men, still labouring on the defences of Cam Hill, worked stripped to the waist under the sun a messenger, covered with sweat and dust, riding a hard-pressed mount, came to Arturo with a message from Count Ambrosius at Corinium.

The north Saxons who held all the shore lands running south from Petuaria on the Abus river to the great fens and marshes below the Metaris estuary, reinforced by sea from the East Saxons of Esc, had broken out of their enclaves and were besieging Lindum and Durobrivae of the fenlands.

That evening Arturo rode out of Cam Hill with two troops of the great horses and two of his original gathering, and with them went a hundred marshmen with Coroticus. Each man took with him his short commons to last until they reached Corinium. Four days later they rode into Corinium as the sun was dropping low over the distant Cymru mountains and took quarters in the camp of the Sabrina Squadron — a camp which Arturo saw at a glance was held by only a beggarly handful of Ambrosius's cavalry.

As he dismounted and Lancelo took the reins of the White One and led her away Arturo saw Count Ambrosius standing at the opening of his blue-dyed square tent to greet him. The meeting was short of ceremony for Arturo was in a mood of angry bitterness which had built in him as he had ridden these past days. He knew his Ambrosius over well now and had easily filled for himself the gaps in the scanty information brought to him by the messenger.

Ambrosius poured wine for him, but Arturo did little more than touch his lips to it. Seated across the table from his commander, he said without ceremony, 'The weather holds fair still — too good for the season — and if we had been ill-prepared at Lindum and Durobrivae it might have tempted the Saxons to break out and breach the line we hold from Lindum to Londinium. But both towns and all the armed camps along the line were left full-manned. What gives them then this sudden courage and hope of success, my lord Ambrosius?'

For a moment or two Ambrosius said nothing. He closed his eyes briefly and breathed deeply. Arturo was all fire and anger and would need careful handling. Even so, he resented his arrogant mood and, but for the tiredness in him, would have bridled it with sharp words. Then, before he could answer, Arturo spoke again sharply.

'I ask, my lord, what gives the Saxons this boldness since between us we had left the line and its cities fully garrisoned and patrolled?'

Smoothing the grey patches of hair over his ears Ambrosius answered, 'The reason, Arturo, lies in the craft of Esc and — I admit it — a lack of foresight in me. He has leagued with the Scotti and they have made landings with many craft from the Mona island as far south as Moridunum and Nidum in Demetia. Without time to warn you I have had to withdraw men from the Lindum line and from here to send west as reinforcements. Would you have done differently?'

'Aye, I would. The Scotti could wait. They have always harried the coasts of Cymru. The mountains would have held them long enough to give time to deal with the Saxons first. You can only hunt one stag at a time. Esc is our stag. The Scotti would take slaves, plunder and cattle and perhaps settle in a few sea valleys to await our coming. What is the last news from the east?'

'That Lindum and Durobrivae are surrounded but still hold. That was seven days ago.'

Arturo stood up 'Then there is no time to be lost. The Companions of the White Horse ride tonight. I pray the gods keep this good weather flowing for us on the ride. What it be when we arrive I care not.' He smiled suddenly, and went on gently, 'There is much to be done, my lord, so I ask your leave to go. We stay but to water and feed our mounts and ride this night.'

For a moment Ambrosius was on the point of finding words to curb the mastery in Arturo and to bring him back under control, and he knew well, too, that the gentleness in his last words held no true respect for him. Then with a tired shrug of his shoulders, he said mildly, 'You will do me one last courtesy before leaving. Drink your wine with me.'

As he reached for his beaker Arturo took his and when they had both drunk Ambrosius said, 'May the gods give you success.'

'If they do not it will be from no lack of manhood in the Companions.'

When Arturo had gone Count Ambrosius poured more wine for himself and sat sipping it. Wine he found more and more these days drove the tiredness of mind and body from him for a short while, but he was under no delusion about the true meaning of its comfort. His days were slipping from him. He had battled and planned and wasted himself in trying to bring unity between so many of his country's chiefs that there was now no true force left in him. He would go soon and Arturo would take his place. No man could escape the toll of his years. He only hoped that the gods would grant Arturo a wide span of life to bring his dream for this country to life.

Then, with a sudden flush of pride, he called for his servant. The man helped him to dress and two hours later as the first stars began to take brightness in the sky, he sat his horse at the great gateway of the Sabrina camp, wearing his plumed war helmet, polished cuirass and greaves, his blue riding cloak over his shoulders and his broad sword held in salute to the Companions as they marched out, near a hundred and fifty horse and a hundred marshmen; the cream of all the fighting men in this country, the pride in them clear as they went under the banner of the White Horse because they knew themselves to be Arturo's men and knew Arturo to be chosen of the gods. But the great gods above, Ambrosius knew, were too remote for man to serve without sight or sound. They needed a man to go before them who was clear to be seen and heard, a god of their own creating.

They were four days on the road to Lindum. On the third day the morning broke with a clear sky and a shift of the wind from the west to the east, a wind that blew strong with an icy, biting savagery as though winter, long deferred, was arrived with a freezing fury at its long delay. Within an hour the roadside ditches were surfaced with ice and the breaths of men and horses plumed in the air and set their sweating beards brittle with its cold grip.

On the fourth day as they came down off the high ground before Crococalana and passed through it they could see, far ahead of them across the flat lands, tall plumes of smoke rising from the direction of Lindum. Now, too, they began to meet people who were fleeing from it with their small possessions hastily salvaged and learnt that after a long siege the Saxons had broken into the city five days ago killing all who could make no escape The garrison had died fighting. The bishop and the monks and nuns had been slaughtered. The Saxons had spent three days ravaging, slaughtering and plundering and then a day and a night of feasting and drinking and were now — three hundred or more of them — moving down the river

Dubglas on their way south to join their fellows — some two hundred strong — who were still trying to take Durobrivae.

Arturo drew his forces off the road to the east and made camp. He sent three of Coroticus's marshmen up the river Dubglas to bring back reports on the Saxons' movements. The river which was close by their camp was slow running and heavily reeded along its banks. Parts of it were already iced over and the soft ground of its marshy verges had frozen hard enough to take the weight of man and horse.

Long before dawn the marshmen returned with their reports on the Saxons. Hearing it, Arturo gave the order at once to break camp and move. Now, he blessed the hard times of night riding and marching at Cam Hill during training. With the marshmen scouts leading them they went five miles northwards up the river and then drew away from it and made themselves ready for the morning light to come. Through the darkness they could see the camp fire flames of the Saxons two miles away in the direction of Lindum. All men stood to their arms and their mounts and long before dawn came there was no troop commander or trooper who did not know the part he must play with the full rising of the sun. Coroticus and his men had already moved off into the night which was bitter with the east wind blowing a gale, setting dust and dead leaves and rushes swirling into the air, and numbing bare hands to a stiffness which only the coming heat of battle was to warm

When dawn came, cloudless and biting cold with the wind, the troopers standing to their horses saw that they were lodged in the cover of a thin growth of pines which covered the low summit of a stretch of heathland a mile from the river. Beyond the pines at the edge of the heathland Coroticus's marshmen lay hidden in the trough of an old road that led down to the river. Three bowshots beyond them, on the slightly lower ground by the river, was the Saxon camp. The warriors were already astir, breaking camp to begin their onward march down the river to Durobrivae and the plundering and ravaging of any farm or small settlement that came between.

Coroticus lying on the lip of the road saw that they were well armed and clothed in heavy furs and thick woollen clothes, and unlike most roving Saxon bands moved in a disciplined manner about their business. Clear in their midst, ordering and command-ing them, was a warrior, tall for his race, who wore a winged helmet and a surcoat of black sheepskin. None of the Saxons were mounted

255

for they had no use or skills for handling horses in battle, but they had with them ponies and mules now being laden with their supplies and spoils of war. From behind him there came clear to Coroticus the signal he awaited; the high, whistling pipe of a greenshank. He rose, but gave no order for all his near hundred men knew their part in Arturo's battle plan. As he stepped into view clear of the sunken road ten men followed him on either side. They walked without hurry towards the Saxon camp, spears slung over their backs to free their hands for the bows they carried. They were so small a party that they excited no great interest, except for a few shouts and bursts of laughter from the warriors who were now forming up raggedly to begin their march.

Within bowshot of the camp Coroticus and his men knelt to one knee and then one after another they shot their arrows. As the flighting hiss of one arrow died so another whistled to life and followed it, and each arrow found its mark in throat or chest or groin. They shot five arrows each and then as the roars of anger and shouts of the wounded filled the air forty or fifty warriors, like a roused swarm of wasps, came running up the gentle slope towards them with swords and spears poised for action.

Coroticus and his men turned from them and trotted without hurry back to the edge of the sunken road and, on the lip of the bank, knelt again and without hurry string-notched their arrows and sent them flighting towards the Saxons. Stung by this taunting affront from so few men the Saxons came charging up the gentle rise, roaring with anger and filling the air with their oaths, leaving eight of their men on the ground behind them. When they were half-a-bowshot away the rest of the marshmen rose suddenly over the edge of the road bank with their arrows ready strung to let them fly into the packed ranks of the attackers. The Saxon attack broke and withered like wheat under the sickle. Then, as another flight of arrows thinned their ranks, they turned and ran back down the slope.

Coroticus licked his lips with pleasure as he saw the fresh stir from the far Saxons as the survivors rejoined them, and grinned at the howling and crying and milling movement in the camp as their black-coated leader began to draw them to some kind of order. Here was, he thought, the beginning of the firing of the wasps nest. He watched as the swarm below took ragged order and then widestrung rank after rank of warriors, led by their wing-helmeted leader, came charging up the road.

The marshmen stood their ground until their last arrow was spent and then, as though content with their wrought havoc, they turned, crossed the road and began to trot for the far cover of the pine-studded heath crest.

Seeing them turn and run the Saxons, breaking ranks and raging to avenge their fallen, came pack hunting after them, swarming across the road.

As the marshmen came through the pines and past the waiting cavalry, Lancelo's horn blew and the long note made the cheek skin of Arturo tighten with joy. Here now was the first day of the Great Horses and the power that came from safe saddles and body-bracing stirrup irons. With himself at the centre, faithful to the White One, they came out of the pines at a growing gallop, Gelliga and his troop to the left and Durstan with his men on his right. Behind them, in a thick driving column, came the long tried smaller horses of the Companions. They burst down on the Saxons who had crossed the road, lances lowered and strongly couched, and Arturo led them, marking the figure of the black-surcoated Saxon leader. The shock of their meeting was like the sudden breaking of an angry sea, and for the first time Arturo and his men knew the real power of their new mounts and horse gear. The Saxon leader ran to meet him and threw up his small shield to hammer aside the lowered lance while the blade of his scramaseax drove hard for Arturo's groin. Arturo dropped the point of his lance and felt the great arm and body shock as it drove through the man's chest. He fell to the ground, screaming, his sword flying from his hand and lay there with the lance spitted through him. As he passed Arturo drew his sword and knew now with certainty that although the lance could only serve but once there was a new strength and sureness in the sword's blade. The battle lust took him and all his Companions as for the first time they knew the bloody, death-giving strength that lay in their sword arms. The swing of the blade which before cut deep, now sheared through flesh and bone like a butcher's cleaver taken to quartering carcasses.

If it was a morning of joy for the Companions in their newfound strength, it was also a morning of blood and relentless carnage, a massacre without mercy to avenge the people of Lindum, a great killing to claim blood price for the murder and rape of the gentle nuns, and a hunt to the death of the sea wolves which would make the memory of the battle of the river Dubglas live for ever. Over the hard, frost-bound river lands they harried the fleeing Saxons, driving them to

259

the water's edge either to turn and meet death or to fling themselves in to sink or swim to the far bank. No mercy was shown. Behind the fast scouring cavalry groups there came Coroticus and his men with their spears and their daggers drawn, seeking the hearts and the throats of wounded and living.

When the killing was done and the last Saxon had found safety across the river, the Companions reformed and buried their dead of which there were few and the march began upriver to Durobrivae, which was to prove luckier than Lindum. The town still held, and the Saxon survivors from the Dubglas battle had reached their comrades with the news of Arturo's coming. The siege was quickly lifted and the Saxons marched in haste to the east and the safety of their flat mere and river-cut lands.

Arturo stayed three weeks at Lindum setting to rights the ordering of the city as the citizens who had escaped came back, reforming the patrols and strong points along the Lindum-Durobrivae line, and pressing to service any youth or man able to bear arms. They would serve until the spring came and then be free to return to farm or settlement; but he knew that there would be no real fighting for them to face. Esc had made his throw and the gods had turned the dice against him. It would be long before he cradled the marked ivories in his palm to make another cast. He left Gelliga in command of the city and the defences of the line with a troop of horse and fifty of Coroticus's men to give heart and fire to the local forces.

He rode back to Cam Hill through Corinium. The news had long been sent ahead of his victory. But there was no welcome for him from Count Ambrosius. He had died of a heart attack two days after receiving Arturo's messenger.

Sitting in the Count's quarters at Corinium with Olipon, the Praefectus Castorum, Arturo asked, 'What was the manner of his death?'

The campaign-hardened Olipon, who now had a real affection for Arturo, though not greater than his love for his old commander, shrugged his shoulders. 'Some men know when their time comes to die. He had a seizure, but he had known them before and overcome them. But this time . . . the wish was no longer in him to live. Two days after your messenger came he died and has been buried at Glevum which was his wish. Long before spring the whole of this country will know of his going.' He paused and grinned ruefully. 'You will then be set high as target for the rivalries and enmities of many chiefs. You must win them by your boldness if you wish for kingship over this country.'

Arturo said curtly, 'There is no lust for kingship in me — only a wish for the return of the greatness of this country and the flowering of peace when we have driven the Saxons from us.'

Olipon shrugged his shoulders. 'True lust or not, my lord — you must assume the shape of it. He who commands must be king for where else does authority rest?' He reached within the loose robe he was wearing and brought out a folded piece of parchment fastened with the seal of Count Ambrosius. 'These are Count Ambrosius's last words to you. Since he wished it I have read them. He speaks as father to son, and he speaks with the wisdom which came with his years and their bitter experience.'

The words of Count Ambrosius, written on the parchment, read:

I salute you:

Be king and above all men. No throne can be shared.
Give your trust to no one except for a season.
The summer of a man's loyalty is often

262

followed by the mischievous winter of his pride.
No matter the warmth of your heart, keep the cold sword always at your side. Treachery respects no blood bonds; look for it even seated at your own hearth.

The gods have claimed you for this country and freed you from the wrack of conscience.
I give you the inheritance of Ambrosius. Enrich it so that in the years to come all men will shout 'Arto' while my name will be whispered like a brief echo, the gentle fall of ash from the fire of your kindling.

# The Holly on the Hillside

Arturo rode back to Cam Hill, leaving Durstan with horses and men to stand in command for him at Glevum and Corinium. His course was set by the words of Ambrosius, all that remained was to test the tides and perils of the voyage ahead. King he would be, but the proclamation should come from others. If any stood in his way they should fall for the gods had freed him from conscience.

The man changed and lived no longer for himself but for his dreams. At Isca he talked long and late with his father who, standing ward for the young Cato, held control of the Dumnonian treasury. Baradoc, knowing the change in him, would have tempered some of his demands but saw the darkness of rising frustration in his eyes and gave him his way. Arturo sent messengers to all the chiefs of the far North as far as the Wall of Hadrian, to all the chiefs of Cymru and the ruler of Demetia calling for their presence at Glevum by the feast of Beltine. He rode to see King Melwas at his winter quarters on the slopes of the limestone hills above the great swamp. When he left Melwas — enriched by presents from the Iscan vaults — it was with the firm promise that Coroticus would come to him in the spring with three hundred armed and provisioned men.

After he had gone Melwas said to Coroticus, 'The old wolf has died. Now the pack gets a new leader but there are many who will wait to tear him down.'

Coroticus rubbed his nose and grinned. 'What other leader is there? There is not a man amongst us who does not know his mind and is with him.'

Melwas grunted. 'I am no fool to sit overclose to the fire and burn myself. I give him the men, but for your glory, not his. *Aie* . . . though, I like him well, and he is no fool to call himself king yet. He will work that royal yeast differently.'

Three weeks after Arturo's return — and he lodged now more often at Isca than Cam Hill — the gods sent him an unexpected gift. A young man who had crossed from Gaul to the estuary of the river Isca with a shipload of horses and returning refugees asked for an audience with Arturo and would name nothing of his business. In the end after much pestering of the fortress guards he was brought to Arturo by Borio who had searched him for hidden weapons.

Arturo saw him in the great chamber where he had once been taken to see first Prince Gerontius and then his son, Geraint. Without opposition from Baradoc Arturo had taken the chamber into his own use.

Alone with Arturo — for he had refused to speak in the presence of any other — the young man said, 'My lord Arturo, I am Oleric, the son of Theodoric from the land of the Visigoths below Gaul.'

'And so?'

'My father's name means nothing to you, my lord?'

'Nothing.' Then seeing the youth's surprise, Arturo smiled and went on, 'In this country we have our own troubles. The Franks, the Goths and the Visigoths are known to me from my studies but of their present men of fame I know little.'

The young man smiled boldly. 'How did you know that I spoke of a man of fame, my lord?'

'Because you stand proudly and speak as would the son of a man of high state. Now give me plain facts and the reason for your coming.'

'I will, my lord. But I should say to you that on crossing from Gaul it was to Count Ambrosius I travelled. Now, since he is dead, I learn, I speak to you who have taken his place, so all men tell me.'

Momentarily Arturo frowned. Then with a shrug of his shoulders he said, 'Speak to me then.'

'Very well, my lord.'

Arturo sat and listened as the youth spoke and, within a very short while, he knew that here being offered to him by this Oleric son of Theodoric was a part of the inheritance from Ambrosius of which he could never have guessed the existence but whose richness made him long for the moment to come when he met the war chiefs of this land at Glevum.

When the youth had finished Arturo said, 'Return to your father and tell him that I accept that which he offers and the first price shall be paid when he comes ashore in this land at the time and the place you have named.'

'I thank you, my lord.'

'My thanks are to you and your father. The gods keep you on your journey back to him.'

A little after Oleric had gone Gwennifer came into the chamber to him. She had been riding and still wore dusty men's clothes, her long hair part-freed from its nape ribbons.

Teasingly she said, 'You look like a cat that has been at the cream bowl, my lord.'

Rising, Arturo went to her and kissed her

hand and said, 'I smile because of the sight of you now, as wild and tousled as the morning you first brought Cabal to me. I smile, too, because it is now hard in me that I have had enough of affairs here and the closeness of this fortress and the streets and the midden smells. Tomorrow we ride for Cam Hill and you come with me. We will lie in our hilltop lodge together and hear the fox bark through the frost-thin air to his vixen and walk by the Cam and see the sun take the silver of the leaping salmon as he comes to the call of Latis.'

They went to Cam Hill where all now was well ordered and sound quarters long made for men and beasts. In the hard bright winter weather they rode by the Cam and sitting their horses by the bank could look down through the clear crystal of the waters and watch the hen salmon arching and curvetting their long bodies as they cut their redds for spawning while the great cock fish kept station at their sides, waiting for the berried moments of seeding and milting, and sometimes, unseen by Arturo, Gwennifer's white teeth would bite frettingly at the inner edge of her lower lip from longing for the boon for her body which was still denied her.

They rode the high downs with Cabal and a span of chase hounds and with the setting up of a winter-coated hare they followed hare and hounds, shouting and calling and laughing as though they were youth and maiden charged with the wonder and passion of a first love which gave all the world a freshness unseen before. For Arturo this time of a few weeks, though not planned from his known need, was a time that his body and spirit needed to refresh him for the days to come. He put from his mind all cares and turned sharply away from the temptation of brooding meditation over the great matters and affairs which awaited him and with the coming of spring. He was a lover with his beloved and the warmth of her kisses and the bonding of their bodies gave him a kingship at night which pushed all thought of far Glevum and of mistrusting, obstinate, and proud war-chiefs from him. Even as the gods now and then turned away from the ordering of men's affairs in this world to days of feasting and nights of revelry so, he knew now, must a great commander seek forgetfulness of his heart's true passion and his iron dedication to his country's desperate needs to lose himself in a skein of simple days and simple delights and simple sights . . . the quick ear-cocking of a wily hare in the moment of sitting upright before breaking to flight, the tolerant complaint in the calling of a diamond-tailed raven as a pack of fork-tailed red kites mobbed it, the rainbow colours the sun's glance gave to an icicle hanging from the lip of a moss-ribbed rock face, the straddled legs and unsteady stance of a new-born winter foal as it rose to face for the first time the new world of light . . . and each morning's unlidding of the blue eyes, clear as the columbine bloom, of his beloved Gwennifer lying with her corn silk hair all a-tousle on the long goose-down pillow at his side.

On their last night at Cam Hill they sat by the turf fire and drank wine, shared from the same cup, and Gwennifer took her harp and played and sang for him and the words that came from her were, he could believe, a gift from the crook-nosed god Maponus who fired the heat of true-tempered words in the minds of all bards . . .

Arto the spearhead in battle
The Saxons will cry woe
As they flee before the Britons
Arto will hunt them down
A pillar of flame, King over men
High the banner of the White One
Under its linen border, great Arto
From Isca in the West
To the great wall in the North
King over men, beloved of all

270

Light-heartedly Arturo said, 'You sing too soon of future things.'

Gwennifer shook her head. 'No, my lord. In men's hearts you are king already. Only the word is lacking and that comes soon. King you will be and sons I shall bear you to be Princes.'

But as the year's shortest day came and went and the feast of the Christos people to celebrate their Lord's birth passed with Arturo joining them in worship — for he would give offence to no god — Gwennifer knew that her deep wish to bear him a child still showed no sign of being granted, and she came fully to believe the truth of the words of Tia which she had overheard. Anger and frustration turned in her like two serpents, so that when Arturo and Baradoc went back to their tribal lands on the north coast below Caer Sibli to order affairs there, she — at her own wish — stayed in Isca There were times then when she paced her chamber restlessly and others when she took her harp and played airs of sweet melancholy so that the tears misted her eyes.

On one such day as the winter-burnished sun hung low, reddening the waters of the Isca in its setting, she sat at her window playing when Borio, now commander of the fortress and its winter garrison, came down

271

the winding stone steps from the broad walks that ran around the fortress walls. Her door was partly open and seeing her playing the harp he stopped and listened. When she had finished and raised her head to see him, he smiled and said, 'You play a sad melody, my lady. But sing no words. Are they then even sadder?'

'Good Borio there are no words to match its sadness.'

'Then it is a tune which must be teased to cheerfulness.'

He came across the chamber, took the harp from her in his big hands, and began to play the same tune in a brighter vein, raising gaiety and liveliness from the same sad notes she had struck, and because the bard's gift was in him and words and music came to him as easily as breathing, he sang:

Her hand and eye are gentle
Walking under the vine
The nightingales salute her
She will come over the high crag
To sit with me under the holly
Until there be no green leaf over us
So long will be the season of love

When he finished Gwennifer laughed with pleasure and went to the table and poured him a goblet of wine. As she gave it to him she asked, 'And where is the one who waits under the green holly tree for Borio?'

Borio's face puckered with a wry smile. 'If she waits, my lady — which I doubt — then it is beyond Deva by the wide sands of the estuary where the wild geese will now be wintering and where — ' his smile broadened, ' — the holly trees are few.' He touched the wine to his lips and saluted her and Gwennifer felt that although his eyes rested on her face only briefly there was in them a rise of boldness.

When he was gone she took the wine goblet and, standing at the window, sipped gently. He had been with Arturo from the beginning; one of the youngest of the Companions. When he was campaigning he grew a beard, but during the winter he went clean shaven, a fresh-faced young giant, big-handed yet with fingers that caressed the harp strings with a light and magic touch to match the easy spring of his gift for words. That far away maiden beyond Deva, she thought, would be a fool not to wait and keep herself for him to bear his children . . .

That night she lay awake for a long time, her mind twisting and turning. The conflict in her between her love for Arturo and her own needs for him and his wide ranging ambitions drove sleep far from her, and sometimes, while her face stiffened in the spasms of her resolution, she felt the touch of tears in her eyes. No man she knew would doubt her honour. No man would talk loosely of her for fear of Arto's wrath and the safety of his own life.

Two nights later when Borio, who had his chamber at the top of the tower above Gwennifer's room, retired he found lying on his bolster a sprig of green holly, its dark leaves silvered by the dim light from a single wall sconce. Because of the poetry and music in him and the memory of the parting look which Gwennifer had given him he knew the meaning of the holly and felt at once the stir of loyalty to Arturo move strongly in him, warring against the sharp onset of his manhood's desires.

She came to him long after the watch had called midnight from the fortress gate-tower. Her hair was braided into plaits, the long tresses coiled in a golden wreath about her head. Her long white gown was close-caught about her neck, but her arms were bare and she moved he thought as swift dryness took his throat, like a golden-crowned swan.

Curbing his troubled spirit, he said gently. 'My lady, you would do me a great honour. But this must not be. Many years ago I came to Arto and pledged him my sword and my faith and swore to serve him with all my honour.'

'You do him no dishonour, my Borio. The gods have brewed the draught of this night's drinking. Arto would have a son to match his greatness when he goes, but there is no living seed in him. Since you have sworn all love for him and I carry none but love for him and his desires the gods have marked us thus to serve him and the secret stays between us for all time.' She came close to him and reaching up touched gently with her fingertips the weather-browned firmness of his cheek. 'Arto's Companions are Arto's flesh, and Arto's wife is the vessel that must hold the everlasting wine of his greatness. The gentle breath of a woman's sigh can blow the candle light to death and darkness. But tonight the boon of darkness lies with you, and I ask it of you from my love for Arto.'

For a moment or two Borio stood, unmoving. The gift of words was in her as in him, but the truth of her words and her pleading was like summer lightning, coming and going in proud, many-hued flames, turning the world to brief wonder and blinding him to set free all the coiling desires of his manhood.

He turned, took three steps to the solitary

wall sconce and blew the tallowed wick to darkness; but, in that darkness as he came to her and his arms went round her and the stir of her body wakened to full life the desire in him, he knew that he did this alone as Borio and for no other reason than Borio's because Borio was a man and Gwennifer was a woman, and both were caught in the snare of the gods.

They were lovers until Arturo's return which was on the last day of the month of the two-faced god Janus. That evening Borio, with Arturo and Gwennifer, ate in full company in the fortress hall. Borio drank heavily to kill the shame in him, while Gwennifer laughed and drank at Arturo's side and teased him gaily. After midnight when, for all his drinking, the gods had withheld from him the least edge of oblivion's cloak, Borio walked the ramparts on his rounds as the rain fell steadily, and — so it was thought when he was found later, though the truth died with Borio — he slipped on the wet planking bridging a parapet gap and fell sixty feet to the cobbled yard to break his neck. They buried him off the roadside along the Isca, where a side stream ran down to serve the aquaduct for watering the horses in the great stockade and where the sound of their neighing and the thunder of their hooves in exercise would reach him. But it was not with this in mind that Gwennifer had chosen it. He lay beneath an old holly tree, its berries red as the robin's breast, red as his blood which had marked the fortress cobbles. But, as Gwennifer was to find as the weeks went by, the sin and the sacrifice found no pleasure with the gods.

★ ★ ★

A few days before the feast of Beltine marking the coming of Spring, Arturo, leaving Gwennifer at Isca, rode north with a full company of Companions drawn from the hill forts and Cam Hill and with three hundred marshmen under the command of Coroticus and the tramp of their going cloaked the young leaves of the roadside growths with dust and made those not in the van of the column draw their scarves across their mouths to save their throats from parching. When they reached Glevum the army of Arturo was camped outside the South gate and close to the river for the watering of horses while the companies and retinues of the war chiefs lay between the West gate and the river. The tribal chiefs and petty kings were lodged in the city in the old half-timbered, half-masonry quarters of the long gone legions which Durstan had put to order during the winter. Arturo himself had quarters in the old basilica which Count Ambrosius had long ago turned into his residence and army headquarters. It was here that the full congress of chiefs took place in the ancient long hall while the townspeople crowded the forum and basilica colonnades to see for themselves the coming and going of lords and princes of the far north-west and north-east and from Cymru beyond the Sabrina, and — from Demetia in the far south of Cymru — the flamboyant figure of Difynwal, young and headstrong and heedless of the distant Saxon threat since his country was still hard-pressed by Scotti invasions and settlement.

In those first days at Glevum there was much coming and going and private meetings between all these men both with and without Arturo. In those first days, too, the magic which already cloaked Arturo and his name grew, flourishing fast among the townspeople, then with the young warriors from the north who each in his bold, impatient heart knew himself to be another Arturo and longed for the liberty to escape from tribe-lands to march and fight and readily to risk any death to snatch at honour and fame. And, in those days, wherever he went Arturo — since

Durstan and Lancelo had their own affairs to marshal — took Pasco with him, Pasco the shabby, shuffling priest whose eyes missed no passing shadow of doubt or shrewdness on a man's face and whose memory held every word spoken in store to be brought out against a man's turn of spirit or to prompt a man from hesitation when fear or greed silently possessed him.

Sitting alone late one night, and seeing Arturo lapse into a rare, silent mood of introspection, Pasco smiled and said gently, 'My lord, you told me once that you honour all gods and given them all worship, and true this seems for they have withheld no favours from you. Now comes the moment when you have to draw these little earthy gods of flesh and blood together and gain their favour. I think you find this a greater matter. Favour one above the others and this pantheon of tribes becomes a squabbling family.'

For a moment Arturo said nothing. Then, loosening the scarf about his throat, for the night was warm, he smiled and said, 'Tis no easy matter, but it will be and must be possible since the truth is that they are all of one family, no matter where their lands lie, no matter the blood lines they carry. They are the family of Britain, Britain which has fathered them. Whoever attacks one member of that family attacks them all. The young wolves fight amongst themselves for leadership. But when winter hunger rib-strakes their flanks they hunt as one. So with these men — they still do not see that there is a hunger creeping over this land which must be stayed — the hunger of the Saxons for land and living space. So long as the Saxons hold their own, then time and the years go with them and against us. Their eyes must be opened. So that the light of truth floods in.'

'And you will do that when the gathering of chiefs takes place?'

'By the grace of the gods, yes — and their grace I have, and for it give humble thanks. This is a gathering Count Ambrosius longed to see. Much he did against me but I would for his honour have him living and be in my place at the meeting to come. Aye — though there is the difference between us that he dreamt of seeing himself Emperor — whereas I dream only of one thing, to be Commander of the armies of the kings of Britain in this war.'

For a moment or two it was on the tip of Pasco's tongue to say that a commander of kings must of right then be the greatest of kings but, seeing the dark intensity of feeling show on Arturo's face, he said mildly, 'And when the great battle is won, what do you do,

280

what will you have become, my lord?'

Surprising him, Arturo grinned and said lightly, 'Why, I shall be my own man again. Free to walk without care through the long summer grasses with my wife, to mark with an untroubled mind the flight of the blue down butterfly, to hold a falcon on my wrist and slip it free to hang high and wait for the flushed wildfowl . . . Aye, free to travel any road or track in this land without fear and to see men smile in good will to one another, and free to hold close to my wife and kin with the humble joy of any ploughman or woodcutter. Men were not born for battle. They were born for the good business of enjoying the fruits and blessings of this earth with which the gods have dowered us . . .

Quietly but boldly Pasco said, 'The gods have always this in their power yet withhold it, my lord.'

'True — but the gods have their reasons which neither the eye nor the mind of man can read. But good reasons they must be and we must await their revelation patiently.'

Four days later the meeting of the kings and chiefs was held in the hall of the basilica. All the men stood and carried their arms and had at their sides a grown son or trusted warrior. Arturo stood at the top of the steps at the end of the hall and four Companions in full war gear stood on the lowest step as bodyguard. They were Durstan, Lancelo, Gelliga and Coroticus of the Summerlands. Bareheaded, wearing the long surcoat given to him by the Bishop of Noviomagus, sword belted about it, Arturo faced them with Cabal couched at his side. Sunlight coming through the high windows of the hall drew rusty glints in his hair and there was a set to his tall figure into which the waiting men, each according to his temper and his own ambitions, read arrogance and pride, the firmness of true authority, or the boldness of courage sustaining a great dream. But there was none that could truly deny the force in the stance of the man and the magic of personality which against all odds had set him where he was that day.

And that day, as he spoke, there was no denial of the gift of tongue which the gods had given him. When he spoke of the Saxons his words were sword sharp; when he spoke of this country, their Britain, it was now the voice of a lover, now the gentle tones of a son to his mother; when he spoke of the need to hold and further strengthen the long line against the Saxons, to give them no westward freedom so that either they must come out in force and make battle or slowly be pressed to the sea, his words were cold, and iron-hard and relentless with the logic of a far-seeing Caesar, and when he came to name them all, one and separately, with the call to be made on them for men and provisions and the duties which they would have to accept he spoke evenly and without emotion as a commander making clear the ordering of the battle lines for the coming clash with the enemy.

When he spoke of the dream of the dead Ambrosius, which was now his dream, he did so with truth, sparing neither fault on the side of Ambrosius nor the arrogance of spirit on his own, and ended with a plea without weakness, saying. 'The like of this day will not come again. The gods in their wisdom send no new day's tide to order the grains of sand on the shore as they ever were before. The great sea tides of this world march under the gods' design, but the full tide of our country's greatness they will hold back forever while there is one least man amongst us who deceives and plots only to feed his own lust for power and riches. Now is the day when the tide of this great country's glory is at the low. But now is the time, and now rests the power in your hands, if you have the courage and the heart and the wisdom, to give me command and men and arms to make battle to win back what is ours. Tread on the adder and it strikes, the wild boar defends its own . . . aye, put your hand under the breast of the gentle dove to rob its nest and it will draw blood with its blows. Are we then to be less than the beasts and to sit quietly and await the slaughter from the east?

Under the gods I say I am not, and under the gods my heart tells me that you are not, for there can be no man here who would wish to be known by his children and their children to come as one who lived and died a craven. You are the kings and lords of this country. Give me the means to bring it back to its true glory . . . '

As he finished speaking, his hand dropping and touching the rough head of Cabal at his side, there was silence in the hall. From outside came the sound of the sparrows quarrelling along the colonnade roof and the rattle of a cart's wheels over the Forum paving stones.

Looking at the gathered leaders, bearded, weathered of face, and most carrying the open and hidden scars of war, their cloaks and furs and robes and kilts making a field of colour, a field at this moment which knew no breeze to stir it to life, Arturo knew the passing of the moments of destiny when all that was needed for his triumph was for one man to stand forward, draw sword or raise spear and cry 'Arto!' His lips firmed wryly at the thought that there had been in his mind long before that such a man could have been bought by him to play this part and with one shout set to work the great yeasting in men's hearts which he must have. But he had set his face against this. Ambrosius would have had it so, but not he. Either the gods touched these men to follow him or he would turn from them and travel his own path and wear down the years of his life with the same spirit and stubbornness that had wrung from him in new manhood the rash promise of Arto.

Then from the front ranks of the company stepped forward young king Difynwal of Demetia, his long black locks greased so that they shone with the bloom of a raven's wing, a gold torque about his brown neck, his stiff beard cropped short to a hedgehog's bristle, and a great chequered cloak of reds, greens, yellows and white billowing over his shoulders and arms and, from the belt about his waist, a short sword hanging from his side. Behind him stood his young son holding the tall standard from which hung the great round shield of Demetia on which was blazoned the fire-breathing red dragon of their country.

Boldly, his voice echoing in the shadowed roof spaces, Difynwal spoke.

'You call for men and arms to come to your command, great Arto. And there is none here with true heart or mind to refuse you this. But what warrior is there who goes to battle with a red heart and an iron hand if he leaves behind him kith and kin in peril? What victory is there when the returning bow or spearman climbs the crag to mountain home or rides the glen to farm and family — and finds death and fire and rapine have gone before him. You would have us face the east and the Saxons . . . *Aie,* that is all our wish. Have you forgotten that your mighty Esc and his chiefs are leagued with the Scotti warriors and shipmen and they raid the coasts of the West from the mouth of the Sabrina river to the headland of Octapitarum in my lands and north to the island of Mona and the straits of Segontium and north again to the Ituna estuary and the shores of the lands of the Novantae? They press us back from our own shores, and when we find strength to press against them they move away in their long curraghs and strike again like a moving swarm of hornets where there are few to make stand against them. The gods have been with you. We all praise your triumphs. We all would cry you Duke of War, Commander of the armies of the kings of Britain, but this cannot be for we have no warriors with the wish to go East to win glory and then coming back to the West find none to share his triumphs, and the nettles and charlock of despair growing through the bones of his loved ones, his hearth cold and open to the sky . . . no joy of wife and sweetheart, no red and yellow cattle in the glen, no proud ram to stand and stamp his foot and marshal the ewes and lambs. Rid me of the men from Erin and you shall have the great part of my men. And know this, I speak not alone for myself.' He half-turned to the chiefs behind him, and cried, 'Look and see those who know the truth of my words and have felt and still endure the suffering of their people. Aye, the gods are with you, but the Scotti are with us and our swords demand their blood!' He drew his sword and raised it and, as he did so, from more than half of the men behind him came also a raising of swords and spears and a swelling roar like the call of a high sea comber in the moment of breaking on the shore.

When the noise had died and the last sword had been lowered and sheathed, Arto spoke and Pasco, lost in the crowd, listened to him wondering at the change in his manner of speaking and in the man himself. He spoke now as though from an age far beyond his years, and with a gentle patience, each word well-honed, but, when he needed, there came the soft burr in his Dumnonian touched voice, now a caress and now a sad chiding, and he began:

'The first man I killed . . . aye, and that long before I found a taste for kissing and cuddling the maidens of my tribe . . . was a Scottus. I cut his throat with a dagger on the sands at night. And when I was youth, I stood and fought the night raiders from the sea with the men of my tribe. With the passing of years, and the growing of my hatred for the Saxon men do you think I have forgotten the Scotti? Do you think I would ask you to give me men to go East and have no care for the West? What great command could I claim from you if I were so stiff-necked and one-eyed that I could not see double danger and turn to meet it? Know this then, without their long-planked and hide-plated curraghs the Scotti are as my Companions would be without horses. When you press them to the sea they take to their boats. But now the days of their boats are numbered. From far Belerium's point there sailed a handful of days ago a fleet of warships, greater in number and size than any the Scotti command, and this fleet will take watch and ward and make battle with the Scotti wherever they be met off our western shores.

And the man who commands them has no more love for Saxon or Scotti than we have. Though — ' he grinned, ' — he is man enough to want payment for his services and the first part of this has already been found from the Dumnonian treasury at Isca. The rest must be met from the war levies laid on us all . . . gold and silver and stores for his ships and harbouring for them. No land grants such as Vortigern gave to Hengist and Horsa. This man lives by the sea and his men are of all nations with their homes far to the south in the country of the Goths below Gaul. This man is Theodoric and he waits now off the mouth of the Sabrina for the beacons on your hills to be fired to bring him into your waters, to scour them free of the Scotti.'

Arto paused and in the silence that held the assembly of chiefs his eyes found those of Difynwal and held them steadily. Then with slow, deliberate words he went on, 'Great Difynwal, I have answered you. I am no beggar to plead with any man for alms for my country. I am no pedlar to haggle over a deal for my country's honour. I seek only the glory which was and must be again hers, and if any in this hall turn his back to me now he turns his back on his country's gods, on his fellows-in-arms against the Saxons. Living there shall be no honour in him and his women and children shall take no joy in him, and dying there shall be no welcome in the Shades for him. I am Arto and have given you my promise. Now, let those who would go tend cattle, lie warm at nights with wives and sweethearts, let them go. I would sooner have a beardless boy with fire in his belly than a grown man whose spirit is a timid hare to send him running at the distant sound of hounds. I am Arto and, with or without you, shall take no rest, nor know any settled hearth until I have done what the gods have commanded me to do.'

For a moment or two none spoke or moved and all eyes watched the two men who had gathered to themselves the ordering of this moment and knew each that the balancing of the future was weighted evenly between them. Against his side Arturo felt Cabal rise to his feet and the soft muzzle came to his hand, while below him Difynwal stood grim-faced and unmoving. Then with a slow movement Difynwal drew his sword, and there were those who thought for bloody work, and he walked up to Arturo and as he came so that only Arturo saw, he smiled, but needed not the smile for Cabal beneath his hand was without sound or stiffening of muscle. At Arturo's side Difynwal turned, raised his sword, and shouted, setting the echoes ringing in the roof, 'Arto! Arto!'

Before the echoes died all men in the hall drew sword or raised spear and the echoes rang again and again, 'Arto! Arto! Arto!'

And Pasco watching, seeing Arturo and Difynwal embrace, remembered the first days of the beginning at the Villa of the Three Nymphs, remembered the marriage of Arto and Daria, the springtime of their love, and the springtime of Arto's manhood; and he knew that now again the season of Arturo's life had changed and, because he gently questioned all God's movements in the affairs of men, yet had no lack of faith, he could find in himself no true happiness for Arturo. From this day he lived apart from men.

# The Immortal Wound

There were no doubts in Gwennifer. Arturo was Commander of the armies of the British kings. It was a title as clumsy and shambling as the movements of a crippled beast unable to fend for itself. The title would die. But not Arturo. King he would be and once named it would be forever. Through his sons his glory would live. Borio had failed her, but there were others and now that she was at Glevum and bore herself like a queen to all men there could be no bar to her desire and no mercy shown to any man, no matter his rank, who should smile out of place or boast with or without truth of her brief and long-spaced favours. Always there was with her Lacus, the groom, to use poison or dagger or the turn of designed but innocent-seeming accident.

But while time and time again she remained barren there were those who knew the truth without sound of words or sight of deed, knew just as rain still a day's coming could be smelt in the wind. All kept their counsel. Arturo stood highest in the land and with the full weight of affairs now on him showed a change under which in a few years the old Arturo was buried to all except a few chosen of his Companions. Only when he rode or made camp for night in some small party with a handful of tried friends would he talk of old times for a while.

In public and campaigning affairs he was ruthless with any who failed him, expecting all men to push themselves to the bounds of their strength and faith as he did himself. And for the most part men did this, for the torch which had been fired in the basilica flared high and bright over the land. For those few whose levies or dues to the war chest fell short there was no mercy. No matter the distance and the days it cost, Arturo would ride with a force of his Companions and there was then no withstanding his demands for now, as many of the shrewder chiefs and small kings had seen without fear, for they had no desire in themselves for it, his power had grown from the day they had acclaimed him Commander. As the years passed he gained an ease and assurance from the knowledge that the men who now served him in the field and garrisons took pride in him, matching their prowess and dedication with his. They were part of him and apart from all men who were strangers to his service. The young sons of tribal chiefs and kings itched to come of age so that they could join him . . .

aye, even if it only meant that they did duty on the Saxon line in idleness during winter cherishing their memories of the scarce summer days of sword-blooding when some rash Saxon warrior had led a foray against them, fretting against the imprisonment of his own enclave. Youth and young manhood held to Arto and many a chief's son shamed his father from trimming his levy or hoarding his wealth when Arto called.

These were years when there were no great battles; these were the years when the slow turn of fortune in favour of the Britons began. The weight of Theodoric's ships and men slowly began to clear the west coasts of the Scotti threat and found them, losing stomach for fight, moving far north to pillage and settle along the shores of the land of the Picts. These were the years when the garrisoning and patrolling of the Saxon line penned in the warriors of Esc and his chiefs and brought to Esc the truth that, with the dwindling of the Scotti threat in the rear of the Britons, the time must come when he would have to march out in force and drive westwards to break the budding might of Arturo for ever. And these were the years when many a night Arturo sat late in his chamber at Glevum or Isca or Deva pondering the reports and messages that

294

came to him from paid or willing place men amongst his Saxon foes. Dead Ambrosius had strung this network and now Arturo spread it wider, and from his gleanings he knew that it would be many years before the itch in his men for true and full battle would be eased by any great march west by Esc. But, though he knew that the time of Esc's coming lay years ahead, Arto lived and planned and worked to strengthen his armies and secure his garrisons and posts as though time were pressing him hard. The gods might at any time ferment the slow yeast to fast rising.

They now had at Corinium near five hundred great horses, manned and equipped and held under the command of Durstan with Gelliga to second him. Lancelo, grown man now, he kept with him as he moved through the country, and it was to Lancelo now, more than Durstan, that he sometimes showed his heart. Towards the end of the year four hundred and ninety as they rode for Isca with a troop of horse Arturo, finding the turning of the leaves as the year died and the soft mists shrouding thinly the countryside moving him to melancholy, felt an unexpected need to ease some of the lone burden he bore. His years were forty now, and with the passing of each year the running out of time seemed to speed ever faster. As a young man a day was an age, giving time for the conquering of a world. Now his days were so hard-pressed that they slipped through his hands like running sand

Riding well ahead of the troop on the White One, the third now of that name, and a new hound Cabal alongside him — for the old Cabal was two years dead, gored to death by a boar at hunting — he spoke to Lancelo without turning to him and said, ' 'Twas this road from Corinium that you rode with your father, Ansold, and your sister Daria to bring them first to the Villa of the Three Nymphs.'

'Aye, my lord. A day when the young beard on my chin was as soft as goslings' down.'

'You have served well, Lancelo, and have always been true Companion, but more — you are my brother through your sister Daria, my true wife. Have you ever turned the truth from me, Lancelo?'

Puzzled, Lancelo said, 'We ride at different gaits, my lord.'

'Aye, but side by side.'

'There has never been else but truth between us. Am I not your man, your brother?'

'You are — and because you are that you would give me no grief or pain. But now I speak plainly and would know a truth and you must answer plainly with no trimming of your words. I walked the rounds at Corinium two nights ago. There was a mist and I heard two guards talking about their fire. That I was there they did not know, that they live still comes from the charity of the gods who stayed my hand. They spoke ill of my lady Gwennifer. Tell me, Lancelo — did they speak the truth?'

Lancelo bit his under lip and was tempted to lie for the sake of their friendship. Then, knowing that a lie from him now would serve no purpose, for truth would come some other road, he said, 'It is the truth, my lord.'

Arturo turned and smiled at him. 'For that I thank you. Look not so glum. I am in good company for many a man from Caesars down to charcoal burners have worn the horns. You should know, Lancelo, that most often when the gods give greatness they season it in a man with a spice of ridicule to curb him from thinking himself more than mortal. Mortal I am and chafe not against it. That the gods spoke for me and made sign when I was born is enough.'

On his first night at Isca as Gwennifer sat at her mirror combing her long hair before retiring, while a south-westerly roared the long length of Dumnonia and shook the closed wooden shutters of the window and the flames of the tall candles swayed in the draughts Arturo, cradling a glass of wine in his palms, spoke to Gwennifer, his eyes on her and no anger in him.

'It was written by Merlin before my birth that I should throw no seed to flower. Merlin whom I have met a few times is a man whose words should always be marked with care. The truth in them is as hard to tell as the counting of the scales on a salmon or the numbering of bubbles in a beaker of cider.'

Gwennifer turned slowly to him. 'You talk in riddles, my lord.'

'No, I talk frankly and without anger. Seed I have and it is good seed and it grew in the body of Daria — but the gods denied it flowering.' He smiled. 'Good Merlin is always a little less than exact and a little more teasing than truthful. The gods have marked me for greatness but for long now I have understood that in their wisdom they will give me no heir in flesh to hold and increase my heritage. Would you know why?'

Firming mind and body now against the unexpectedness of this talk, but grateful for the lack of anger in him, Gwennifer said, 'Yes, my lord, I would. If greatness is your part why should there be none of your blood to inherit and increase it? There is shame in me, but that it was done, this thing I did, then it was done to cheat the gods and glorify your name when you were gone. In that lies all my love for you.'

'Your love for me is clear but ill designed. That you have not borne a child to foster on the world as mine lies in your own barrenness. My seed is good but at its first shooting the gods would wither it and the womb that held it. You wonder that I am not angry with you and send you from me?'

'Yes, my lord, I do, for I have deserved both.'

'No. What you did was out of love for me. But now there must be an end of it for there is no ripeness in you. Wife you are, but never mother . . . ' He stood up and went to her and she rose from her stool to him. Facing her, he saw the slow start of tears in her blue eyes and his nostrils were full of the perfume of her tall, slender body and the candlelight streaked her hair with soft shadows. He took her in his arms and held her to him and against his cheek he felt hers touched now with the dew of her falling tears and her body shook with the slow rack of her sobs.

Later in the darkness, as they lay abed with the night full still of the great shout of the gale winds, Gwennifer said, 'You would have told me why the gods who give you greatness give you no heir to inherit, my lord.'

'And tell you I will, but you must mark my

words as you would those of a Merlin. I am not born in this land for the first time. This country has known me before in its hour of need and I have given it peace and greatness, and shall give it that again during this life and then dying shall rest in chaos until I am called again to restore its glory . . . ' He was silent for a while and then, with a little grunt, went on, 'You think that both a puzzle and a dream? Well it may seem so, but it is also a truth beyond explaining. Some men there are who are marked by the gods with an immortal wound. They die the death of this earth but not the death of the gods . . . and they sleep a while until the gods call them from darkness to know the joy again of the rising sun, to hear the neighing and tramp of the waiting war horses in the meadow, and the cries of misery from their oppressed countrymen whose ills they must set to flight again . . . ' He yawned suddenly and then laughed. '*Aie* . . . I was long a-seeing it — but true it is.'

He put out an arm and drew her to him and kissed her tenderly and then as he felt the tips of her fingers caress his forehead, he went on, 'So take no fear from me. Tomorrow you are born again and we shall ride out on the water meadows into a new world to watch the fall of the red and brown leaf, the flick of the white scuts of the moorfowl in the sedges, see the great oaks wrought black like shaped iron against the rising sun, and I shall be your love and you mine and we shall both be content to live under the will of the gods whose judgement is beyond any man's knowing.'

★ ★ ★

In the year, that followed, old Ansold the swordmaker, the father of Daria and Lancelo, died sitting at a tavern bench in Isca after a heavy day at his smithy. He finished his mead sitting among friends and then, as though the drink had fuddled his head, he bent forward and rested his forehead on his arms. Thinking him sleeping his friends laughed and talked teasingly to him until one touched his shoulder a little roughly and the old man slid sideways from the bench to the ground. He was buried not far from Borio above the horse grounds and close to his smithy where the sound of hooves on the ground and hammers shaping the iron for stirrups kept him company. Two months later Lancelo married a young woman from Corinium called Hylda whom Gwennifer took as a companion and found no envy against her when she was soon pregnant, took pride in all knowing it, and had no shame when the child

301

was born six months after the marriage.

In that year as the campaign season opened with the firming of the ground and the dying of floods from the valleys, Adipo, the son of the chief of the Durotriges and the husband of Arturo's sister, Gerta, came to Corinium with the levy of warriors from his father. With him came Gerta and their ten-year-old son Mordreth, who spent his days with the troopers on the cavalry grounds of the Sabrina Wing, learnt fast all barrack talk and oaths, and loved horses with a passion untouched by fear. He worshipped his uncle Arturo and found quickly a way to his heart and favour for he was the nearest to a son, Arto knew, that he would ever have. He set him up on the broad back of the White One with a wooden sword in his hand and let him circle the tan bark ring, shouting and calling. When the White One half bucked playfully from the laughter and the cries of the troopers he fell heavily only to pick himself up, his small dark face straining to hold back cry or tear, and demanded to be remounted. Arturo came to love the boy as near son — and shrugged off the sharp talk from Gerta at his indulgence of the boy.

In that year too, beginning with the lesser chiefs who had favours to seek for the placing of their sons or, since the times were quiet, asked leave to stay men from their levies for sowing and cropping and cattle-minding, there were those who addressed him as 'Royal Arto' and — since they were seldom refused their wishes — the habit spread. Arturo kept his pleasure to himself and was content to let the gods shape the weather of his ambitions, knowing that king he would be since they were willing it and the country — as Ambrosius had long ago seen — needed a man to stand above all others in sovereignty.

In that year too Cerdic of the West Saxon settlements stirred again and Arturo sent word to the Bishop of Noviomagus and the Chief Citizen of Venta to keep him supplied with all they could find of Cerdic's thinking and planning, and was content to wait until that tree was in full bearing before he should cut it to the ground. He knew, too, that Cerdic was in full league with Esc and could be watched as a weather gauge to the coming moves of the Saxon leader. That the move would not now be long delayed, he knew to be true for in all the Saxon enclaves men were restless and called for an end to their penning and craved the liberty to move west to the days of fighting and plunder and the nights of drunken boasting.

In that year, too, Oleric, the son of Theodoric, married a daughter of king

Difynwal and was given a land grant in Demetia, and many of Theodoric's men married girls from the towns and settlements of the sea coast of Cymru so that the fleet was slowly being bonded to the land with ties stronger than any stout hempen hawser. The valley of the Tamesis was peaceful except for a few small bands of cut-throats and outlawed men, both Britons and Saxons, who gave sport and good training to the unblooded and untried young men of the levies who were sent there. Londinium began to prosper but few men chose to live within its broken walls except merchants and traders and craftsmen and that these made trade with Esc's people gave Arturo no worry. That the Saxons should buy where before they had robbed was no pleasure to Esc or his chiefs and must shorten their tempers and the days to come before they moved in strength.

In the summer of that year Baradoc, now near his sixtieth year, took Tia with him to Aquae Sulis where he was working on the defences of an old hill fort to the east of the town and they were lodged in the old villa of her uncle, the long dead Chief Centurion Truvius. They would eat in the courtyard under the shade of the great sweet chestnut tree, the courtyard in which they had been married. One evening sitting there Tia looked across at Baradoc, weathered, stiff-armed, hair now greying, fast, and teasingly she said:

'Over the silver stream hunts the four-
    winged fly
Each eye holds a thousand eyes
But he sees not your beauty'

Baradoc spooning up from his bowl wild raspberries laced with sweet wine smiled. 'Prettily said. After a day in the sweat and labour of digging, with one's ears deafened by shouts and hammerings, there is no balm like the music of poetry.'

Tia ran the tip of her tongue between her lips to stay her laughter and found more words for him:

'I would have built for you a house with
    a roof of green rushes and a flower-
    pied floor.
A thousand seabirds would have greeted
    the golden girl with a brow like a lily,
    the young queen who rode the peril-
    ous paths without harm or hurt.'

Baradoc looked up, his face a little puzzled, and wiped fruit juice from his mouth with the back of his hand. 'I praise the man who made the words. I would like to have shaped them

305

myself and spoken them for you . . . *Aie*, there was a time in my youth when I could sweet-talk my love.'

Tia hid her smile behind her hand for the words were his and belonged to the days when they had travelled to Aquae Sulis and had stayed in this villa. But they were gone from his memory. Man wooed and spoke love words but when the wooing was done the years took their words from them. The past was a load which could not be carried forever by them, unlike a woman who hoarded its rare treasures never to lose them. Yet, as the thought ran with her, Baradoc suddenly shook his head, laughing, and he rose and came to her and kissed her on the forehead and said, 'Aye, now I remember. The last of the words I wrote here in this yard by moonlight for you . . . on . . . on, yes, the wax of your uncle's old ivory tablet.'

The next morning as she lay abed by herself, Baradoc having ridden away to work before dawn, she listened to the screaming of the swifts as they hawked over the river below the terrace slopes and the calm joy on her face moved suddenly to a tightening wince of pain. Her hand went to her right side, pressing against it to ease the sharp bite which with the passing of this last winter had begun to assault her more and more. The gods, she knew, had nearly marked the full tally of her days and she would share the secret with no one. She died in the autumn while she made visit with Baradoc to his tribal lands on the north coast of Dumnonia, moving to sleep in his arms at night and passing to the Shades before dawn broke.

She was buried on the clifftop under a high cairn of boulders in sight of distant Caer Sibli where she had brought Arturo into the world, buried with the purple bloom of the heather moorland behind her and before her the tall cliffs rising over the gold and white sands where the seabirds wheeled and called and the red-legged choughs scavenged and quarrelled along the rock faces. She was of full Roman blood, rare now in the land, and her only living son was Arturo to whom the news came a month later as he rode south from Eburacum to winter at Glevum.

That night in camp on the road, Arturo walked through the willows of the riverside grove where they rested, alone except for Cabal, and knew the regret that all men have for the passing of a loved mother, and regret, too, that time and affairs had forced them apart. Daria and his mother he had now lost. Loneliness and loss was the constant lot of all god-touched men for they had a greater family to serve. There was a shame in him,

307

too, that evening as he walked by the riverside, his face brushed by the passing of the night moths, his eyes and ears aware of all sound and stir, the splash of a foraging water rat, the brief gleam of a glow-worm under a dock leaf and the screech of a little owl, for, there was a part of his thoughts which rode free of his grief because with the news of Tia's death had come also news from his spies who served him from the lands of Esc. With the coming of spring Esc meant to move out against him, but not with a full force, to test his readiness and the quickness with which he could marshal and move men against him. To crush such a move ruthlessly he knew would defer Esc's full effort for years. The Saxons should be encouraged to think that for all his strength he lacked the skill to manage it quickly. Esc should be encouraged.

That winter at Isca the young Prince Cato, not much older than Mordreth, began to show a rebellious, imperious nature, resenting the wardship of Baradoc. He had the courage of his father but not his understanding, and the arrogance of his grandfather but an ambition which was far narrower, seeking only pride and pleasure and power for himself. Mordreth was brought to Isca to keep him company and there were few weeks when they were not in disgrace. They were young hawks eager for the onset of their moult to adult plumage. For only one person were they gentle and obedient to hand, and that was Gwennifer who saved them many a beating and days of sour bread and water for their escapades. It was, too, through the unruly boys that Gwennifer met Merlin for the first time.

She was riding down the river towards the horse enclosure one afternoon of frost-bright sunshine when she heard cries coming from ahead. Breaking from a small alder growth on the river bank she saw Mordreth and Cato shouting and laughing as they danced around a brown-cloaked man with long black hair and an unkempt beard. They were pelting him with addled eggs from an ancient and spring-deserted swan's nest which they had found in the reeds. As soon as the man rushed at one, striking out with his staff, the other attacked him from behind, and both the boys were too nimble and alert to take any harm from him.

Setting her horse to a canter she bore down on the boys who, seeing her coming and recognizing her, ran away up the hill-slope and disappeared over the road towards Isca. As she pulled up in front of the man he plucked a handful of browned dead grasses and began to wipe egg mess from the front of his robe. Looking up at her as he did this, he grimaced wryly and said, 'You came at a good time, my lady Gwennifer. A few more moments and I would have lost patience with their antics and cracked their skulls with my stave.'

'You would have needed their nimbleness.'

'And could have found it. But I was content to mark them and make some study of them.'

'Why so?'

'Time will show why.'

'You talk in riddles.'

'When I need, my lady. But I can beg alms or a night's lodging boldly like any homeless man. Nay, reach not for your belt purse. I need no alms from you, my lady.' He picked broken egg shell from his beard, wiped his messy fingers on his robe and went on, 'You are fortunate to stand up wind of me, my lady Gwennifer.'

'To right the ill done to you, you shall come to Isca and be given fresh clothes and lodgings — and the boys shall be whipped.'

Merlin laughed. 'I need neither clothes nor lodging. But see the boys whipped. It is time their hides were seasoned. And give my good remembrances to your husband, Great Arto.'

'How shall I name you?'

'You know not that already, my lady?'

The truth came slowly to Gwennifer and with it she felt the mantling of blood in her cheeks. 'You are the one who wrote — His glory an everlasting flower . . . He throws no seed.'

Merlin smiled. 'With a fine pointed slate in his hand and a bare rock face before him . . . aye, why then I am the kind of man who itches to fill its smoothness with words. I could have as easily written — Fish with a feathered hook in these waters and the gods will give you jade-flanked mackerel.'

'But you did not.'

'All poetry comes from the gods and we must abide their choice of the moment. Time is a succession of small accidents arranged by the gods.'

'And why have they arranged this time and chance to bring us together?'

'Could it be that, no matter the truth of the words on the rock, you would have cheated them?'

Angry, Gwennifer said, 'You talk over boldly now, master Merlin. Yes, I would have cheated them, and if there were new hope to show him my love would cheat them again. Men have many gods but a woman has only one — the man she loves.'

'Well spoken, and true.'

'Against all the gods I say that Arto will be

311

Great King of this country and should have sons to harvest the fruits of his victories.'

Merlin put a hand up to the muzzle of her horse and gentled it as it stirred restlessly under her. 'There are no fruits of victory with the sword. Seasons of quiet, yes. The real conquest comes not from the men who invade a country or the men who defend it. The good earth of the country, shaped by the rains and rivers and the seasons, is always victor. It is the land and the seasons over it which conquer — not the warriors.'

'Now you talk in riddles again.'

Merlin shrugged his shoulders. 'It is a simple one, my lady — except that you would have to live all the years of your life and a thousand more to know it.'

Angry still and now impatient with the man, Gwennifer said sharply, pique strong in her voice, 'I think you are no more than a fool who makes idle play with the first words that come into your head. So be it — and now, go tell the gods, who made me barren for their sport, that they have my curses!' Then, as she wheeled away and was poised to set her mount to a gallop, she called back over her shoulder, 'And the boys shall not be beaten!'

Smiling, Merlin watched her go and disappear down the road to Isca. Then holding his nose to shut out the stink of addled egg he went to the river to wash, chuckling to himself at the flash of fire there had been in Gwennifer's eyes. No matter her deeds she was true wife to Arturo and the gods would take her curses indulgently.

# The Breaking of the Saxons

In the early spring Arturo went north to Glevum leaving Gelliga in command of very much reduced forces both at Isca and Cam Hill and the other fortified camps. Before he went he spoke alone with Gelliga at Cam Hill, the two of them sitting in the strengthening sunshine outside his quarters where none could overhear them. Gelliga's face grew doleful as he listened.

'They will come this year, and long before summer. Esc's men from the east, keeping south of the Tamesis and there will be a joining with them by Aelle and Cerdic from the south. You will call your men together from the forts. But make no great haste in the matter, as though the surprise of their coming has left you in doubt whether you should make full battle with them or wait until you can get help from me from the north.'

'That gives me a bitter taste in my mouth even now, my lord.'

'Then swallow it. I want Esc to think that these past years of success have turned us too confident and slow to act. Harry them and harass them, but make no stand to block their

314

way. They will only come so far to test us — and I want them to find us surprised and slow to act. By the time I come south they will be on their way back to their own lands, and Esc will think that in a few more years he can come again in full strength and overrun the whole length of the Tamesis valley . . . aye, and press on to Aquae Sulis to split the country in two and so gain the rich southern half for himself. Where the young wolves wanton this season, the whole wolf pack will come in later years — and we shall then make the full killing.'

Gelliga sighed. 'You live ahead of me, my lord. I am still in the old days when if the Saxons moved we went to meet them with the sword and lance.'

Arturo plucked a young grass stalk and chewed on it. 'No more. In these days if a commander has true cunning the battle must be won before the first sword is drawn and the great horses put to the gallop. All I say here is between us. If men speak against me saying I left you ill prepared and came late to your help . . . well,' he grinned, sliding the grass stalk to the side of his mouth, 'agree with them and grumble a little with them. There will be much spoken against me and I want the sound of it to reach Esc.'

Gelliga laughed. 'Arto the bear, men call

315

you. But you have learnt the cunning of a serpent. Aye, I will make hard words against you my lord, but only from my mouth, not my heart.'

There were a few others to whom Arturo spoke as he had done with Gelliga; Difynwal of Demetia, Loth the father of Gwennifer who was marshal now of the far northern forces, Baradoc his father, and the father of his brother-in-law Adipo, the chief of the Durotriges who held the country west of the Vectis sea . . . all men in whom he had trust.

And that year the Saxons marched as he had known they would. They came three hundred strong from Esc and were joined by two hundred men from the West Saxon shore, and they spread death and took plunder and slaves along the Tamesis. Aelle and Cerdic, ignoring Noviomagus and Venta, went close about the western end of the forest of Anderida and joined Esc's men at Calleva and rumours and tales of bloody slaughter went winging like black crows over the country. Among Gelliga's men as they rode and shadowed the Saxons, harrying and harassing them when they could but too weak to oppose them boldly, there was grumbling at and some scorn for Arturo who was slow in coming down the old road from Glevum, through Corinium and Spinis to Calleva with

the great horses and his foot troops. When he
arrived, to find the Saxons long on their way
back to their lands and no hope left of
catching and bringing them to battle, there
were even those among the most faithful of
the Companions — Lancelo and Durstan and
others — who found their loyalty to his good
name and leadership hard pressed. This
Arturo suffered for he knew it would pass. It
was better to lose a little of their love and
faith for a few years than to give them the
truth to spill when the drink ran in the halls
at night and so find its way to Esc.

With Prince Cato and Mordreth, youths
now, there was anger in the one and
disappointment in the other. Sunning themselves one afternoon on the Isca fortress
parapet walk Cato said angrily, 'He grows
lazy and too content with the thought of his
coming kingship. Aye, and look how he bears
himself here. Am I the Prince of Dumnonia
or is he? Dumnonia's money, not his, has
paid for Theodoric and for the breeding and
manning of the great horses.'

Mordreth said loyally, 'All money well
spent. And I think you talk too soon — like a
cock deceived by a late moonrise. There is
more in all this than can be openly read.'

'You share his blood and so you stand for
him.'

Pugnaciously Mordreth answered, 'Aye, I do. And if you call him badly without truth — then I will spill yours!' He moved towards Cato, his fists raised ready for fight.

'Then try it — for I tell you blood he will spill in time. And that mine. With me gone he will call himself Prince of Dumnonia, name his blood royal, and so use me as footstool to climb to kingship.'

Moving close to Cato, Mordreth, his body taut with anger, said, 'You speak so because you itch for your wardship to be ended. So now take back the words for nobody to my face links Arto's name with murder.'

For answer Cato spat in Mordreth's face. They fought, rolling and tumbling on the parapet, their angry shouting sending the jackdaws skyward and eventually bringing a guard and Master Ricat, old now but far from lacking strength and authority, to pull them apart and clout their heads. Of their quarrel Ricat asked nothing for scarcely a week went by without a fight between them or the two of them falling into mischief.

Gwennifer knowing the murmurings against Arturo understood his mind without need for telling from him. In some ways she had the mind of a man and could guess the thinking of Arto. Knowing his love of his country and its people she knew, too, the hardship of his feelings and the depth of his compassion for the men and women who had been exposed to the Saxon march and who had been pillaged and killed to make the coming bait for the trap he would set. Battle was in Arturo's blood but beyond this he was, unless the gods called for it, a hoarder of the lives of his warriors. That autumn when he came to her at Isca there were times when she woke late at night and knew him to be lying alongside her untouched by sleep. Without need of words she would rest her cheek against his bare shoulder and his arm would go round her taking the voiceless comfort she offered.

The next year as though he feared that Esc would strike again, Arturo moved the main part of his forces eastwards, splitting it to stand in readiness in the south below Londinium and in the north based on Ratae and Durovigutum. But no move came except for a few small raids and attacks made by wayward and venturesome Saxon parties. The following year he did the same as though to stamp on Esc's mind that he had learnt the lesson of unreadiness and would not be caught again. But that winter he set the trap for the taking of the Saxons.

Through the merchants, traders and people of Londinium he started the rumour running that the Picts in the far north were massing to move south with the Spring. By packman and pedlars and paid agents he fed the tale of the coming of the Picts to the Saxon enclaves, and long before the turn of the year he began to send men and horses north to Glevum, stripping forces south of the Tamesis ruthlessly from the march line which Esc must take to gain a lasting hold on the country. Men and horses went north. They were raw levies, barely trained, but they made a marching show for men to see, and the news of their going ran fast to the Saxons. But at Glevum he held the Companions and their great horses, over a thousand of them, and Coroticus with his marsh bow and spear men numbering near another thousand. They camped south of Glevum spread down the river Sabrina below the high scarp to the east. At Glevum Arturo sat and waited for the coming of Esc and for the first smoke and flame of the warning beacons that stretched from the heights above Londinium to run from hill and scarp and downland crest westwards to the last great beacon of piled brushwood and resin-sapped pines on the lip of the scarp south of Glevum. A pillar of smoke by day, or a great finger of flame by night; when the sign came Arturo would know that Esc and all his confederates were on their way to split Britain apart, to butcher it and to flay it like a heifer in a slaughterhouse. But if the grace of the gods ran true then Esc would find that the butchers were to become the butchered.

Six days before the feast of Beltine Arto was sitting in his room at Glevum, the window shutters open to the mild evening air so that he had sight of the southward curving river over which swung a long skein of winter geese disturbed from their feeding on the flats by some hunter. The long sharp scarp of the hills was warm-lit by the light of the setting sun when Gwennifer, who had lodged with him that season at Glevum, came into the room.

With a shadow of a smile touching the corners of her mouth, she said, 'My lord, there are two young warriors who would speak with you.'

Looking at her and sensing her half-teasing near to laughter mood, he asked, 'And should I see them?'

'I think you should, my lord. They come to ask service with you.'

'Then send them down the river to Durstan.'

'They ask for you, and I think they have claim to that right.'

'And since you ask for them they are fortunate. I will see them.' Before she could move away he stretched out his hand and, taking her by the wrist gently, he looked into her clear blue eyes touched now by the finest web of lines in their corners and he knew that she was one of the rare women whose beauty, though changing with the years, would never diminish. The gods had taken Daria from him and given him her in place. This wisdom and kindness of the gods he had long come to know. They had set him to live a life apart, given him grief to try his faith in his dream and then sent him Gwennifer to test his compassion, a compassion which had long ago turned to true love and worship. He kissed the palm of her hand and then said, 'I think these warriors will be no surprise to me — for I was of their age once and know their feelings.'

'Then be good to them for my sake.'

She left him and a few moments later Prince Cato and Mordreth came into the room. They had grown from boys now to well-set youths who held themselves with the fast-coming stance of manhood. They were dressed in tunic and trews without distinction and belted with short swords and side daggers and as they stood there Arturo caught from them the smell of sweat and horse. He welcomed them and then said, 'You should both be at Isca working in the schooling pens.'

For a moment they were silent, each waiting for the other to speak, then Prince Cato said, 'I have but two years of wardship to go, but am only a few months short of the right to bear arms. For the sake of standing on the order of those few months, my lord, would you have me miss the great battle which comes?'

Not answering him, Arturo turned to Mordreth and asked, 'And you — who lack even more months?'

Mordreth smiled. 'My lord, I lack any good reasons except that I would serve with you as groom, servant, or ride messenger and if call arise draw sword to defend myself. Hard words have been said against you, my lord, in these past years, and said by Prince Cato and myself — but now we know the truth. We would be with you in the day of your triumph.'

Knowing the feelings which ran in these two because he had known them himself long ago, he said, 'Men go to battle but the gods ordain which side triumph shall bless . . . ' Then with a grin and a shrug of his shoulders, he said, 'Let it be so, then. Ride down river to Durstan and tell him to give you service fit for your years.'

'Fighting service, my lord?' asked Cato.

'Can it be avoided if the gods throw it your way?'

★ ★ ★

A week later, a little before sunset, the beacon high up on the ridge flared into life, its flames rivalling the glow of the setting sun, its long tail of resinious smoke rolling westwards across the river in ragged plumes. Then began the long wait which, although all now knew its reason, set men itching for the move to come against the Saxons. Soon fast-riding messengers, covering the country in relays, began to arrive at Glevum and on the great war map long ago painted on the wall in Ambrosius's counsel chamber the fine-pointed charcoal sticks marked the slow movement of Esc and his warriors.

They came westwards through the country south of the Tamesis and when they were at Calleva they were joined from the south by Cerdic and his men. Here, under the deliberately scant forces of Gelliga, they were met. Before their strength Gelliga could do nothing and turned away from them, riding west, drawing the Saxons on and convincing them of the weakness of the forces in the south. When they reached Spinis, and it was clear that they were driving for Aquae Sulis to reach the Sabrina river beyond it at Abona and so split the country, Arturo moved.

He sent Durstan with five hundred horse

and two hundred of Coroticus's men to move down to the headwater lands of the Tamesis and the Abona rivers north of the Cunetio-Aquae Sulis road. With the rest of his army he went south from Glevum down the Sabrina river road to Abonae and then turned back east to Aquae Sulis. Beyond Aquae Sulis he drew off the road to Cunetio into the wooded slopes and waited for the coming of Esc.

In the years to pass the men who fought in the great battle of Mount Badon which crushed the power of the Saxons for a hundred years to come each told the story they knew. But there is no man in battle who knows its full shape and the terrors and triumphs of all its movements. Each man fights his own battle, lost in a small world of violence and death and maiming. To a Coroticus marshman, arrows ready notched, lying screened by the thickets of the slope above the road, there was nothing at first except the distant cloud dust from the marching, unwary Saxons. The droning of the honey bees working the blooms of gorse and harvesting the pollen from the clumps of purple marjoram and the pink-flushed flowers of the convolvulus rose higher than the distant stir of tramping warriors. When the dust cloud became men — axed and sworded, unkempt from days of marching, sunlight flashing from spear tips and bronze armbands, a great snake of warriors crawling towards him, men without care, victory under their belts, and a greater victory to come — then he picked a man, worked his left hand fingers gently on the smooth mole-skin grip of his bow and lightly began to flex the drawcord, his eye never leaving his mark, his lips drawn back over his teeth which held his second and third arrow, and waited for the low whistle of command to sing down the line of his hidden comrades. And when the signal came and his arrow sped high and curving, flighting now with a hundred others, searing the air with sharp-honed tip and stiff flight feathers, his battle had begun and the gods would give him either the mercy of safe sleep that night or the ease of the gentle voyage to the Isles of the Blessed.

In the trees on the slope above the marshmen, each trooper and Companion sat his horse, the great beasts' heads tossing against the summer flies and the quiver of muscles, nerved by the communion with their riders, twitching their smooth hides. The same tremor held the body of each waiting trooper, lance lowered and cloak belted back to free the quick drawing of sword from its scabbard when the lance had done its work.

Then was the moment when the Saxons halted under the rain of arrows and confusion held them briefly and each trooper lost all thought of gods or sweethearts or family and, hearing the high call of the battle horns and trumpets, pushed horse to gallop and went streaming down the hillside, leaving marshmen to lie flat and let them through while ahead went the White One with Arturo and at his side rode Lancelo. Following them to join the marshmen came the foot levies from Cymru and Demetia, from the tribes of the north and the south of the land, a moving hillside, an avalanche of Britons to sweep the Saxons back. Red were the swords that day and swift the horses and fierce the spear and lance thrusts and bright under the sun the coloured surcoat of Arto carrying the figure of the Blessed Mary.

The Saxons stood and fought but when they saw the great crescent of Durstan's horses thundering down the far slope to take them from behind hope went from them. They scattered like a vast flock of crows disturbed from a new sown corn field and, seeking escape from the cavalry, turned south away from the road and climbed the steep scarp of Mount Badon to seek the sanctuary of its ramparts which still waited final ordering at the hand of Baradoc. But there on the level land beyond the summit lay Gelliga and his horse to pen them back or to ride down any that looked for escape. Lucky were those Saxons who broke through to pass back along the road to Cunetio, and luckier still those few who pony-mounted rode into brake and woods and found escape, among them Esc and his son and the bastard Briton Cerdic.

Unlucky were those who found the shelter of Mount Badon's ramparts for there was no water hole or spring to slake their thirst, and the bite of thirst is harsher and speedier felt than that of hunger and soon drives a man to desperation. For three days the sun was brazen in a cloudless but not barren sky for the eagles and kites and the crows and ravens swung in a dark circus above them waiting in patience for the feasting to come.

At sunset on the third day the Saxons broke in force from the hill top down the steep scarp and the Britons hunted and harried them on foot and on horse through the long night and the following day. When the sun went down that day the Saxon might and threat was broken and tamed for a lifetime and more. Victories and conquests when all who lived that day were dead would take strange and wayward paths which unborn men would follow not knowing the shape of the destiny the gods were slowly working for their land.

During the days and nights of the battle and the siege of Mount Badon and the harassing of the retreating Saxons many things happened the memories of which would either be lost or changed by time. Prince Cato and Mordreth killed their first Saxons and with each telling the count rose a little higher. Mordreth's horse stumbled as he tried to force it up the steep scarp to the hilltop in pursuit of the Saxons and youth and beast fell and Mordreth broke his right leg which being set badly always afterwards marked him with a limp. Prince Cato riding hard down the Cunetio road reined-in to lance a wounded Saxon lying on the ground and gave chance to a gut-ripped Saxon lying by to throw with his last strength an axe and mark the youth's face with a long scar from the side of his mouth to his ear.

On the evening when the penned Saxons on the hilltop, made bold and desperate by thirst, broke out, Baradoc, fighting on foot on the steep scarp side, wielding his sword in his left hand, was beset by four Saxons and killed three before the fourth ran him through with his scramaseax and sent him to the gods to join Tia, granting him the only death which he would have wished. He was buried on the vine slope outside old Truvius's villa at Aquae

Sulis where the four winged dragon-flies hovered and darted over the yellow flags and the kingfishers flew low like moving fire over the clear waters.

In those days of battle and siege nine hundred and more of the Saxons died, and two hundred of the Companions, troopers and marshmen and foot soldiers of Arturo, among them Marcos who with his long dead brother, the dumb Timo, Christos men both, had been the first to join Arturo and go with him to the Villa of the Three Nymphs. Garwain died when his horse was cut down, and many others long tried by service to Arturo. Among those that buried and mourned their dead were few without wounds to show as small price for the victory which the gods had sent them.

In the first charge down the hill slope to the road Arturo took his own wound a spear thrust that glanced off his saddle bow and took him above the groin on his left side, a wound ignored until the evening of that first day when Pasco bound it with cloth strips while Arturo made light of it. But men said in the years that followed — though not to Arto's face — that the wound reopened always on the morning of the day of remembrance for Mount Badon and ran blood until sundown.

Three days after the battle Gwennifer came

from Glevum to Aquae Sulis to Truvius's villa where Arturo had made his headquarters and where there came to him the news of the continuing eastward flight of the Saxons, harried and hounded by the forces under Durstan and Gelliga. Gwennifer dressed his wound and as they sat under the covered way above the courtyard she played her harp for him. Knowing the turmoil in his mind, the lasting heat of victory in him still, and the strengthening of his dreams for the years to come, she sang:

The great horses of Arto have broken
    the sea-men
Now he is king of the star-bright King-
    dom
A lamp to outshine them, an eagle
    screaming above the crags
Over this land now the brown leaves
    that fall are gold
The white waves are silver on the shore
The mist rises from the meadows of red
    clover
And the misery of years lifts from the
    hearts of men

Arturo, hearing her words, remembered the first time she had played for him at Lindum and how, though he had taken pleasure in her and her music, he had not known then that she would be wife to him. The gods held the future from men, to let men dream their own future and labour to create it. At Mount Badon the work and dreams of years had been brought to fruiting, and each year had levied its own cruel cost. But there was with him at this moment a wisdom deeper than any he had known before. The Saxons were broken, and would lick their wounds for years. But some small part of this country they had made their own and he knew that there could be no pushing them into the sea. They must sit where they were and slowly the seasons and the slow shuttle of daily affairs would mould their ways and loyalties to the great shape of this land. Warriors took victory by the sword, but the gods guided a slower and secret battle. He was now in his forty-fifth year and knew that the temper of freedom in a land called for more than the simple acts of warfare which brought peace. War had bonded this land together by the sword. Under the gods he must find the means to hold it so in peace. If the gods still loved him he would find a way and already in his heart he knew that it was a way which he would walk alone. Men needed gods no matter how they named them, but a land and a nation needed a man to be seen and to act like a god.

Cold with a sudden loneliness he put out a hand gently and stayed Gwennifer's playing by touching her arm. He said, 'My lady Gwennifer, play me no song of war and kings. In this courtyard my father and mother were married. She lies by the sea and he by the river so there is always the blue water path of joining between them. Play me a song of small delights.'

Gwennifer smiled and took his hand and kissed it. 'I have no great gift with words, my lord.'

'Then give me a small gift.'

She sipped her wine for a moment and then took the harp and played:

I ask the gods small bounties
A secret hut in the wilderness
A moss-lined well beside it
And a thicket for the singing birds
Within a row of tall, bright candles
And under their light the face of my
    love
Her eyes the twin stars of constancy
Drawing me to the smooth haven of her
    arms

As she played the thought came to her that long dead Borio would have shaped the words with truer pace and sweetness and there was a quick wonder in her that the woman of those days was long dead too. The gods could be cruel in their brief designs but once the due course was run they could sweeten life with new joys. Arturo would be king, but she was content to know that she had long been his queen. The coming years would change him, but nothing in her would alter for her constancy and love was hard set against any change of season.

# The Dream and the Dreamer

Arturo rode down the Cam Hill with six mounted Companions behind him. Autumn sunshine was mellow over the land. The White One now and then tossed her head to shake away the teasing flies. Cabal, the last of the great hounds to bear the name, moved at the mare's side, limping a little from the stiffness in his right foreleg from sinews torn by a dog otter's bite in his younger days. From the high branches of a great poplar a red squirrel scolded their passage, and hearing the sound Arturo smiled to himself, for the squirrel had been in the dream of this day to come, the dream which the gods had sent him seven nights before. It had possessed him with a living, undeniable truth and there was no flaw in his memory of it, and no turning from it to find escape. The will of the gods would run its course this day and there was a weariness in his body and heart which gave welcome to it.

In the dell on the hilltop the willow herb flowered between the cairn stones of Daria's grave, and the stones were thick mossed and almost hidden by the spread of ivy growth.

Great hart's tongue ferns grew in the shade of a white thorn tree, bird-seeded years ago. The gods had given him the love of two women to comfort and ease the march of his years. Daria lay beneath the berried thorn and Gwennifer, spared the sharing of this day with him, rested at Eburacum to spend the winter with her aged father. The gods had worked the weaving of her days with kindness to take her from his side on this day of golden fruitfulness which was to die into the long darkness of the rest they decreed for him. There was no flaw in the memory of the dream. The flashing of the white rump of a bullfinch flighting across the path had been there, and the rustle of a grass snake through the new fallen leaves that carpeted the bottom of the dry ditch at his side.

In the twenty years since Mount Badon he had given himself to this country and had learnt the art and cunning of being many men, and finally no fixed man to himself. Emperor he had called and made himself to give no rankle to the country's kings. He smiled to himself hearing the name coming from Difynwal's tongue in the old language of the tribes . . . Amerauder. In twenty years the Scotti were tamed, the whole of the North recovered. Londinium and other cities flourished, though not fully as they had in the last days of the legions. He had forced formal treaties on the Saxons and they lived like docile cattle in their shrunken enclaves. And he had taken great Camulodunum, the first city of the Romans, to split the North and Middle Saxons from the South. Cerdic and his West Saxons lived on sufferance in their land, and all the provinces of the country had their governors and law givers and suffered sharply if they failed him or their duties. To bring peace to a country had been the first part of his life work, to keep that peace he had had to shape himself anew and found many times when the iron of his pitilessness seared him more sharply than his victims. Men told and sang the stories of his deeds and his wonders and coloured them bright and let truth lie unseen like a mouse in a corner while legend flew high like a red dragon over the land. He let the silvered tongues of bards and singers run free for he knew that, while the gods were always above men, men had need to make of one of their own a god of flesh and blood. He had long ago lost the pathway of true life and rode the shining way of myth. This the gods had decreed for his life, and now they had marked him for a death as unreal as the last great span of his life had been.

They came down the scarp slope to the

water meadows of the Cam that ran its crooked way seaward and they rode its bank westward to find the road to Isca. But as he moved to the easy motion of the White One, a man deep in his sixties, tawny beard grizzled with the frosts of the years, the lean face weathered and furrowed, and his body held a little bent to ease the old and constant bite of the wound he had taken at Badon, his eyes were soft with a rare joy. He knew that this day of the coming true of the dream was the one which would take him to the long rest of body and spirit and to the peace at heart which had gone from him on that day on the downs above Cunetio when he had killed his first Saxon. He reached his right hand across and touched the hilt of his scabbarded sword and slipped it a little free to prove its readiness for many a brave but careless Companion had died on hard weather campaigning from the tight grip of rain-swollen wooden scabbard on the wanted blade at the moment of peril.

On a rise in the ground as they left the river the twin green hills of Ynys-witrin showed jewel clear through the bright air. Coroticus reigned there now and called himself Melwas after his dead father, and Coroticus had lost three fingers of his right hand at the battle of Celidon Wood in the far north, long after Badon; Coroticus who had always been true to him and read a fuller understanding of his ways than any other. After this day there would be bitter blood between Coroticus and Prince Cato.

Breasting the rise Arturo marked ahead the pine wood that stood above the road to Isca. It stood now as it had in his dream, even to a kestrel hovering to one side above the harvest stubble of a corn plot and a tethered goat with three free kids watched by an old woman who sat teasing and spinning wool from her hand spindle. A blue skein of smoke rose from a hollow that hid a settler's hut.

After his death peace would slowly die like a great tree being eaten away by rot and beetles; after his death, for his honour and glory, the bards would call this day a day of battle for although many emperors had died by poison and assassination the gods would have for him the glory of death in battle. In the affairs of the gods and emperors truth might serve for a day but the bright, ringing falsehood would quickly flower to ennoble for all time the way of his going.

As Durstan rode silently at his side he was tempted not for the first time since the coming of the dream to turn to him and the other Companions and send them away for their deaths, too, had been marked in it. But

339

there was no power in him to speak the words for he rode under the gods as he had done all his life and was their creature.

He looked ahead at the pines again and saw the kestrel slip sideways down the breeze to hover over the trees and then turn away in rapid flight. He knew that the bird had taken alarm at the men and horses hidden within the wood. Prince Cato would not be there with his envy and malice and fears for the curbing of his gluttony for power. There were others like him in the land and there would be feasting when he was gone. Man's nobility under oppression and peril grew feeble after victory. Those who worshipped him after Mount Badon would now see him gone and the gods for their own reasons would not stay their hands. Mordreth, poisoned from long service and boonship with Cato, would ride with the sword drawn to lead the handful of men behind him, Mordreth who through his mother Gerta was part of that flesh of Baradoc and Tia which framed and filled his own body in full descent, Mordreth, whom he had banished in perpetuity to the lands of the people of the Enduring Crow for trying to lay hands in drunken lust on the lady Gwennifer at Isca, would come to give him death and to meet his own and forfeit all reward from Prince Cato.

Durstan at his side looked up and said, 'The sky clouds and there is the smell of rain coming from the West.'

Arturo nodded and said, 'Aye . . . Latis will begin her weeping and the lakes and rivers of the Summerlands will rise and over-run their banks.' The rain would fall on him, but not on the living Durstan for there was half a day to go yet before the first heavy storm drops would fall to mark the end of the dream and the onset of the long darkness which awaited him.

Mordreth and his men came when they were within a bowshot of the pines, but before they showed he knew their coming for the old woman untethered her goat and led it away with the young kids following, and so earned her handful of coins for making the signal of his arrival. They rode without haste to raise no alarm, ten mounted men with Mordreth at their head and no hand lying ready on sword pommel to signal ill intent. It was then that he turned to Durstan and spoke the last words to him which had marked his dream.

'My good Durstan, stay by me this day as you have stayed by me since the night we rode from Isca into outlawry. Dumnonia which claimed our beginnings now goes to brand itself with lasting shame at our ending,

341

but it is an ending which shall bring you into the everlasting glory and companionship of the gods.'

Then as the horsemen coming to them broke into a gallop and the drawing of swords flashed like the soft play of lightning, Durstan smiled and said, 'I am with you, my lord, and without sorrow for from this day on there is finer and truer company to be found in the shaded halls of the gods than here among mortal men.' Then he grinned and spat and, drawing his sword, went on, 'But let us give ourselves the pleasure, dear Arto, of colouring our blades with the blood of traitors . . . *Aie,* tis a far better way to end than by poisoning or midnight dark strangulation.'

They fought without give or flight, the seven against the eleven, numbers which men's pride and the warping and swelling of memory and time would mount twentyfold. They fought stirrup to stirrup, knee to knee, and their movement was the dark swirl of a whirlpool encircling violence, sucking to its centre men and horses. Hooves trampled the fallen and dying. Blood ran down the fair quarters of the White One, shone like dew on the proud neck of Durstan's black stallion, and was trampled beneath hooves to give a darker hue to the red earth of the rich western soil.

They fought from the high pitch of their saddles, and when their horses were cut down or threw them in the rising panic which took the beasts, they fought on foot and no side showed mercy and no man sought flight. It was a time of blood and death under the slow clouding sky and none marked it to live save the old woman and her husband who lay low behind the brushwood fence of their steading and peered through the dead twigs and wished themselves dead for they had not known that the riders from the east would be Arto and his Companions.

Durstan died of a sword slash across his throat from behind for his body to fall and be trampled by the hooves of the horses. The call of a raven, the first of the birds of prey to arrive overhead, gave him farewell. Unmanned horses swirled in the circle until they were spun off like sparks from a grindstone to canter away or stand with their heads lowered in heavy breathing. And when to the raven overhead had gathered the first of the kites and buzzards, there rested living only Mordreth and the last man of his band and Arturo. Then the two rode him down, passing each on either flank of the White One, and as Arturo took the blade of Mordreth's man on his own and swept it aside to free his sword point to drive true into the man's throat to give him death, so Mordreth's sword drove into his left side at the place of his Mount Badon wound. But the pace of his mount, and the sudden swing of the White One's haunches as she bucked free of the fallen man under her rear legs, broke Mordreth's hold on his sword and it fell from Arturo's side to the earth.

Knowing it must happen, the dark strung moments of the dream sliding by under the casting hands of the gods, Arto pulled the White One round and rode against Mordreth who had jumped from his mount to take a sword from the side of one of the dead. He rode him down, driving the full weight and run of the White One into him, and as he lay on the ground Arturo turned and rode him down again, the pounding hooves of the White One battering his body and breaking his bones and his screams came wailing back in dying echoes from the tall stand of the close-by pines.

Arturo rode back to Mordreth and dismounted. Standing over the son of his sister, blood of his blood welling from the slack mouth, he took his dagger — for there was no honour in the man to warrant the nobility of the sword — and mercifully slit his throat and gave his slipping spirit easier and faster passage to the darkness of the limbo which waits to meld into nothingness the souls of those whom the gods reject. Then he mounted the White One, scabbarded his sword, kicked her into slow gait and then dropped the reins loose about her neck and let her have her own way.

She moved and turned her head to the north to follow the path of the dream. As she went Arto took from around his neck his red and white scarf of the Companions. Wadding it he thrust it under his tunic and held it tight against his wound to stem the steady flow of blood.

\* \* \*

When he came to the edge of the marsh lake, through which the river Cam ran, the light was going from the sky and the rain was drifting over the land in thin, soft veils, shrouding close by Ynys-witrin, and pocking the smooth face of the water with its gentle touch. He dismounted, loosed his sealskin travelling pack from behind his saddle, and sat on it to await the coming of the man who had saved his life from bleeding away in the Circle of the Gods from his first wounding by a kinsman. Inbar of his own blood, who had lived between good and bad, now lay dead many a long year; and now Mordreth was shapeless flesh and bone to make quarrel among the birds of prey. The man would come but there would be no saving; Merlin who had said long ago . . . *there will come a day when I shall be with you in an hour of your own choosing when the war horns shall blow neither for victory nor defeat, but to set the echoes rolling for evermore over this land to give your name everlasting life while you take the long sleep which the gods have decreed for you.*

From the fringing lake reeds a bittern boomed and through the veiling rain a marsh harrier drifted over the waters like a lost spirit. A frog croaked a slow complaint and a shoal of minnows broke through the water like a silver cloud as they leapt to escape a marauding pike. The White One, unscathed, her smooth hide stained with the running scarlet of his own blood, cropped the sweet turf. There was a slow weariness working over his body that numbed him against all pain. The blood ran slowly over his hand that held the wadding to his side and he knew that as it ran so would run his dream, and knew more, that the ending of the dream he had dreamt was no ending for it had faded on a moment bereft of death's last ease . . .

Cabal came and sat by him, pushing his muzzle fretfully against the back of his free hand. He teased the hound's ears, thinking of the puppy hound that Gwennifer had ridden from Lindum to present to him. In Eburacum now she was safe. There were many sides to love and no man or woman could claim to know them all. She would move in beauty through the years left to her and find strength to bear the sorrow of his going.

The soft rain thickened and fell hard now to beat the lake water into a hissing froth. Through it came a narrow flat-bottomed boat of the kind which the marshmen used for duck hunting and fishing. A man sat in the stern and paddled it gently, a brown-robed man, black-bearded, his head uncovered to the fast falling rain. The prow of the craft drove through the reeds and grated on the gravelled bank. The man stepped ashore and then sat on the prow with his feet resting on the gleaming stones of the lakeside. He nodded his head to Arturo, smiling gently, but said nothing.

Arturo said wearily, 'So here the dream comes to an end. What lies beyond it?'

Merlin rose then and coming to him answered, 'Latis weeps for you. She is the gentle-hearted one among the gods, but seldom knows the full truth of her sorrow. The waters are rising for you to make a moving pathway without beginning or end.'

He wiped his hand across his beard to free it of rain and fingered his dark eyebrows to clear them of their heavy dewing. 'But you will not lack for company. There are others who move on it. The good and the bad. Some long distant Caesar, a drunken poet with a head full of Spring music and words that touch the heart before the mind. Maybe a few priests who have come close to knowing the purity of the God who stands above all other gods, and some great bishops who handled charity as though it were a sword. The gods stock the pens of time with all sorts of human cattle.'

'Cattle?' The twist of a smile touched the corners of Arturo's mouth.

'Aye. Men are but cattle of a kind and the gods herd them.'

Arturo rose and would have walked towards the boat, but Merlin held up his right hand. 'There is no moving out on to the waters until you have done the two last things of the dream.'

'My dream ended with your coming.'

'But the dream runs on through all time and now you must shape it for yourself. Before you move on the waters you must finish the earth dream from your own fashioning.'

Arturo closed his eyes and swayed a little

from the weakness in him growing from his wound. Then he turned and walked to the White One. She raised her head and he stroked the velvet of her mouth and he remembered the first White One, she whom he had caught and tamed from the great woods above the Villa of the Three Nymphs. Blood from the tearing of his flesh as he had ridden her through thorn and briars and the thick lattice of brakes and undergrowth had streaked her hide that day. His own blood this day stained this mare's hide with a ragged poppy bloom.

Moving from her with Cabal limping at his heels, the hound whining, sensing strangeness and distrusting it, he walked to the water's edge and drew his sword from its scabbard. Holding the bloodied blade before his face he kissed it and then threw it far out on to the waters. Its great splash disturbed a feeding mallard and the bird took flight through the rain, trailing feet and wing beats marking a foam-flecked path into the growing darkness.

Behind him Merlin, with laughter in his voice, said, 'Tis no great loss. Until mankind reaches true manhood there will be no lack of swords in this world.' Then, as Arturo turned from the lake and went to his rain-sodden campaigning pack on which he had been sitting while he awaited Merlin's coming, the man rose and joined him.

Arturo knelt, swift pain unexpectedly scything across his left side, and unfastening the strapping of the pack took from it the silver chalice which had always travelled with him since the day that golden-haired Gwennifer had used it for her salving ointment. It was tarnished and dull but the falling rain fast pearled and dewed it with clinging drops which broke and ran to puddle thinly within it. He was tempted to cup it in his hands to see if the growing water within would turn to the blood colour he had known at the Circle of the Gods. But Merlin reached out and took it gently from him, saying, 'Nought will happen, my lord Arturo. On another age and in another's palms the turning will be seen again.' Chalice in hand he went to the boat.

Arturo followed him. Merlin pushed the boat free to rock on the waters which were now loud with the pulse of the heavy rain. Arturo stepped into the boat and sitting took the paddle. Cabal would have jumped in with him but Merlin touched the hound's head and Cabal sat, shivering and whining. Looking at the man Arturo, eyes half-closed with pain, said, 'So the dream goes. But before the waters take me, I ask you one last grace.'

Merlin smiled. 'There is no need for asking. From here I shall go to Cam Hill and make simple prayer for you and Daria. And when I come to Eburacum I will give comfort to your lady Gwennifer.'

'My gratitude. And the gods go with you.'

Merlin's face twisted wryly. 'Aye, I fear they will. But I would give much for the long sleep into which you now drift.'

He put his foot to the prow of the boat, sent it free on the waters, and stood watching in the rain as Arturo with his left hand made stroke or two with the paddle to send it out into the river current that now ran with growing vigour through the lake. Arturo dropped the paddle and sat without movement. He drifted on the surge of the growing current into veils of rain and darkness which slowly enshrouded him and hid him from the sight of Merlin.

At his going the White One raised her head high and whinnied loud. Merlin laid his hand gently on the neck of the shivering hound, speaking softly to it as the rain gathered fast in the bowl of the chalice on the ground at his side.

# List of Place and Tribal Names

*Abona* R. Avon
*Abonae* Bristol
*Abus* R. Humber
*Anderida* Pevensey
*Antivestaeum* Land's End
*Aquae Sulis* Bath
*Ariconium* Weston-under-Penyard
*Atrebates* Middle Thames Valley tribe
*Belerium* Land's End
*Belgae* West Country tribe
*Brigantes* Tribe holding lands north of York from coast to coast
*Caer Sibli* Lundy Island
*Calcaria* Tadcaster
*Calleva* Silchester
*Camulodunum* Colchester
*Cantawarra* Canterbury
*Cantiaci* Kent tribe
*Catuvellauni* Essex tribe also holding lands north-west of London
*Causennae* Ancaster
*Clausentium* Bitterne
*Corinium* Cirencester
*Coritani* Lincoln-Leicestershire tribe
*Cornovii* Cheshire-Staffordshire tribe
*Crococalana* Brough
*Cunetio* Mildenhall
*Cymru* Wales
*Demetae* South-West Wales tribe
*Deva* Chester
*Dubglas* R. Witham
*Dumnonia* Cornwall and Devon

352

*Durnovaria* Dorchester

*Durobrivae* Rochester

*Durocornovium* Wanborough

*Durolipons* Cambridge

*Durotriges* Somerset-Dorset tribe

*Durovernum* Canterbury

*Durovigutum* Godmanchester

*Eburacum* York

*Erin* Ireland

*Eurium* Usk

*Glevum* Gloucester

*Gobannium* Abergavenny

*Iceni* Norfolk-East Anglia tribe

*Ictis* St Michael's Mount

*Isca* Exeter

*Ituna* Solway Firth

*Hercules Promontory* Hartland Point

*Lactodorum* Towcester

*Lavobrinta* Forden Gaer (Wales)

*Lemanis* Lympne

*Lindinis* Ilchester

*Lindum* Lincoln

*Londinium* London

*Lugovalium* Carlisle

*Lutetia* Paris

*Metatis* The Wash

*Mona* Anglesey

*Moridunum* Carmarthen

*Nemetostatio* North Tawton

*Nidum* Neath

*Novantae* Dumfries tribe

*Noviomagus* Chichester

*Ocelli* Flamborough Head

*Olicana* Ilkley

*Octapitarum* St David's Head

*Ordovices* North Wales tribe

*Parisi* East Yorkshire tribe

*Petuaria* Brough (Humber)

353

*Picts* The Scots
*Pontes* Staines
*Portus Adurni*
Porchester
*Ratae* Leicester
*Regnenses*
Hampshire-Sussex
tribe
*Rutupiae* Richbor-
ough
*Sabrina* R. Severn
*Salinae* Droitwich
*Scotti* The Irish
*Segontium* Caernar-
von
*Sorviodunum* Old
Sarum
*Spinis* Speen

*Tamarus* R. Tamar
*Tamesis* R. Thames
*Tanatus* Thanet
*Tisobis* R. Glaslyn
*Trinovantes* Essex-
East Anglia tribe
*Turius* R. Towy
*Vectis* Isle of Wight
*Venta* Winchester
*Verlucio* Sandy Lane
*Verulamium*
St Albans
*Vindocladia* Badbury
Rings
*Vindolandia* Chester-
holm
*Ynys-witrin* Glaston-
bury

We do hope that you have enjoyed reading this large print book.

Did you know that all of our titles are available for purchase?

We publish a wide range of high quality large print books including:
**Romances, Mysteries, Classics**
**General Fiction**
**Non Fiction and Westerns**

Special interest titles available in large print are:
**The Little Oxford Dictionary**
**Music Book**
**Song Book**
**Hymn Book**
**Service Book**

Also available from us courtesy of Oxford University Press:
**Young Readers' Dictionary**
**(large print edition)**
**Young Readers' Thesaurus**
**(large print edition)**

For further information or a free brochure, please contact us at:
**Ulverscroft Large Print Books Ltd.,**
**The Green, Bradgate Road, Anstey,**
**Leicester, LE7 7FU, England.**
**Tel:** (00 44) 0116 236 4325
**Fax:** (00 44) 0116 234 0205

*Other titles published by*
*The House of Ulverscroft:*

## THE CRIMSON CHALICE

### Victor Canning

When a party of marauding Saxons destroy her father's villa, young Roman girl Gratia, 'Tia' escapes. She comes upon the body of the heir to the chieftanship of a British tribe in the west. Baradoc, a prisoner of Phoenician traders, was sold as a slave and is also escaping the Saxons. However, after being attacked he was left for dead by his cousin, the next heir. Tia nurses him back to health, and they continue together to the safety of her uncle's villa in Aquae Sulis . . . Their son, Arturo, inherits his father's desire for uniting Britain against the Saxons.

# THE CIRCLE OF THE GODS

## Victor Canning

Arturo's dream, like that of his father, Baradoc, is to unite Britain against the marauding Saxons. Always a wild and arrogant youth, he grows up and leads a rebellion against Count Ambrosius. He raises a small force of men which attacks Saxon settlements. Then, with Durstan and Lancelo to lead the troops, Arturo's great campaign begins . . .

# BIRDS OF A FEATHER

## Victor Canning

A fortunate man, Sir Anthony Swale is married to a loyal wife; he lives in a grand house in Somerset and leads a very privileged life. He devotes most of his time to collecting rare art treasures, particularly from behind the Iron Curtain. And he will pay any price for the right piece — including treason. But then his treachery is discovered — and agents working for the Government decide it is time to take discreet action . . .

# THE BOY ON PLATFORM ONE

## Victor Canning

Cheerful Peter Courtney, a fourteen-year-old, is an unusual boy. Exceptionally gifted, he's able to repeat, fully, any text which is read to him once — even in French. When his widowed father's business fails, he takes Peter around London's social clubs to perform professionally. Because of his skills he finds himself involved with the Secret Service. He is required to use his gift to receive important information regarding traitors to the British and French Governments — but this places Peter and his father in danger. Now they must escape and leave everything behind . . . in hiding from an assassin who is thorough and systematic.

# TALES OF MYSTERY AND HORROR: VOL.III

## Edgar Allan Poe

These *Tales Of Mystery And Horror* include the story of Bedloe, a wealthy young invalid, who has a strange tale to tell his physician, after he experiences a form of time travel, in *A Tale Of The Ragged Mountains* . . . And *The Conversation Of Eiros And Charmion* is a very strange tale of a comet approaching earth, causing it to contain pure oxygen. The result of this has a devastating effect on people . . .